SOMEONE
KNOWS

ALSO BY VI KEELAND

Thrillers
The Unraveling

Romances
Indiscretion

What Happens at the Lake

Something Unexpected

The Game

The Boss Project

The Summer Proposal

The Spark

The Invitation

The Rivals

Inappropriate

All Grown Up

We Shouldn't

The Naked Truth

Sex, No Love

Beautiful Mistake

Egomaniac

Bossman

The Baller

Beat

Throb

Worth the Fight

Worth the Chance

Worth Forgiving

Belong to You

Made for You

SOMEONE KNOWS

A NOVEL

VI KEELAND

EMILY BESTLER BOOKS

ATRIA

New York   Amsterdam/Antwerp   London
Toronto   Sydney/Melbourne   New Delhi

EMILY
BESTLER
BOOKS

ATRIA

An Imprint of Simon & Schuster, LLC
1230 Avenue of the Americas
New York, NY 10020

This book is a work of fiction. Any references to historical events, real people,
or real places are used fictitiously. Other names, characters, places, and events
are products of the author's imagination, and any resemblance to actual events
or places or persons, living or dead, is entirely coincidental.

First Emily Bestler Books/Atria Paperback edition June 2025

EMILY BESTLER BOOKS / ATRIA PAPERBACK and colophon
are trademarks of Simon & Schuster, LLC

Simon & Schuster strongly believes in freedom of expression and stands against
censorship in all its forms. For more information, visit BooksBelong.com.

For information about special discounts for bulk purchases,
please contact Simon & Schuster Special Sales at 1-866-506-1949
or business@simonandschuster.com.

The Simon & Schuster Speakers Bureau can bring authors to your live event. For
more information or to book an event, contact the Simon & Schuster Speakers
Bureau at 1-866-248-3049 or visit our website at www.simonspeakers.com.

Interior design by Davina Mock-Maniscalco

Manufactured in the United States of America

1   3   5   7   9   10   8   6   4   2

Library of Congress Cataloging-in-Publication Data has been applied for.

ISBN 978-1-6680-4749-1
ISBN 978-1-6680-4751-4 (ebook)

With love to Chris

CHAPTER

1

May 20th. The date printed at the top of the newspaper startles me, and I drop it like it's a hot coal that's burned my hands. It falls to the floor in a scattered array of ink-stained stories. The man behind the counter frowns.

"Sorry," I offer as I bend, then do my best to shuffle the pages into order and place the paper back on top of the *New York Post* pile before moving to the magazine rack. *Sports Illustrated* has a racehorse on the cover. Mr. Hank, my old landlord, will like that, so I pluck it from the pile and head to the register to pay.

It's the third time I've been reminded of the date since I woke up, and it's only 4 p.m. Normally, when I'm teaching summer classes, like I am now, I only go in twice a week, so I don't even know what day it is. But May 20th isn't just any day, I suppose. It's the twenty-year anniversary of the day I'll *never* forget.

I leave the bodega and decide to walk the fifteen or so blocks to Mr. Hank's assisted-living facility, rather than taking the subway. It's beautiful out, and I still need to stop and pick up donuts. Plus, I don't want to see him until I can clear my head. He's struggling through dementia, so the last thing he needs is me bringing my anxiety for a visit. But my mind whirls as I walk, and not even the bright pink blossoms of the magnolia tree in Union Square Park can soothe the melancholy that lingers in my heart.

I pass the High Note, the pub where I met Derek, the guy I used to hook up with before Sam, and look through the front window. Derek was a fireman. A few guys are sitting at the bar, probably firemen, too. They seem to occupy the place most evenings. I don't have any desire to go in, but it gives me an idea, reminds me there's a way to loosen the tight knot in my neck and take the edge off all the anxiety I feel today. So I reach into my pocket, pull out my cell, and type as I stroll past the bar.

Elizabeth: Up for hanging out tonight?

"Hanging out" sounds so much better than *fucking me until I can't think straight anymore*. But running five miles this morning didn't clear my head, and I'm sure Sam won't mind. He's always been the initiator of our get-togethers and has mentioned more than once that I could reach out to him, too.

Fifteen minutes later, I arrive at Park Manor Nursing Home. I still don't feel great, but Sam's enthusiastic response to my text has helped, smoothing the edges of my jangled nerves. He's working tonight, though, so I won't see him until tomorrow.

I check in with the nurse at the desk on the third floor, and she hits the button to unlock the door to the memory care unit. It's easy to find Mr. Hank—he's laughing uproariously at the television in the lounge. The hearty sound lifts my mood more than anything else today. As I approach, he catches sight of me, his eyes twinkling with recognition.

"Elizabeth!" he says. "C'mon over here, young lady."

The warmth of his greeting thrills me. Despite the fact that he saved my life when I first moved to New York—two days shy of twenty years ago—by giving me a discount on rent and telling me where to look for a job, he sometimes can't recall who I am now. I hurry over, give him a big hug, and offer the bag of donuts I picked up from his favorite street vendor. They're chocolate, also his favorite—that's one thing he never forgets.

"Oh, you didn't have to do this."

"I wanted to." I smile, holding out the magazine and daily racing form I picked up at OTB earlier. "I shouldn't encourage your habit, but I thought you might like these, too."

Mr. Hank has been a gambler all of his life, mostly on the ponies. He can't go outside without the assistance of an aide anymore, and he refuses to use anything but a landline phone, yet somehow he's figured out how to create a FanDuel account on his iPad so he can bet ten dollars a day on horse races.

"You're too good to me." He pulls a chocolate donut from the bag and licks his lips. "You know, I used to make chocolate donuts. Just like this. Only better, of course."

I smile. "Of course. Your bakery was voted best donuts in New York City, eighteen years in a row."

He takes a bite, chews slowly, and I can tell he's savoring it.

"I was the only baker in my neighborhood to keep making them by hand after the donut machines came out." Another bite. This time with a groan of happiness as he chews.

Mr. Hank looks good today. Not all that different on the outside from twenty years ago, though maybe some wrinkles have grown deeper. I wish I'd appreciated how special he was when I first moved here. Sure, I knew he was helping me— and I said thank you, and I truly was grateful—but you never realize how much you appreciate someone until they're gone. Of course, he's still here. Most of him, anyway.

"What block was your bakery on?" I ask, even though I know the answer.

He chews, polishing off the last bite of his donut, and

something shifts in his eyes. He looks right at me and tilts his head. "What bakery?"

My heart sinks. "Oh, never mind. How was your donut?"

"Delicious. Want one?" He holds the bag out. "I made them myself. Hand-rolled, not by some machine."

Usually, I'd say no. But he has such hope in his eyes, I can't refuse. "I'd love one. Thank you."

"How are your studies, missy?"

I smile, say something about how they're going great, even though I've been the teacher for fifteen years now, not a student.

He nods. "I always knew you were a good one. Could tell from the moment I met you."

My heart squeezes. He was the only one who thought that back then.

"How's Walter doing?"

God, the brain is such a labyrinth of complexity. Precious memories fade like whispers in the wind while the worthless ones stay anchored. Walter was some jerk I dated briefly when I first moved here. But I've learned that it's best for Mr. Hank if I don't correct him and just continue with the conversation. So I force a smile. "Things are okay."

He makes a grunting sound. "I think it would be best you date men your own age. Older men have agendas."

This time my smile is real. Some things haven't changed after two decades. Sam is ten years older than me.

Forty-five minutes later, it's dinnertime for Mr. Hank. He opens his arms for a goodbye hug, and I step in, inhaling the scent of chocolate donuts and Old Spice. The smell is uniquely him. When I pull back, he clutches my arm for a second, gives me a big smile. "I love you, kid."

I press a kiss to his cheek. "I love you, too."

———

Two hours later, I'm soaking in the bathtub with a glass of wine. The stress I've felt all day dissolves like a sugar cube in a hot cup of tea, and I barely remember my name, much less today's date. I should have done this earlier; maybe I would've finished the work I need to complete before it got so late. I only teach two classes at Pace University during the summer, but one of them is an online yearlong fiction-writing seminar that just started, and it requires a lot more time than the English 101 course, which meets in person twice a week. There are two dozen first chapters of books waiting for me to read and critique. I'm the only professor who volunteered to take on the class when the school started offering it a decade ago, and it's a lot. But every once in a while, I find a diamond in the rough, a student who shows promise, and it makes all the extra hours worthwhile.

My iPad is on the bath mat, so I reach over the tub and grab it, along with my reading glasses, and press the button to fire it up. I preferred the days of students handing in papers that were on actual *paper*—much gentler on my eyes and easier to scribble a note in the margin with a red pen. But I'm a dinosaur at thirty-seven now.

I call up the first submission and read through the chapter. It's written well enough, but it doesn't grab my attention, doesn't make me excited to turn the next page or anxious to read the whole book. Polishing it likely won't make it a diamond, but I add a few comments, note a few suggestions to pick up the pace, and hit send.

I open the next file, sip my wine, and sink deeper into the warm tub. The document opens to a title page—*The Reckoning* by Hannah Greer. My course syllabus suggests not attempting to come up with a name for the book until the first draft is completed—so the title can capture the true spirit of the novel. But every year, one student does it anyway. The next page even has a dedication—that's something new.

> To anyone who has done something evil in the dark
> and believes it will never come to light.
> You're wrong. Your day of reckoning is coming.

Wow. Dark. Though it certainly has piqued my curiosity as a reader. I scroll to the next page and expect the creepy vibe to continue. But it doesn't. Instead, it opens with a prologue, a beautiful discussion about coming of age when life isn't so easy. It might not be what I expected with that title and dedication, but it's a strong start nonetheless. Immediately, I have a sense of the character—a young woman questioning her self-worth, on the cusp of going out into the world. I can identify with that. I add a quick comment, suggest the student describe the face her protagonist is making, rather than *tell* me she's sad.

I keep reading. The main character is a girl in her senior year of high school. A girl who looks at her *male* teacher differently than the other kids do. It sounds like she might have a crush. She's daydreaming, looking out the window at a yellow finch—

A yellow finch.

My breath comes up short.

My heart pounds.

I close my eyes and manage to shake it off, laugh out loud at myself even. I'm being ridiculous. It's just a bird. And find me a high school kid who doesn't stare out the window daydreaming at some point. I'm just being paranoid.

I read another paragraph, then another, but the farther I go, the more I realize I can't shake it off anymore. A sheen of sweat forms on my forehead, though the bathwater has grown cool. I read rapidly to the end and swallow.

This isn't fiction.

This is a real story, a *true* story.

But that's not possible. Is it? Maybe it's just . . . similar.

I wipe my forehead, grab my wineglass, and gulp the rest

down. Then I flip back to the beginning and read again. It's just a first chapter, but the names, what the teacher does, it's . . .

Definitely not fiction.

And while I might've only read the beginning of the story, I already know the ending. Mr. Sawyer has an affair with my best friend, Jocelyn, and winds up dead.

Because *I killed him*. Exactly twenty years ago today.

CHAPTER

2

Chapter 1—Hannah's Novel

Jocelyn stared out the window, watching as a bright yellow finch landed on a branch, bringing its nest full of babies their regurgitated meal. It was supposed to be innate, wasn't it? The nurture of a parent—feeding, bathing . . . physical affection. Yet this morning *she'd* been the one to wake her mother, make her breakfast, help her into the shower. Then again, finches couldn't stumble to the liquor store and pick up a plastic bottle of vodka that made them forget their role in life.

"Miss Burton . . ." Her teacher stopped at her desk. "Are you with us this afternoon?"

She blinked a few times and cleared her throat, feeling her cheeks turn pink. "Sorry. Yes."

Mr. Sawyer placed a packet of stapled papers face down on her desk—*her graded assignment*—and waited until she looked up at him. "See me after class, please."

Great. Just great.

Jocelyn glanced once more at the finch before forcing her attention to the front of the classroom. Her eyes landed on Mr. Sawyer's ass as he continued down the row, handing papers back. It wasn't her fault her gaze lingered. The man had a good body—way better than the boys her own age. She chewed her lip, contemplating how many hours of exercise her English teacher must do. to look like that. Firm and fit, his ass complemented the rest of the man—broad shoulders, a narrow waist, and a smile that belied the sternness of his voice.

Her friend Ivy leaned over and whispered, "Close your mouth. You're drooling."

Jocelyn squinted. "I am not."

Ivy chuckled and turned over her own paper. C−.

And Mr. Sawyer hadn't asked *her* to stay after class . . .

Jocelyn had thought she'd nailed the assignment. She drew in a deep, steadying breath before flipping it over to check her grade. A+ was written at the top in red, a big fat circle around it.

Oh, wow.

Ivy leaned over again and snuck a peek, rolling her eyes.

After that, Jocelyn managed to pay attention for the rest of class. When the period was over, she approached Mr. Sawyer's desk. Without looking up at her, he shuffled some papers and gestured to the first row. "Have a seat."

Once the last students cleared out, he closed the classroom door and leaned a hip against the front of his desk.

Jocelyn sat up a little taller.

"Talk to me." Mr. Sawyer folded his arms across his chest. "Do you have an interest in studying writing in college?"

She shrugged. "I'm not sure I'm even going to college."

"Why not?"

Jocelyn's eyes shifted to the window. She couldn't see the finch now, but it was on her mind. She didn't want to say her only goal in life was to find a job that paid enough money to get the hell away from her mother, so she said nothing.

"Jocelyn?"

Her eyes jumped to meet Mr. Sawyer's.

"Look at me when I speak to you."

She nodded. But instinct drew her eyes down again, so it wasn't as simple as it sounded. Especially not when Mr. Sawyer—her secret crush—held her gaze in silence for a full minute.

Eventually, he smiled. "Thank you. I think you're an excellent storyteller. Do you enjoy writing?"

Jocelyn nodded.

"Speak, Miss Burton. Use your voice. You're not a bobblehead."

She met his eyes once again. "Yes."

"Yes what?"

"Yes, I enjoy writing."

"Excellent. Tell me what you do in your free time. Do you write for fun? Do you keep a daily diary?"

"I don't have a diary I write in every day, but I keep a notebook that I like to write random things in."

"The yellow one with a butterfly on the front that sometimes you have out during class?"

Jocelyn looked down. "Sorry."

"I'm not looking for an apology. Good writers write when it strikes them. Tell me, what kinds of things do you write about in your notebook?"

Jocelyn shrugged. "I don't know. Stuff."

"Do you write about boys?"

Her cheeks grew warm. "Not usually."

"Do you have a boyfriend?"

"No."

"Ever had one?"

"Not one that's worth writing about."

Mr. Sawyer's lip twitched. "Do you write about your friends?"

"Not really."

"So I'll ask you again, Miss Burton. What is it you write about in your journal, if not boys and friends?"

"I don't know. I guess I mostly write what I'm feeling."

"And what is it that you feel?"

Jocelyn's pink cheeks burned crimson. "Angry."

"Good. Now we're getting somewhere. Angry about what?"

"My mother. She's a drunk."

"What about your father?"

"I've never met him."

Mr. Sawyer rubbed his bottom lip with his thumb as he stared at Jocelyn. His eyes were a deep, intense green. They seemed to darken as the seconds ticked by. It made Jocelyn want to squirm in her seat, but she knew he'd see it, probably call her out on it, too. So she did her best to stay rooted in place.

"Williamsburg College isn't too far and has a creative writing scholarship. The top submission gets a full ride. Second and third place receive partial tuition funding. I can help you improve your writing. It's not something I do for many students. But I think you might be special. However, you'll need to work on becoming more disciplined. You're easily distracted."

"How do I do that? Study more?"

Mr. Sawyer's eyes gleamed. "Discipline doesn't have to be about studying. It can be learning self-restraint in general. For example, you fidget a lot and often stare out the window."

"How do I fix that?"

"We'll work on it. That is, if you're interested in my help."

Jocelyn couldn't nod fast enough. "I'm interested."

A ghost of a smile tugged at the corner of his lips, and he pointed a few rows away. "Good. Meet me here Friday. Four o'clock."

CHAPTER

3

It's a bright spring day, warm air floating between campus buildings, navy-and-gold Pace flags fluttering in the wind. Usually, I'd grab a coffee and sit and enjoy the sunshine, or maybe finish up grading on a park bench. But today, I have a singular goal.

The registrar's office is in a big, modern brick building with a glass front. I find the entrance, step through the automatic doors, and come to a stop. To my right, there's a student help desk, but I need more than they can give. My purse vibrates as I look around. Digging my cell from inside, I find Sam's name flashing on the screen. We have plans for tonight, which I forgot all about until this minute. It seems impossible that it was only yesterday I texted him. Yesterday, when my biggest problem was that the date on the calendar read May 20. Now there's someone who knows *what happened* leading up to that date twenty years ago, someone who has threatened *a reckoning*. I ignore Sam's call, too anxious to get the information I came for to let anything else distract me right now.

The main office is a DMV-like setup, with seating to wait and numbered stations, staff calling up students. I peer around for someone to help me. Of course, only two of the stations out of twelve are currently staffed with employees. One of them I recognize. The twentysomething doesn't just work here. Eric's also a student. He catches my eye and smiles. I've dealt with him a few times before, when I had scheduling issues and errors in my class roster. He's the sort whose eyes rest on you too long, who remembers your name and classroom when he shouldn't. And every single time I've spoken to him, he's given me a compliment of some sort. But that might work to my advantage today.

He finishes with a student, so I step up to his station. "Hi, Eric."

"Aaron," he corrects, yet smiles. "But how are you, Elizabeth? It's been a while."

I should remind him it's Professor Davis, not *Elizabeth*, but instead, I smile. "Right, of course. Aaron. I'm doing well. How about you?"

"Can't complain." He eyes my hair. "I've always wanted to ask you . . . Is that your natural color? Usually, red is sort of orangey, but yours is more like a cinnamon."

Who asks a woman if she dyes her hair? Certainly not a student. Yet I twirl my hair like some flirty teenager and lean in, because I'm not above anything today. "It is. Do you like it?"

He leans closer, too. "It's beautiful. Makes your green eyes stand out."

Oh God. It's difficult not to roll those eyes. I need to cut to the chase. "Listen, I need help, Aaron. Do you think you can help me?"

"Of course. Whatever you need."

Perfect.

"I'm having trouble reaching a student. She's not answering her student email, so I was hoping she might have another email listed in the school's records? Or a phone number or an address? Some other method of contact."

"Oh, that's . . ." He swallows, looks down at his hands. When he looks back up, he won't meet my eyes. "I'm afraid it's against policy to give that out to anyone, even professors." Aaron fidgets. "I'm sorry."

"It's really important," I press, dropping my voice. "She could fail the class if I can't get ahold of her. I would feel really awful. Aaron?"

"Yes, ma'am?" He looks up, locks eyes with me.

"I think this once we could make an exception, right? Help out a fellow student. And because we're friends. Right?" Another smile, just between us.

"Well . . . okay. But don't tell my boss, all right?"

"Oh, I thought you were in charge." I slide him a paper where I've written down what I know about Hannah Greer. "This is her name and student number."

"Let me . . ." He types away, clicks the mouse, then pulls the scrap of paper toward him and scribbles a Gmail account. "Oh, interesting," he mutters. "This might be why you can't get ahold of her."

My ears perk up. "Oh? Is something wrong?"

"No. But she's a visiting student." He slides the paper back. "Nonmatriculated. It looks like yours is the only class she's taking."

I pause, sirens blaring in my head. So "Hannah" could be anyone, anyone who *only* signed up for my class.

"Thank you so much, Aaron. I owe you."

Stepping outside lets me breathe a little easier, but not for long. My nerves come back full force as I glance down at the sheet. *Hannah Greer*. I have a Gmail now. I would have preferred an address. I've slowed to a stop, lost in thought, staring down at the scrap of paper, when someone bumps into me.

"Excuse me," the man mutters. He's tall, wearing a dark jacket, and continues striding down the sidewalk. I look up, watch him go. There's something familiar about him, but then again, I've had hundreds, thousands of students here. Of course I recognize some. I glance over my shoulder, cross the street, and hurry toward my office. I can't help it—once I'm across, I look back one more time. The man in the dark jacket, he's stopped. And he's looking right at me.

Is he *watching* me?

Did he bump into me on purpose?

Could *he* be Hannah?

No, no, no. I'm being paranoid. Have been since I read that damn chapter. The chapter that's a *coincidence.* A very big one, but a coincidence nonetheless. It has to be. Once I sort out who this student is, I'll know for sure.

Back in my office, I pull off my jacket, unwind my silk scarf. They both go on a hanger, and I adjust my blinds so the outside is blocked—as if someone might want to see what I'm doing. I sit down to type at my laptop, speedy pecks of keys, entering the Gmail account and hitting search. I already know from my Google research this morning that the name alone returns millions of hits. It's too common. *Maybe that's the reason they chose it.* But nothing comes up with the Gmail account, either.

No social media tied to it. No image of a person.

I huff in frustration and repeat the same search, this time adding the name Hannah Greer to the Gmail account—still nothing usable comes up. My phone vibrates from my purse, and I pull it out, annoyed by the interruption.

Sam.

Again.

I need to cancel tonight, so I swipe to answer.

"Hi, Sam." I stare at the tiny cactus on my desk, the one that's shriveled into a collection of brown, dead spikes—a sign that I should not be in charge of the care of any living creature.

"Hey. Sorry to interrupt your day, but I thought I'd see if maybe you wanted to come to my place tonight," he says. "I can cook us some dinner. I've been told I make a mean chicken piccata."

Sam and I don't have that type of relationship. He's a nice guy, a handsome police detective who will probably make some lucky lady a great boyfriend or husband someday, but that's not what I'm looking for, and I was up front about that from the beginning. He's been good with our arrangement, too. Though lately, I've suspected he wants more. "I think I actually need to cancel tonight. I have a lot of work to finish up for this class I'm teaching."

"Oh. Then maybe we can just hang out like usual and do dinner another night?" A car door slams shut, and the city sounds in the background go quiet. "I caught this call last night. I'm going to be pretty busy with it for a while, at least once the autopsy comes back in tomorrow."

The word *autopsy* makes me go still. "Someone died?"

"Well, yeah. It's New York City. We average more than one homicide a day."

My voice climbs an octave. "That's . . . that's awful."

"You get used to it, sadly," he says. "Looks like an older-man-younger-woman thing this time."

My eyes flare. "What happened?"

"The suspect was his mistress. We can't find her. She took off, but no one else had motive."

I swallow back the rise of fear. "How much younger was she?"

Sam chuckles. "Not getting ideas, are you? Killing an older man you're sleeping with?"

"Of course not." I force humor into my voice, levity. Inside, though, I'm sinking deeper into a dark place. Nothing about the last twenty-four hours feels like coincidence right now. "How would I ever get that home-cooked meal then?"

"I could make dinner at your place while you work to-night. You gotta take a break to eat sometime, right?"

I open my mouth to tell him I can't. The last thing I need is to spend time with a police detective right now, but the scrap of paper on my desk catches my eye, gives me an idea. "Hey, I have a question."

"What's that?"

"Is there a way to trace an email address?"

"Just an email address? Or an email received?"

"The address."

"An email address by itself can be tough. But you can usually trace an email received back to the approximate location of the sender using their IP address, as long as they're not using a VPN. Though you would need an incoming email for that." He pauses, and the wheels turn in my head. "You need to track someone down?"

"Just wondering." I chew the end of a pen, practically hearing the curiosity on his end as silence fills the line. "One of the students in my fiction-writing class had a character track someone's location from their email in their story. I didn't know if it was accurate or not."

"Oh, gotcha."

"Listen, Sam, someone just walked into my office," I lie. "So I have to run. Maybe we can get together next week?"

"Yeah, okay."

"Good luck with your . . . homicide."

We disconnect. My brain tingles with the information he's given me. I want to think about the woman murdering the older man, but I've got other things to keep me busy.

I pull up a new email, type in the address Aaron provided, and compose yet another lie:

Hannah,

I received the chapter you submitted through Blackboard. However, for some reason I was unable to open it. It's a system glitch, which happens occasionally. Can you please email it to me directly? At this address would be fine.

I stare at the screen. Hit send. And the wait for a response begins.

CHAPTER

4

Normally, on Thursdays after I've finished teaching, I head to the yoga studio across from campus, but today I skip exercising. I also haven't been running every morning like I usually do. It's been almost a week since I emailed the student who submitted the ominous chapter, and I can't seem to quell the unsettled feeling in the pit of my stomach.

I've considered calling Ivy. The three of us—Ivy, Jocelyn, and me—were inseparable back in the day, the three musketeers. A trio of lost souls who bonded over being dirt-poor and neglected by our alcoholic, single moms. Or in Ivy's case, alcoholic *and* drug addicted. We told each other *everything*. So it's hard to believe it's been twenty years since I've spoken to either one of them. I know where Ivy is at least. Jocelyn, though, she disappeared the day I did, two decades ago. I went north, and she went south to Florida, and that's the last I heard of her. I'm not sure whether I should try to make contact with either of them. What if someone is trying to smoke us out, cause us to make mistakes? No, it's best to keep to myself. Besides, it could all still be a coincidence, couldn't it? I once read an article about identical twin brothers separated at birth. They never even knew about each other, yet they married women with the same names and gave their firstborn children and dogs the same names.

It's not impossible.

That's what I keep telling myself.

But today I need to do a little more digging, a little more research—though not from my laptop this time. Everything we do in today's world leaves an electronic footprint, and one can never be too careful.

My eyes are alert, scanning face after face as I walk to the library. Three kids fresh out of high school kick around a hacky sack to the left, a redhead twirling her hair and making googly eyes at a nice-looking guy with broad shoulders sits on a bench to the right—he's too busy to notice, checking out the ass of every woman who passes. Before last week, I wouldn't have seen a single face, but suddenly everyone is a suspect to rule out.

Inside the library, I take the stairs to the second floor. My pulse quickens as I approach the bank of cubicles, each equipped with a desktop available for anyone's use. There are more than a dozen, yet only one is occupied. Everyone has a laptop or iPad these days.

I choose the workstation farthest from the woman working and glance around before pulling out a chair. No one seems to be paying attention, so I hit the space bar to wake up the screen and jump right into it, clicking the Google icon from the menu bar, then typing:

D-A-M-O-N S-A-W-Y-E-R

My hand shakes as I hit the enter key. It's a name I'd managed to not think about in a very long time—almost two decades—until last week.

The search return at the top of the page is the website of Chapman and Sons Funeral Home. Obituary of Damon Sawyer. I've read it before. Hundreds of times, a lifetime ago. But I click into it and read.

Damon Sawyer passed away tragically at age thirty-nine on May 20. He is survived by his devoted wife, Candice,

and a seven-year-old son. Damon was born and
raised in Minton Parish. Upon graduating from the
University of Southern Louisiana with a degree in
secondary education, Damon returned home to
Minton Parish to become a teacher at the local high
school he had attended. He was a beloved member of
the teaching community and earned the title of Teacher
of the Year three times—a testament to how much he
gave to his students.

How much he gave . . .

Scrolling the rest of the results, I find most of it vaguely
familiar—a few mentions from Minton High School, an old
article from the *Minton Herald*, triathlon results from twenty-
five years ago. I guess when you're dead, very little gets added
to your Google search. At the bottom of the page, though,
there is something new—another obituary on the website
of Chapman and Sons Funeral Home. Obituary of Candice
Maynard-Sawyer.

His wife. I click into it. It's dated five months ago.

Candice Maynard-Sawyer passed away at age
fifty-eight on December 13. Candice met the love of
her life, Damon Sawyer, while attending college at
the University of Southern Louisiana. Together they
had one son. Candice was a Eucharistic minister for
more than thirty years, bringing communion to elderly
church members who were unable to attend mass. Her
yearslong battle with heart disease ends only for her to
be reunited with her beloved husband and our Father in
heaven.

Beloved. What a joke.

The nerves I felt typing Damon's name are suddenly replaced by anger. I tug at the neck of my blouse. Why is it so

damn hot in here? I need some fresh air, so I close out of the web page and gather my things. But as I start to get up, I think better of it. There are other names I haven't searched in a long time. So I type:

I-V-Y L-E-I-G-H-T-O-N

Unlike Mr. Sawyer's, this name comes back with a ton of hits—the first of which is from Minton Parish Child Protective Services. A few years back, I had a rare, lucid conversation with my mother, and she mentioned that Ivy had become a social worker. The irony isn't lost on me that the child who used to get removed from her home has now become the remover. Curious, I click into the web page, and I'm taken aback when a picture of my old best friend pops up. She hasn't aged so well, but there's no doubt it's her. Plump face, tired eyes, gray-streaked frumpy hair—the same gummy smile that shows off the tiny chip in her front tooth she got when we were riding bicycles at seven. I read the bio and stare at her for a while. She lives in Clarion, a stone's throw from where we grew up and where she apparently still works. But it couldn't be Ivy who sent me the chapter, could it? She's the only person in the world who stands to lose almost as much as I do by dredging up things from the past. Plus, she has *five* kids. She wouldn't have time to dig skeletons from closets. But before I click back, I jot down her email and telephone number—just in case.

I look around before typing again. The one woman using a computer isn't paying me any mind, and other than her, it's a ghost town up here.

My eyes well up as I type the next name.

J-O-C-E-L-Y-N B-U-R-T-O-N

More than seventeen thousand hits. I try adding *Florida* at the end, since that's where she went after leaving Louisiana, but it doesn't narrow it down much. So I spend the better part of three hours scrolling page after page, looking for anything that seems like her. But I come up empty.

I slump back into the chair and sigh. *Where do I go from*

here? I want to reach out to Ivy and Jocelyn, but we made a pact before I left—never to contact each other and never to talk about anything that happened with anyone. Jocelyn was adamant that we never cross paths again, and it looks as though she made sure we wouldn't.

As if on cue, my phone vibrates. It's Sam. I haven't heard from him since I canceled getting together last week.

Sam: Any chance you're free tonight?

My first instinct is to say no. But then I glance again at the screen in front of me. Seventeen thousand, one hundred and forty-eight hits for Jocelyn Burton. There must be a better way to find her, and to find Hannah Greer. Who better than a police detective to give me some guidance? I nibble on my lip, debating for a few minutes, before finally typing back.

Elizabeth: Sure. My place or yours?

I wind up meeting Sam at a restaurant, rather than one of our apartments like we usually do when we get together.

"This is nice, isn't it?" He smiles as we eat. "I mean, what we usually do is pretty damn nice, too. But I like taking you out. We should do it more often."

Shoot. This was a mistake. I knew it when he suggested meeting for dinner, but I didn't push back. Sam seems like a great guy. Not once in the few months we've been getting together has he shown any red flags. He's been a perfect gentleman, except in the bedroom, where he's aggressive, which I rather like. But I learned years ago to be up front with the expectations I have of men. Most are thrilled to find a woman only looking for sex. Once you take the next step, it's difficult to pull back without upsetting the other person.

After we've finished, I look him in the eyes. "I like you, Sam. You seem like a genuinely nice guy."

He frowns. "I hear a *but* coming . . ."

I smile sadly. "But I'm not looking for a relationship."

"It was just dinner."

"I know. But I want to be up front with you."

He sighs. "Is it me?"

I shake my head. "No, it's me."

"We haven't talked too much about our previous partners. Did something happen to sour you on relationships?"

You mean like a deadbeat dad, a string of "uncles" who used my mother, and a teacher who abused the trust of my best friend? Yet I shake my head. "No. I just like to keep things simple."

Sam rakes a hand through his hair. "All right. If that's the way you want it."

"I'm sorry."

"It's fine." He smiles, trying to make light of the moment, but it doesn't quite reach his eyes. "The alternative isn't a bad consolation prize."

A few minutes later, the waitress brings the check. Sam takes out his credit card and sticks it in the leather padfolio.

I hold out my hand. "I'd like to pay half, if you don't mind. I'll give you cash."

Sam frowns. "Really? You can't let me pay for one meal? Do you want the receipt for the condoms, too? Maybe we can calculate how much one from the box costs and you can leave the cash on the nightstand before you slip out each time?"

"I'm sorry. I didn't mean to upset you. I just prefer to pay my own way."

Sam says something under his breath and tosses a few twenties into the check holder, taking his card back out. "Whatever. It's fine."

I open my wallet and count fifty dollars. But as I pull the cash from the compartment, something tucked between the bills falls out—a slip of paper. It floats to the floor, closer to Sam's feet, and he reaches down and picks it up, extending it to me across the table.

"Louisiana, right?" he says.

I freeze. "What?"

He looks down at the ink on the paper, at Ivy's phone number. "The area code. It's Louisiana, isn't it? My ex-partner retired there to be near his kid who went to college at Tulane and stayed. His area code is 337."

I snatch the paper back. "Yes, it's Louisiana."

"That's where you were born, right?"

I blink a few times. There is no way in hell I told him that. I don't tell anyone where I'm from. "How do you know that?"

Sam looks away, clears his throat. "You must've told me."

"I absolutely did not tell you."

His shoulders slump, and he hangs his head. He knows he's been caught in a lie. "I, uh, ran you when we first started dating."

"Ran me? What does that mean?"

"Through the system. At work. I do it to everyone I date. You can never be too careful, especially in New York."

"You *investigated* me?" My heart thumps around in my chest, but not just at the indignity of being spied on. *What if he found something about what happened before?*

"Not investigated. Just punched you into the system. You know, to see if you had any priors or anything. System also gives all last known addresses. It showed you grew up in Louisiana. I was surprised. You don't have a Southern accent."

It feels like I've just had my clothes unwillingly ripped from my body, and I'm standing naked. I should have known better than to date a *detective*. Of course he'd look me up. My head spins while I take in the fact that Sam has known where I grew up for the three months we've been spending time together, and yet never once mentioned that he knew I'd lied to him about being from New York. Paranoia creeps in. I start to remember other things—like that time we were at his apartment and I went to the bathroom. When I came out, he had my phone in his hand. He claimed he'd picked it up instead of his by accident. Was he lying? And another time when he stayed over, and I found him looking through the end table drawer in my living room. He claimed he was looking for the remote, but the remote was sitting right on the coffee table.

The waitress comes over to collect the check, but I haven't yet put my half inside. The cash is still in my hand. I open the padfolio, then look up at Sam's face. "On second thought . . ." I shove the bills back into my purse. "You can pay the whole damn bill."

"Elizabeth—"

Sam says more, but I don't stick around to hear it. I'm already out of my seat and taking long strides toward the restaurant door. He catches up to me outside, just as I lower my arm and a cab pulls to the curb.

"Elizabeth, wait!"

"No, Sam. I'm leaving."

"Just come home with me. Let's talk about this. It's really not a big deal."

I ignore him and climb into the back of the cab, slamming the door shut.

"Twenty-Second and Second, please," I say to the cabbie.

He looks in the rearview mirror. "The guy outside is still talking to you."

"Just drive. I'm done talking to him."

CHAPTER

5

I *don't even like roses.*

I pluck a petal from one of the flowers and briefly consider texting Sam to provide him with my thoughts on the originality of this delivery, which arrived three days ago. But that would mean answering one of his four apology texts, something I'm far from ready to do at the moment. I still can't get over that he *investigated* me.

"Hey. You want to grab a bite to eat?" Aiden's belt jingles as he walks from the bedroom to the living room, buckling it. Or maybe his name is Cayden? I'm not actually sure.

"That's not necessary. You can go."

He chuckles. "*Damn.* That's cold. I guess you really meant it when you said you were looking for a quick hookup only."

I smile politely. "Yes, I did."

"Can I see you again?"

"I doubt it. But thank you. I had a good time."

The guy shakes his head. Though at least he doesn't argue. Aiden or Cayden *or whatever the heck his name is* grabs his jacket from the chair and heads for the door. "Take care, Emily."

I don't bother to correct him. Once he's gone, I latch the chain on the top lock and fill the kettle with tap water. My insomnia is back. It's been years since I had trouble sleeping, but I still remember all the remedies I used to try. I've been drinking lavender relaxation tea every night for the last week. It didn't work half as well as my Tinder date to relieve the stress knots in my neck, but maybe the combination will finally allow me a good night's rest. Sleep has eluded me since that mysterious chapter arrived ten long days ago. It doesn't help that I still haven't heard from the student who turned it in.

While I wait for the water to boil, I pluck more petals from the roses. Three flowers are completely dismantled now, and I leave their barren sticks in the vase and the petals strewn all over the kitchen counter. The look is more interesting than the original.

Once the kettle sings, I steep the tea bag and decide I'm not tired enough for bed yet. So I grab my laptop and a stack of English 101 exams I've already marked and sit down on the couch to enter the grades into Pace's system. My computer fires up to the last page I've visited—the one I've stalked all week—my email. Nothing new has arrived since the last time I checked a few hours ago. At least that's how it looks until my email syncs, and then suddenly it shows a new message on the screen.

It's from her—Hannah Greer.

My heart pounds so hard that I have to shut my eyes and take a few deep breaths before I'm calm enough to read. When I click to open the message, I think I stop breathing altogether.

Professor Davis,

I apologize for taking so long to respond. I hadn't checked this email until now. I assumed any correspondence would come from the school email students are instructed to use, not my private one. Attached please find the original file that was

submitted. Please let me know if you have any
difficulties opening this one.

Thank you,
Hannah Greer

The message is innocuous enough, a typical response a *real* student might send upon receiving an email from a teacher. But the response isn't really what I'm after. I've already memorized the steps required to determine the location of the sender of an email, so I go right to the header, click to the received line, hit reply, and select show original to open full details on the origin. Once I find the IP address, I copy it and open a new window with the IP-lookup tool I've bookmarked. Instantly, a map pops up with a red dot planted on the United States. I can easily tell the sender is not in New York—the mark is too far south—though I have to zoom in to see exactly where the email has been sent from. When I do, my heart stops.

Saint James, Louisiana.

There's a scream building in my lungs, and I swallow hard to keep it down.

Saint James is not far from Minton Parish. I click on the map's plus sign to zoom in closer, see exactly how far it is. There isn't a scale, but knowing the roads and surrounding cities, I'm certain it's not more than a ten-minute drive. My eyes trace the journey, lingering on the small town I'd hoped never to think about again. But then they catch on something else—a city an equal distance from Saint James, but in the opposite direction. *Clarion.* Where Ivy's bio said she lives. I gnaw on my lip, considering . . .

An advertisement on the IP-locator page snags my attention. It's for a VPN service—virtual private network. I read about them recently, too. For eight bucks a month, anyone could have sent the email I just received from anywhere in the world and made it look like it came from Louisiana. A VPN establishes a digital connection between a computer and a remote server, masking the true IP address. Disguising your location can be as simple as clicking a box and picking a city. For all I know, the sender could be sitting in the apartment next to me.

Or in Clarion, Louisiana.

Or in the precinct a few blocks away.

Sam.

My mind keeps circling back to him. A skilled investigator would know how to hide anything. And apparently Sam has known I'm from Louisiana for months. Could he be part of some large, multistate investigation—the New York arm supporting the two-man Minton Parish police department? I think about the day we met. I was at a movie by myself—the cinema in the Village that only shows classics—watching *Citizen Kane*. He struck up a conversation at the concession stand and paid for my popcorn. After the movie, he found me again and asked if I wanted to go for a drink. Could he have been following me back then? We'd been seeing each other once a week for three months now, and, come to think of it, he's never mentioned going to see another classic. In fact, most of the movies he's mentioned watching are the polar opposite of old-time black-and-white films. He seems to have a penchant for action movies and sci-fi.

I eye the mug in front of me—*calming tea, my ass*—and get up and dump the contents into the sink. This is a job for whiskey. So I pour two fingers into the still-warm mug and knock back the amber fluid like it's medicine. It burns as it slides down my throat, but I like the way it feels.

Pain and pleasure are like darkness is to light. One precedes the other.

I remember Jocelyn mumbling that over and over the day I found her, beaten and bloodied.

It's amazing the memories that come flooding back when you least expect them. I pour more whiskey, sit back down with my laptop, and do what I do best: talk myself down from the ledge.

That chapter is just a crazy coincidence.

I bet a teacher grooming a student is not even that uncommon, sadly. There's probably a handbook that lays out all the steps:

Step 1. Form a bond. Find common interest and hobbies—writing perhaps.

Step 2. Strip them of all dignity and reduce them to their most vulnerable self—kneeling while reading their biggest fears aloud is a handy-dandy instrument here.

Step 3. Fill a need; provide comfort.

Steps 4, 5, and 6. Isolate. Control. Begin next level of abuse.

It's just a big, fat, screwed-up coincidence. The product of someone's imagination—a *twisted* imagination, but imaginary all the same. When the next chapters arrive, the characters' paths will diverge. I'll be chiding myself over how paranoid I was, how much time and energy I wasted worrying about something that didn't exist.

I close my eyes and inhale deeply. *Just a fluke.* Happenstance—the story, the location of the sender, a detective knowing more about me than he's let on . . . all of it. After a while, I start to feel a little better, a little calmer. But then my laptop chimes, alerting me that another new email has arrived. I click over, and whatever peace I've managed to muster disappears faster than the color from my face.

Professor Davis,

I thought I'd send the next assignment, which is due in a few days, just in case you have trouble opening my document through the portal again.

I hope the story has caught your attention and you enjoy how it unfolds.

Thank you,
Hannah Greer

CHAPTER

6

Chapter 2—Hannah's Novel

"Oh my God, that's exactly what she sounds like."

Jocelyn shut her locker, laughing at a joke Lucas had told. They weren't a *thing*—but a few weeks back, they'd fooled around. Even though Lucas's home life was shittier than hers, he always seemed to have a smile on his face. Jocelyn appreciated that quality more than most girls her age, who were focused only on looks. She found Lucas unconventionally handsome, with his shaggy hair, prominent nose, and wiry frame.

"I gotta run," Lucas said. "My class is at the other end of the building, and Dickson locks the door if you're one second late. I already have detention twice this week."

"See you later."

Jocelyn had finished packing her books into her book bag when she felt a presence come up behind her, just before a heavy palm wrapped over her shoulder. Somehow, she knew who it was.

"Hello, Jocelyn."

"Hi, Mr. Sawyer." She turned to look up at him. His presence made her feel calmer. And yet nervous, too. How was that possible?

He lifted his chin down the hall. "Who was that?"

"Lucas."

Mr. Sawyer was silent, yet the tension set in his jaw spoke volumes. He was waiting for more.

"He's just a friend."

The muscle in his cheek ticked.

"My . . . ummm, friend is sort of hanging around with him. He was looking for her."

Mr. Sawyer's face softened. "Keep your focus on your schoolwork. Not boys."

Jocelyn nodded. "I do."

He smiled. "Good. How are you today?"

Her insides grew warm. No one ever cared to ask how she was doing. "I'm okay." The memory of how she'd felt alone in the classroom with him the other day hit, and she lowered her gaze to stare at his shirt. A crisp button-up, ironed, neat. It made her realize she should be trying harder, in her slightly rumpled secondhand clothes.

"Good. I have an assignment for you."

She couldn't help it—her eyes shot up, meeting his, wide with curiosity, excitement. But she immediately grew nervous that she might disappoint him. "Okay." Her voice was tentative.

"I'd like you to write an essay for me on how your mother's drinking makes you feel. Really . . ." He paused, gave it a moment's thought. "Pour all your heart and emotion into it. Strike to the bone. Understand? I want *all* of your emotion. Don't leave anything unsaid." His hand touched her shoulder again, and a jolt shot through her body. She liked it, hoped he'd never move.

But a moment later, it was gone. Cool air filled the space between them. A slam of a nearby locker brought her back to real life.

"Yes, sir," she murmured. "I won't leave anything unsaid."

"Good. Now get to class. Keep under the radar. Don't look for trouble."

That night, Jocelyn set aside everything—even eating
dinner—to write. And write she did. Every time she paused,
she remembered the way Mr. Sawyer had looked at her, the
way her skin lit up when he touched her—thinking about
it, goose bumps sprang up all over her body. She forced
her focus back to the task at hand and let emotions pour
from her. Words flew from her keyboard like nothing she'd
experienced before.

The following day, she waited until after school,
then went to Mr. Sawyer's classroom. She knocked quietly
on his door, and he opened it immediately, like he'd
been waiting for her to arrive.

His dark eyes studied her. "Yes?" he asked curtly.

"I have it." She held up the sheaf of papers, neatly
stapled together. "The assignment."

"Good." He opened the door, allowed her entrance.
Jocelyn took a few steps in and paused, feeling a thrill
run up her spine when she heard the loud *click* as he
engaged the lock on the door behind her.

Her stomach swam, but not with nerves this time—with
excitement, even if she didn't fully understand why.
She *did* know this meant they couldn't be interrupted.
That she, alone, would receive his attention until he
dismissed her.

Mr. Sawyer stepped in front of her—right up in her
space. Like sunshine, he made her warm, and she wanted
to bask in the glow.

She lifted her paper. He looked at it but didn't take
it from her hands. Instead, he turned on his heel, went
back to his desk, perched on the edge, and studied her. She
blushed under the intense scrutiny. And suddenly, she
remembered how much truth she'd put in the paper she'd
written. How much of herself—her cringeworthy, true self—
she'd written into each page. What would he think of her
after he read them?

Her mouth opened—she was going to tell him that,

actually, she should edit it one last time, or that
she'd realized she forgot something or—

"Please kneel, Jocelyn."

Her body froze. *Kneel?* She laughed nervously. "You're
joking, right?"

But there wasn't a trace of humor in her teacher's
face. Mr. Sawyer pushed off the desk, rising to full
height, which now seemed taller than she'd ever noticed.
"I will not repeat myself, Miss Burton. When you're in
this classroom, receiving my help, you'll do as I say.
Is that understood?"

"Uhh . . . yeah."

"The word is *yes*, not *yeah*."

"Oh. Yes."

"Yes, what?"

"Yes, sir."

He smiled, and Jocelyn's eyes locked with Mr. Sawyer's
once again. A shiver ran up her spine—not the creepy-
crawly kind, but the kind that comes from a surge of
excitement pulsing through your body. She liked the way
he looked at her. She liked having his sole focus, as
being the object of attention was an honor rarely be-
stowed on her.

"Very good. Now . . . right there." He pointed to the
floor next to a desk. "Kneel, keep your eyes down, and
read the essay to me aloud."

Again, she almost questioned him—why did she have to
kneel? But his face was stern, and he was waiting, so
instead, she swallowed her words. After all, she'd come
here. She wanted his help and had agreed to write this
thing. So she couldn't back out now.

The hard laminate floor was cool against her knees.
She cleared her throat, traced the first printed words
with her eyes. Was she really going to do this?

"'My first memory of my mother . . .'" she began.
And suddenly, she was reading. Remembering each moment
she'd written into this essay, how alone she'd felt. All
the nights she'd cried herself to sleep, wondering if

when she woke, her mother would be home. And if she was home, if she'd still be alive, or if she'd have killed herself with alcohol and drugs. Before she knew what was happening, Jocelyn was sobbing through her words, hot trails of tears streaking down her cheeks, no doubt marring the eyeliner she'd put on just for Mr. Sawyer.

Eventually, Jocelyn got through all six pages. She read the last line, the last words, and stifled back a last sob, embarrassed at herself—how weak she was, how she couldn't even read the paper she'd written aloud without turning into a baby.

Mr. Sawyer remained at his desk, unmoving. Watching her. There was a gleam in his eyes, something that made her think he liked the essay—but then his jaw hardened.

"Where are you supposed to be looking, Miss Burton?"

She instantly bowed her head again, looking back at the floor, at her inked pages covered in splotchy tears.

"That was very good," he said. And her pulse quickened. He thought her writing was *very good*. "But," he bit out, "you need more discipline. Stay on your knees. Eyes down."

She waited for further instructions, but there were none. She didn't dare look up, but she could hear him, moving about the classroom, jostling things at his desk. Five minutes passed, then ten. Fifteen, twenty. Her knees ached, her palms were sweaty, and her throat felt swollen. More than anything, she wanted to stretch her legs out, just for a moment of relief. But still, she stayed there.

She wanted to please Mr. Sawyer.

Eventually, shoes came into view. Shiny, leather, expensive-looking ones. So much nicer than her grubby sneakers.

"Jocelyn, stand up."

She wobbled as she rose, a steady hand on her elbow keeping her from toppling over. Mr. Sawyer gently touched her cheek, and she nearly flinched in surprise. But when he stroked her skin with his thumb, she leaned into his palm. It felt so good, like he cherished her.

"You are beautiful, Jocelyn. Do you know that?"

She didn't believe him, but she didn't want to challenge his words, either.

"You did very well today. I'm very happy with your efforts."

"Th-thank you," she managed. Inside, she felt like she was trembling. Or was she trembling on the outside, too? Shit, she didn't want him to see. But still, his hand on her remained steady. Whatever he saw, he liked. And she wanted him to like her.

"I look forward to next time." His words were soft. She waited, hoping he'd say more, hoping he'd say when "next time" might be. Instead, he reached into his pocket and took out something small, something shiny. "I have a gift for you."

"For me?"

His warm voice cooled, turned clipped. "Don't be an echo. Be a voice, Jocelyn."

She wasn't even sure what that meant, but she didn't want to ask and sound stupid. "Okay."

"Okay what?"

"Okay . . . sir."

Mr. Sawyer placed a small pendant in the palm of her hand and closed her fingers around it. "Good girl. You may go." He went to the door, unlocked it, and opened it for her. But as she approached, he put his arm out, stopping her from passing. "Next time, you will not question my instructions. Do you understand?"

Jocelyn nodded. "Yes." Mr. Sawyer continued to stare at her until she realized what he was waiting for. "Yes, sir," she added.

He removed his arm, allowing her passage, but caught her eyes one last time. "Good. Because in the future, Miss Burton, failing to obey will have consequences."

CHAPTER

7

I should go home. Or go for a run, or to the gym at least. Instead, I stare out at my empty classroom, folding and unfolding the piece of paper I've had for two days. I fold it one way, and the details disappear—no name, no email. I fold it the other, and they're cut in half, the four in Ivy's phone number becoming two little lines. I give it a spin, a flick, let it float to the ground, where I'll inevitably pick it up, because what else can I do?

There's really only one option.

I push away from my desk, scoop up the scrap, and shove it in my pocket as I grab my jacket. Outside, I stride to the nearest train and hop on, not bothering to check where it's headed. It doesn't matter, anywhere distant will do. The stops speed by. New Yorkers herd on and off like cattle. The power flickers, someone turns their music on too loud, someone else speaks what I think is French into their cell on speakerphone. I ignore it all. Being single-minded, goal-oriented, is what's gotten me this far. When the twelfth stop comes, I stand and step off as soon as the doors slide open, taking the staircase up to the street. A bodega stands on the corner, and I go in, grab a prepaid cell at random, and slide cash across the counter. Credit cards are traceable.

Only when I'm back outside, in the fresh, warm air of late

spring, do I pull out that slip of paper and squint at the numbers. I type them in, hit call, and take a quick look around me. Lots of people are hurrying one place or another, but no one too close, no one listening.

The phone rings twice before a vaguely familiar voice comes on. It's changed some—deepened over the years. "Hello. You've reached Ivy Leighton at the Louisiana Department of Children and Family Services. If the reason you have reached out is not urgent, please leave me a message, and I'll return your call as soon as possible. If this is an emergency, please hang up and dial 911 or contact the twenty-four-hour Child Protective Services Emergency Hotline at 337-555-0100." My heart sinks. I can't leave a message. I think the recording is about to end, that I'll have to try again later, when she adds, "You may also reach me on my cell phone," and gives another number. I scramble in my purse for a pen and scribble it beneath her work number.

This one, I don't call. Instead, I text the briefest of messages:

Call me at this number from an untraceable phone. —E

Then I wait, pacing up the street, getting a coffee from a street vendor, drinking as I alternate between checking the phone every few seconds and glancing around me—making sure no one's watching. I could try harder to find Jocelyn, too. Google was a bust, but maybe Sam can do some digging and get me a phone number. The police have access to that type of stuff, don't they? But even the thought of that makes me nauseated. The fewer people I talk to about what happened, the better. Plus, the IP address came from Louisiana, not far from Ivy, and I never heard Jocelyn came back to town.

After twenty minutes of my mind racing, a jolting realization hits me. I'm not sure what took me so long to think of it, but what if Ivy doesn't realize it's *me*? We haven't spoken in twenty years. She might think it's some weirdo whose name begins with the letter *E*, might delete the message without a second thought. She works at CPS, for Christ's sake, has gotten married, had *kids*. There must be a million other things on her mind.

But no . . . she'll know. Hopefully.

I hurry to the train and take it back toward home.

I would certainly know it was her if I got that text signed with an *I*.

———

I'm one glass of pinot grigio in when the phone rings—a strange, shrill jangle that confuses me until my gaze falls on the prepaid. That area code I'd recognize anywhere. I grab the phone, press it to my ear. "Hello?"

"Elizabeth—"

"Wait." Words threaten to spill from my mouth, but first I have to be sure. "This is a safe line?"

"I borrowed my mother-in-law's phone. She's practically a saint."

My blood pressure comes down a notch, but still, I reach across the table for my wine, take a swig.

"What happened? Why . . ." A pause. "*Why?*" she says. "We made a pact."

I knock back another swallow of wine. Good thing I opened a fresh bottle. I steel my nerves and just say it. "Someone knows. Someone besides us."

"Someone—" Her voice cuts off.

The silence between us feels heavy.

"That's not possible," she says. "You know it's not. It was only me, you, and—well, he certainly can't tell anyone." In the background, a child yells—a reminder that she has a life. A life she wants to protect. Surely she wouldn't have told anyone, right?

"I would have said the same thing until a couple weeks

ago." I give her the abbreviated version—that I'm teaching a class, that first chapters came in, that a Hannah Greer just *happened* to write the story of what happened all those years ago and all of the details are the same as what Jocelyn described, down to the yellow finch. "It's exactly the same. *Exactly*. And I looked up her IP address. You can see where someone's sending an email from, like their city. It's . . . it's close. To where we lived."

More silence.

My wine is gone, and my eyes stray to the refrigerator, where the rest of the bottle awaits.

"I think . . ." Ivy stops, clears her throat. "I think your imagination is running wild. The details probably aren't *all* the same. How can you even remember the specifics when it's been more than twenty years?"

"Have *you* forgotten any of them, Ivy?"

"No. But—"

"I'm not imagining anything. Even the names of the characters are the same—Ivy, Mr. Sawyer, Jocelyn, all of it. *Someone knows*."

"But that's impossible." She sighs. "Wait. Hold on a second." Again, a child's voice whines in the background, this time closer. There's the sound of a door shutting, other noises fading into the background. "If the #MeToo movement showed us anything, it's that basically *all* women have been harassed or assaulted or—"

"These chapters have more than that. They have details. *A lot* of details."

"But . . . who would do something like this after twenty years? And why? And how would they have found out? It doesn't make any sense. Why would they enroll in your class and send it as a story? Why not just call the police?"

My mouth goes dry. Her questions are valid, and I *do* probably sound paranoid. Who would go to all that trouble?

Someone who wants revenge.

The words streak through my mind so fast, I gasp.

"What? What happened?"

"Nothing." I get to my feet, cross to the kitchen, retrieve the wine bottle from the fridge. It makes a glugging sound as I fill my glass and stare out the window, lost in thought. I'm sure something more is happening here, and I feel the need to convince her.

"It's not a coincidence," I say. I'm still staring out the window. But in my mind, I'm picturing something else. Something small that would fit in the palm of my hand, something that my friend wore every day during senior year. "It was the same story, Ivy—not just a student-teacher fantasy that plenty of people probably have. I'm telling you, there were details. Even the . . ." I inhale. "Even the silver pendant he gave Jocelyn."

It's her turn to gasp. "Saint Agnes?"

"Yes." I chew my lip. "Ivy?"

"What?" Her voice sounds distant, like she's now grappling with what I've dealt with for these past weeks.

"Is it you?"

A beat passes.

"*What?* Why would you ask me that? Why would I do that to you? Do that to *us*?"

"No one else knew. Who could it be, then?"

"Is it *you*?" she counters.

"Of course not!"

"Then who the hell is it?" Her voice goes up a notch, filled with fear. "I have as much to lose as you do. I have a *family*, a *life*, a *career*."

I press my lips together and don't point out that I have a life and a career, too. And my life isn't worth less just because I chose to not have a family. "There's no statute of limitations on mur—" I start to remind her why I'm so freaked out, what's at stake here. But the word gets stuck in my throat. I can't say it.

"Oh God."

"We need to think, Ivy," I say. "Who else was there?"

"I don't know." She's upset. Even through the phone, I can tell tears have streaked down her cheeks. Ivy was the last person I really cared about, really loved, and it makes my chest clench to hurt her.

"What about Wendell Unger?" I say. "Is he still around?"

"The police chief?"

"He investigated what happened. Maybe he found something we don't know about?"

"They never even questioned us twenty years ago. And why would the chief of police not arrest you, not arrest us? Instead, he pretends to be a student? That makes no sense."

She has a point. "You never told anyone? At all?"

Silence. A silence that *means* something. Anxiety spirals through me. Anger, too. We *promised*. We swore up and down we'd never tell a soul.

"*Who?*" I demand before she can answer. "Who did you tell?"

Ivy's shuddering breath comes through the line. "I told Father Preston. Not details! I just . . . I confessed my sins a year later."

"Are you freaking kidding me? Why would you do that, Ivy? It's our *lives*!" I clench the phone so hard the plastic shifts. I bang my fist on the table, making the wineglass jump, creating tiny ripples in the liquid. Then I'm on my feet again, pacing. "What did you say? What did you tell him?"

"I'm sorry! I didn't tell him who or any details of what happened—just that . . . that a friend of mine had done something bad, and I'd helped cover it up. I didn't even say why we did it."

I scrub my hand over my face and force slow, deep breaths. She didn't tell him details. That's good. That means he doesn't *really* know, right?

"Did you mention the Saint Agnes pendant? Jocelyn? Mr. Sawyer?"

"No, definitely not."

"How can you be so sure? It was twenty years ago, Ivy!"

"Because I was careful. And I remember every detail of that conversation. I swear, I didn't tell him *anything* specific. No name, no location, I never even said what the bad thing I'd covered up was."

She's sobbing now, and it hurts my heart. I wouldn't have gotten through that day if it weren't for Ivy. I'd dragged her into the mess. "Okay, okay. Just . . . don't do anything strange now, like go see Father Preston and ask him about it. Don't talk to anyone about it. Okay? I'll . . . I'll figure this out. I have to."

"What are you going to do?"

"I don't know. But I'll be in touch again soon."

I hang up, set the phone down, and stare at it. I think I believe Ivy. But if she only told one person—a priest who's taken a sacred oath to not reveal what is said in confessions—and she didn't tell him any details, it must be someone else.

There's Sam, a man who has been quietly poking around my life. I need to dig a little deeper there. And the only other person I can think of is the one person I've refused to let myself consider would do something like this. But maybe I have to.

I lied to Ivy. She isn't the only person who told someone what happened twenty years ago.

CHAPTER

8

I have to be honest, I was surprised when I got your text."
Sam lifts a hand, calls the waiter over. "I didn't think I'd
ever hear from you again, especially not to meet for dinner."

He's not the only one surprised we're on a date tonight.
If none of this were happening—I wasn't being haunted by
the past and hadn't found out he'd *investigated me*—I would
probably never have spoken to him again. But I need to feel
him out more, see if he has anything to do with what's going
on. Keep your enemies near and all . . .

My list of suspects has grown as fast as my paranoia—
Ivy, Chief Unger, Father Preston, *the man sitting across from
me*, not to mention the person I should never have told. After
my conversation with Ivy a few days ago, I decided I need to
rule them out methodically, one by one, and get to the bottom
of this.

Sam orders a bottle of wine, makes some small talk. A few
minutes later, the waiter pours us each a glass of pinot noir.
I stare at the deep red color, swirling it around, watching the
legs streak down the glass.

"So tell me," I eventually say. "What else did you learn
about me from your investigation?"

Sam frowns. "I told you, I didn't investigate you. I ran a
simple report."

I wave my hand. "Semantics. Tell me what this report contains."

He shrugs. "Basic background data."

"Where does the data come from?"

"The NCIC database—National Crime Information Center."

I've been relatively calm since we sat down, even knowing I might be sitting across from a man who holds the keys to my future, but the mention of the word *crime* makes my blood pump faster. It swishes through my ears, leaving me instantly off-kilter.

I swallow. "And what does 'basic background data' contain? Do you now know the PIN to my ATM card? What about my bra size?"

"It just lists things the police department would want to know about someone—if you've ever been arrested or had a warrant issued, prior addresses, stolen property reported, known gang affiliations. For you, the only thing that popped up was a list of prior addresses."

"Ah. And that's how you found out I grew up in Louisiana?"

"Yes."

"Tell me, Sam. If you've known I grew up there since shortly after we met, why didn't you call me out when I told you I was born and raised in New York?"

He shrugs. "I assumed you had your reasons. You don't talk about your family, so I thought maybe you had some difficult memories from that part of your life and preferred to not speak about it."

"Difficult" is putting it mildly.

Sam gestures to my forehead. "I didn't push for the same reason I didn't push when I asked you how you got that faint scar on your hairline and you ignored me. You have a way of getting your point across without saying much, Elizabeth." Sam sips his wine, watches me over the glass. "Is that what it is? You don't want to talk about the past, so it's easier not to open the door at all?"

I look away, debate how to navigate this. "My mother's an alcoholic. So, yes, it's a topic I prefer not to delve into."

Sam reaches across the table and takes my hand. He squeezes and waits until I meet his eyes again. "Thank you for sharing that just now. I truly am sorry for running you. It wasn't cool."

"No, it wasn't. I feel violated. An unspoken trust between us has been broken."

He hangs his head, rubs the back of his neck. If he's full of shit, this man should get the Academy Award for feigning guilt. "I understand."

I count to ten in my head, try my best to keep focused, and take a deep breath. "Look at me, Sam."

He stares straight into my eyes.

"I prefer when someone has questions that they go straight to the source. Is there anything you want to know about my past? Anything at all that your background investigation didn't tell you?"

He shakes his head. "No. I don't need to know about your childhood with your mother or anything from your past you don't want to discuss."

I watch him deliberate on saying more, the debate playing out all over his face. Fear of what will come out of his mouth next prickles up my spine, makes the little hairs on the back of my neck stand at attention. *Is he Hannah Greer or just a cop whose job has made him suspicious about everyone, and he thinks it's okay to investigate every woman he meets?*

After thirty seconds that feel more like thirty minutes, he takes a deep breath. "Bottom line, I like the woman you are today, and I'd like more with you than just the occasional hookup. You've made it pretty clear that isn't what you want, but you're asking me for honesty, and that's the honest truth. I like you, Elizabeth. You're smart, funny, independent, and all of that is wrapped in one hell of a package on the outside. I think there's something here, something more than just great chemistry in bed. Though if my choices are keeping things casual or nothing at all, I won't push, and we can keep things the way they are."

My eyes jump back and forth between his, searching for any sign of insincerity. But I find none. Sam is telling the truth. I'm 99 percent sure. I should be relieved, but it just means the devil is someone I *don't* know intimately, at least not anymore.

"I realize that today is about groveling," he continues. "And probably tomorrow and the next day, too. Because I fucked up. Royally. But if I expect to ever earn your trust again, I need to come clean about where I am with this."

I'm not sure he could earn my trust again. I have issues that have nothing to do with what Sam did. To me, trust is like glass. Once it's broken, even if you glue all the shards back together again, it's never the same. On some level, I can almost understand why Sam would do what he did. Hell, I've googled men I've dated before—isn't that almost the same thing? I just didn't have access to the database that Sam does.

But even putting trust issues aside, things inevitably get messy when two people want different things from a relationship. Though . . . my gut tells me I should keep him close a bit longer—just in case—even if it's wrong to string him along. "I need some time to think about things, Sam. We've hit a hurdle I'm not sure I can get over, much less keep running forward."

He nods. "I understand. Take all the time you need."

The rest of the evening goes by pretty much pain-free. We share a meal, talk about New York City politics and the effect it's having on the police department and school funding, and pretty soon the waiter brings the check.

Sam opens the padfolio. "I know you like to split the bill, which kills me. Will you at least let me pay for it this time as part of my apology?"

I shake my head and pull three twenties out of my wallet.

"I'll let you put in an extra five since I don't have change. How's that?"

He smiles, plucks his American Express from his wallet, and stuffs the cash in. "It's a start. I'll take what I can get."

The waiter comes a minute later and disappears with the card. While we wait for him to return, Sam's phone buzzes. It's face down on the table.

He picks it up and swipes. "It's my captain, reminding me to get the paperwork in to block off my vacation time. The old-timers get first pick, before the new guys. I always forget."

I nod. "My vacations are when the university tells me they are."

"How long is the summer session?"

"It runs through the end of July. But I get a short break in about a week."

"You have any plans? I should be able to take some time off. Maybe we can go away to the Caribbean or something? Work on rebuilding the trust I've lost while sipping margaritas." Sam sees my face and holds up a hand. "That's not exactly giving you time. Forget I mentioned it."

I smile. "I've actually been kicking around the idea of going home."

"To Louisiana?"

I nod. "It's been a while."

Outside, I walk to the curb, lift an arm to flag down a cab.

"You want to go to your place or mine?" Sam asks.

"I think I'm going to head home by myself tonight."

Sam's shoulders slump, yet he nods. "All right. Can I call you in a few days?"

I force a smile. "Sure."

CHAPTER

9

Maybe I should have taken Sam up on a trip to the Caribbean.

It might be ungodly hot there, too, but at least it wouldn't be filled with memories the way Louisiana is. The Toyota Corolla I rented doesn't drive quite right—a typical airport car, used by too many people who didn't give a damn as they hit a curb or slammed on the brakes. It's the alignment, I think. Right now, I just hope it doesn't putter out and die, leaving me stranded in a mosquito-riddled field in ninety-degree weather with high humidity.

"I hate Louisiana," I mutter as I stab a finger at the audio console. The Bluetooth doesn't seem to work, either, which means I can't connect my phone and listen to a podcast. Instead, I'm left with scratchy country-music radio, a man's voice wailing about love unrequited. It's only a matter of time before he starts in about his truck and his dog. I huff out a breath and shut it off, looking out at my surroundings as I try to relax and feel *at home*.

Though I didn't feel at home when it *was* my home, so it's futile.

But as hot and muggy and uncomfortable as it is here, I need to get to the bottom of things. I can't continue to live with so many unknowns hanging over my head. And all roads in this mess I'm in point to this little town—the IP address, Ivy, the *scene of the crime*. I don't even have a real plan for what I'll do while I'm here yet, other than to talk to Ivy, but my gut tells me if I'm going to find clues about who Hannah Greer really is, I'm in the best place to find them.

Twenty minutes later, I park in front of a familiar house, except the yellow paint my mother swore was the color of sunshine has faded to off-white, and it's peeling. Moss grows fuzzy in the cracks of the roof, which looks a lot like it's sagging in the middle. The once-trimmed green grass rises nearly to my knees as I pull myself from the car, lift my hands over my head, and stretch one way, then the other.

For a second, I wonder if my mother even lives here anymore. The place looks abandoned. Then I spot the cross hanging on the door. I remember her buying it, remember the day she hammered a nail into the wood and hung it, proclaiming, "This household belongs to God."

It wasn't the first sign she'd gone a little off the rails with religion. Nor would it be the last. I glance at my phone, but no notifications have popped up. I'm desperate for a distraction, a reason to wait a little longer before I go up to that door and knock.

It's been nearly twenty years. Yet, sadly, not long enough.

Mom and I trade occasional phone calls. They used to be more frequent, at least on the big holidays and birthdays. But that's fallen off over the years. Her slurred words and preaching were too much to handle. So I stopped calling as often, and she either didn't notice or didn't care. Now it seems the only time we speak is when family members are having babies or someone's died.

I still send cards on her birthday and at Christmas, even though hers have stopped. It's just as well, because the last few she sent me were full of shame, full of judgment—reminding me what Christmas was about and questioning whether the life I was living as a single woman in the big city was honoring Christ's sacrifice for me.

I take a breath and force myself to put one foot in front of the other. At the door, the cross now hangs crooked. I can't help it—I reach up and straighten it before my knuckles rap against the door.

"Come in!" someone wheezes from inside.

I pause. Maybe someone *else* lives here. Or maybe she has a roommate now. Maybe . . . I reach for the knob, twist, and creak the door open. "Hello? I'm looking for Ther—"

"Elizabeth?"

I swing the door the rest of the way open and catch sight of a woman on the same couch we had when I was a kid. It's tan and sagging, now worn to a shade that's closer to gray. And the woman is gray, too. Sallow and bony and—I swallow. *Oh my God. It's my mother.* Not as I've ever known her, but it's really her. My suitcase drops from my hand and thumps to the floor. "Mom?"

"You born in a barn? Get in here. Close that door. You're letting the cool air out."

I step inside quickly, like I would have when I lived here. Old feelings rush back. I'm a little afraid of her, aware she isn't above the type of harsh discipline she received as a girl. It's dim, the light mostly coming from the television and an ancient-looking computer monitor sitting on a folding table nearby. And it's the same television we had before—the boxy kind, no flat screen—after more than twenty years. I stop, absorbing it all. The house smells off—almost sour, like bad food, maybe urine, too.

"Mom?" I say again, because I can't quite believe my eyes. My mother was once a woman proud of her curves, frequently declaring, "God made me this way," and that she had "good child-bearing hips."

Now she looks like an image from a magazine—a starving child, maybe a person who lives somewhere riddled with disease. Skin and bones. Cheeks hollowed out. Blond hair stringy, limp, and dirty. I can't quite understand what's going on, what's *happened*, but of course, it's been a long time. A lot can happen in twenty years, and apparently it has . . .

"You just gonna stand there?" she snips.

"Um . . ." I blink again, then cross through the kitchen into the living room, over the threadbare imitation Persian rug, which is also more than two decades old. I nearly trip over an empty bottle of what is likely gas station whiskey and offer her a one-armed hug. This close, I can hear the wheeze in her chest, smell a sickly scent of . . . I'm not sure what. But something isn't right. I slowly sit down in the chair across from her.

"Mom?" I ask, forgetting all about the reason I came here. "What's . . ." I flush, aware that I'm close to telling her she looks like shit, the sort of thing that would have gotten me slapped when I was a kid. But I'm not a child anymore, even if it suddenly feels like it. I take a deep breath and continue. "You seem sick. What's going on? Why didn't you call?"

She gives me a long look. Even her eyes are off, the whites having turned an unhealthy shade of yellow. "You have your own life. You don't want to be a part of mine. Besides, I have the church. I didn't need you."

Ouch. Cut to the bone.

I stare at her. "What's wrong, though?"

A heavy sigh. "I'm dying, Elizabeth. Isn't it obvious?"

Her words echo in my head, cause a clench in my stomach. Like someone's punched me in the gut. I barely speak to her anymore, and yet . . . she's still my mother. I search for words but come up empty-handed.

"Pancreatic cancer. I have one, two months to live. Tops." She reaches for a glass of amber liquid that I'm sure is liquor and takes a big gulp like it's lemonade. "So, to what do I owe the honor of your presence?"

Straight to business. As if she didn't just drop a bomb on me. I open my mouth, thinking of saying *to visit you, of course*, but we'll both know I'm lying. So I don't. I let the silence settle between us.

"Well, if you're just gonna sit there, can you at least hand me those?" She gestures to the coffee table, to a dozen orange prescription bottles sitting between us.

My gaze falls on them—the names are all twelve letters long, practically another language. But I do recognize one—oxycodone.

"Mom, you shouldn't be mixing this with—"

"I know, I know. Heard it from the doctor. I don't need another lecture, especially from you. Just give it to me."

I guess I can't blame her. If she's dying anyway, why bother stopping a lifetime of trying to kill herself? I gather up the pill bottles and move them to where she can reach.

"Did you get a second opinion?"

"Got three. It's too late. It's spread all over."

I swallow and try to imagine a world without my mother. It should be easy, because at this point, she's barely part of my life. And yet the idea of her being gone, completely gone, and me unable to pick up the phone and call her . . . leaves me feeling unmoored. She's all I have, even if we don't really have each other anymore.

"Mom, maybe you should come up to New York. See some doctors up there?"

"Shut up, child. I don't need any such thing. You think you're better than me living in that highfalutin city of yours, that the doctors know more because they pay ten thousand dollars a month to live in a shoebox? You know what that makes them? *Dumb*. My doctors here—where we take care of each other—are just fine. I'm dying, and there's nothing anyone can do about it. It doesn't even bother me anymore, because I'll be with Jesus soon, and then nothing will hurt ever again. When was the last time you went to the Lord's house, anyway?"

The God talk already. I'm all about people having their religion, but there's going to church every Sunday, and then there's being a full-on righteous zealot who preaches to everyone while not looking inward at your own behavior. It's a good thing she believes God will save everyone, because she never did a damn thing to take care of herself—or her child, for that matter.

I went to church every week with her when I was little—wearing my best dress, helping my unsteady mom to a pew. The same woman who didn't come home most nights because she was screwing every loser in town. Church seemed like a scam to me. A way of getting people to part with their hard-earned money.

The priest had a new house located on the manicured church grounds. Most of his congregants, meanwhile, lived in this sort of place. A tiny two-bedroom down a dirt road. Dogs chained outside. Porches falling apart. Kids in hand-me-downs that rarely fit properly. I didn't see the priest caring if I ate, and God certainly didn't save my friend when she needed saving in high school.

"I choose not to go to church, Mom."

She shakes her head. "You'll never have good in your life without God."

"Really? Have you considered that your God made you an alcoholic? And is now letting you die alone in this house?" The words slip from my mouth before I can stop them. I've never been good at not speaking my mind. Being in New York, away from this place, has only strengthened that. New York and I are a good fit—there, people respect raw honesty. Here, though, it's expected that you shut up and keep your thoughts to yourself. Unless you're my mother, of course.

"You ungrateful little brat. God loves me despite my

sins. He forgives me—Father Preston told me. *Here, look!* I wrote them all down so I wouldn't forget to confess any." She thrusts a ratty piece of paper into my hand. It's written in clunky pencil, handwriting shaky like a child's.

Drinking

Fornication

I stop reading right there. I've lived her sins. I don't need the reminder. "Mom, look, I'm sorry. But—"

"*You* should be reconciling *your* wrongs, missy. Before it's your time, so you can spend an eternity in heaven, too. Look at that list—look at all the things I've never shared with anyone. We all have secrets, don't we?"

My body stills at the word *secrets*.

When I look up, she's peering at me. *Glaring* at me.

"I know you've been a sinner, too. You never know when your time is. You should repent. Ask forgiveness. You never know when the past might creep up on you."

Despite the old air conditioner keeping the house below eighty degrees, I go hot with sweat. It dampens my hands, makes my skin feel slick.

I've always sworn I never told anyone. But I did tell one person.

My mother, the night it happened. I came home shaking, in tears, and for once, she held me, hugged me tightly, and it spilled out. It's one of the rare memories I have of her being *loving* toward me. I was just a kid who had done something unthinkable, and I couldn't help but confess. In the morning, I woke with a violent start, realizing the mistake I'd made. But when I went to check on her, she was passed out—still drunk. Which meant she'd been drunk the night before. I broached the subject when she got up later that afternoon. "About what we spoke about last night . . ." But she didn't seem to remember a thing. That was normal for her. Blackouts were a common occurrence. I never mentioned it again, chalked it up as lost to alcohol. It made sense. After all, she'd been drunk enough to pretend to love me that night.

Now, though, as I stare across the coffee table at her, as she suggests that *we all have secrets*—I have to wonder if she's told someone my sins, too.

CHAPTER

10

It seemed so much bigger back then.

I stand looking up at the second floor of Minton Parish High School—a certain window, third from the end. It's not like I've grown. I've been the same five foot six since ninth grade. Yet the building felt more substantial to me at seventeen, more intimidating.

"Can I help you?" A woman's voice startles me, pulls my attention from the second floor. She's petite, older than me by twenty or thirty years, with thick-rimmed, dark glasses that are too big for her tiny face, and a blunt pixie cut.

I'm not even sure where she came from. Inside? She's standing in front of the main entrance, so that seems logical, but the door is shut, and I didn't hear it creak open or clank closed.

As if she can read my mind, she gestures behind her. "My desk is in the main office, next to the window, so I spend a lot of time looking outside. We took the channel letters with the name of the school down a few days ago. Finally getting new ones after thirty some-odd years. I thought maybe you weren't sure if you were at the right building because of that."

I hear every word, yet it takes a few seconds for what she's saying to register in my brain. "Oh. Yes," I lie. "I was trying to figure out if this is still the high school."

The woman smiles like she's proud she just solved a riddle. "Yes, ma'am. You've reached the right place." She fans her face. "Lordy, it's hotter than a blister bug in a pepper patch today, isn't it?"

Now, *that's* a phrase I haven't heard too often since moving to New York.

"What can I do you for?" she asks.

"I, um . . . I lost my high school diploma and was wondering if I can order a new one. I need to prove I took some advanced classes and graduated." I force a smile. "I'm going back to college at my age."

She returns the smile. "We're never too old to learn. I can print you an official transcript. It'll note all your classes on it. Would that do?"

"I think so, yes."

She waves me toward her. "Come on inside."

I look up at the second floor, the third window from the left, and swallow. I hadn't planned on going in. I'm not even sure why I'm here, but my pulse speeds up at the thought of getting closer. "Great. Thanks."

In the office, my eyes rove over the tall counter that separates the staff from the visitors, the frosted door to my left with Principal on it in thick black letters, the rows of mailbox slots to my right labeled with teachers' names. I scan them one by one, left to right, until it's clear they're in alphabetical order. Then my eyes drop down to read the last row—Mr. Parker, Mrs. Pearlman, Miss Rojas, Mr. Santoro, Mr. Tambar. I'm relieved one name is missing, even though of course it would be.

The woman settles at her desk on the other side of the counter. "What's your name, sweetheart?"

"Elizabeth. Elizabeth Davis."

"Last four digits of your social?"

"Five, four, six, four."

Her nails clack against the keyboard as she types.

She smiles. "Here you are. But just to be sure, what's your address?"

"I don't live here anymore, but it was 21 Julep Road."

"Davis on Julep Road? Your momma wouldn't happen to be Theresa Davis, would she?"

I purse my lips. The pastime in this small town is hearing a name and playing six degrees of separation. If someone doesn't know you, they know someone you're related to, or their sister or brother does. "Yes, it is."

The secretary's face falls. "I go to Saint Matthew's Church. I'm sorry about her illness. Her spirit is so strong, though."

Why am I surprised that strangers knew before me? I shouldn't be. That's how my mother operates—put on your Sunday best and gossip with all the other *good Christians*. Save the ugly for at home.

"Thank you."

"Do you live nearby?" the woman asks. "I don't remember seeing you at Saint Matthew's with your momma."

I shake my head. "I live in New York."

"Well, she must be happy you're here now." The woman returns her attention to her computer screen, clacks a few more keys, and the printer spits out a few sheets of paper. "Here you go." She slides two pages across the counter and points to a box at the top right corner. "Your graduation is noted right here. If that's not good enough, I can order you a new diploma, but usually this is more than sufficient."

"Thank you. I appreciate it."

An earsplitting bell rings. Seconds later, a teacher comes into the office with a student, and then two more people file in. The secretary, whose name I still don't know, sighs.

"Do you mind showing yourself out, Ms. Davis?"

"Of course not. Thank you very much for your help."

Apparently, security hasn't changed much in Minton Parish. Who lets a virtual stranger loose in a high school these days? The hallway outside the main office is a sea of teenagers. They walk in clusters, gossiping, or by themselves, staring down at their cell phones. I might as well be invisible. Which gives me an idea . . . I turn right out of the office—walking the way I came in—but when I reach the entrance, I head in the opposite direction to the main staircase, blending into a crowd of students. Once I reach the second floor, I glance down the hall. Teachers are standing in front of their classrooms as students enter. They won't be as oblivious to a stranger wandering the building. So I duck back into the stairwell, turn my back to the students rushing to get where they need to be, and pretend I'm scrolling on my phone. Minutes later, another bell rings, and the few stragglers still coming up the stairs pick up their pace and jog the rest of the way to their destinations. If I remember correctly, there's another bell—the late bell—so I wait. Sure enough, it rings through the hallway speakers, and then there's the sound of doors closing, and the second floor goes quiet.

I wait another few minutes before peeking my head out to make sure the coast is clear, and a rush of adrenaline sends my heart racing as I step out into the empty hall. I take a deep breath and tiptoe down to the third classroom from the end. The door still has the same small window. I close my eyes and remember the way I used to look at Mr. Sawyer when I passed by, before everything happened. I thought he was so handsome—most girls did. That makes me feel sick, and I open my eyes to force my mind back to the present. I peer through that same window now, and there's a woman— a young teacher at the front of the classroom. But no matter how hard I try, I can't stop myself from visualizing the vivid description on the pages of the last chapter I received from Hannah.

Kneeling.
Staring down at the floor.
A caress of the cheek.
Good girl . . .

I blink open my eyes and the young teacher is gone. Instead, I see Mr. Sawyer and my best friend, Jocelyn. I know it's not real, but it knocks the wind out of me just the same. I'm still seeing them when a voice breaks in.

"Ma'am? Can I help you?"

The teacher. She's in the hallway now, wearing a look of concern. When I don't answer, she takes a step closer.

"Are you okay, ma'am?"

I take a deep breath. "I'm sorry. Yes. I . . . I was just leaving."

I don't wait for a response before I turn and walk quickly down the hall, rush down the staircase, and fly out the front door of the school. I keep running until I'm in the parking lot, locked inside my car. My hands shake as I attempt to put the key in the ignition, and I still can't catch my breath.

It was a mistake to come here. To the school. To Minton Parish. To Louisiana.

Yet I can't stop myself from going to visit the spot that is *the biggest mistake of all*.

———

The Memory Haven Motel has changed even less than the high school. The neon sign that flickers intermittently is still missing half the *M* in *Motel*, so it reads as "Memory Haven *Notel*," which is fitting. It's concealed from the main road by overgrown trees, and its peeling brown paint seeks attention about as much as the people who frequent the place.

I watch as a man parks in front of room 112. He exits his car and looks around before slipping inside the room. Heavy drapes shroud the windows, and I imagine the stench of stale smoke and mold. Not long after, a brunette pulls into the parking lot. She drives around to the side of the building and parks her car, then walks with her head down to the same room. She knocks and the drapes move, allowing a peek outside, before the door opens and she ducks in.

A little while later, an 18-wheeler pulls in. The driver doesn't get out. Instead, a woman pulls in next to the truck. She parks and climbs up into the big rig. I can actually see her head bobbing up and down from where I'm parked. *Good to know the place is as classy as it was in high school.*

I sit in the parking lot with the engine running for a few hours, staring at the last room on the second floor—the one farthest from the crappy little office downstairs. I'll probably run out of gas soon, but I can't make myself leave, and it's too damn hot to turn off the car. No one has gone in or out of 212 yet. I'm half tempted to go in and say I need a room, see if they'll give me that unit. But I don't really want to. I've let in enough memories these last few weeks. I'm just about to call it a day when a knock on my car window makes me jump. I see the brown police uniform and holstered gun before anything else.

"Shit," I breathe, holding a hand over my heart.

The man bends, showing me his face. Is that . . . Wendell Unger? The police chief?

I haven't laid eyes on him in twenty years. The face is older, weathered and wrinkled, but I really think it might be him. He gestures for me to roll down my window, and my heart feels like it might leap out of my chest as I press the button to lower the glass.

Where the hell did he even come from? I didn't see anyone approaching my car.

"Good afternoon." He nods. "Didn't meant to startle you. Just noticed you sitting here for a while and thought I'd check to see if everything is all right."

"Everything's fine, Officer." My eyes drop to his name tag. Unger.

"Good. Can I see some ID, please?"

"Did I do something wrong?"

"Just a precaution," he says. "You've got out-of-state plates, and you're sitting in the back of a parking lot—like you want to see something but not be seen. Just doing my job, ma'am."

I reach for my purse on the passenger seat. "Of course."

Digging out my wallet, I extend my driver's license through the window. Chief Unger takes it and holds it with extended arms, like he should be wearing reading glasses.

"New York, huh? A long way from home, aren't you? What brings you to Minton Parish?"

"I'm visiting my mother."

He looks at the license again. "Elizabeth Davis? Theresa's daughter?"

"Yes, sir."

His eyes roam my face. "You sure are. It's been a long time. But I remember you."

"You do?"

He leans down so we're eye to eye, only the car door separating us, and offers me back my license. "I'm sorry to hear about your momma."

I swallow and take my ID. "Thank you."

"You might want to head home soon. This area of town isn't the safest."

My eyes slant to look at the last room on the right up on the second floor, then back to Chief Unger. He's watching me, quietly observing—a lot like Sam always has. Only I never gave it any thought until recently. It makes me feel restless.

"I was just about to leave anyway."

He offers a curt nod. "You have a good night, Elizabeth."

I roll up the window and wrestle the car into drive as fast as I can. It's only when I reach the exit to the motel parking lot that I allow myself to check the rearview mirror. And I wish I hadn't, because a chill crawls up my spine from the way the chief of police is watching me leave what was once the scene of the crime.

CHAPTER

11

It's still dark the next morning when I park the rental car and kill the engine. My back is aching from all the sitting—in New York, I walk most places or take the train. I'd forgotten what a drag it is to drive everywhere. I take a long pull of coffee and let the dome lights shut off as I watch the house on the corner. It's 5 a.m. here, which makes it 6 a.m. in New York. Still early, but not as painful as it would be for a local. And it's a local I'm here for.

Ivy's house sits just a few yards away. Her address wasn't hard to find. I did a quick Google search of her name again last night, and any crazy person could find her—perhaps she did. *Me.* A woman who works for CPS should be more careful. I'm sure people aren't too happy when she removes their kids. The lights are all off, which means she's probably not awake yet, which is good. I want to see what she's up to these days, from the start.

Sure, I could go knock on the door. But I've already spoken to her once, and she denied being behind the story. I need to watch her, see who she spends time with, where she goes when she thinks no one is paying attention. And her guard will be lower if she doesn't know I'm here in Louisiana. Though the way Mom gossips, and given her obsession with going to church, maybe the point is moot. Maybe the whole town already knows of my arrival. I frown, considering that possibility.

Twenty minutes later, a light turns on. I jot down the time in the notes on my phone. I don't even know why I do it. But there's so much going on in my head, I don't want to forget any details. An hour passes, and Ivy makes her way to her car, parked haphazardly in the grass. Why is that a thing here? Parking on the lawn. There's another car in the driveway, I assume her husband's. Why not park behind him or in the street?

I attempt to take a gulp of my now-empty coffee. Being here has me on edge. If I'm honest, it reminds me of who I used to be, and I don't like it. I earned who I am today and everything I have. I worked hard to put this life behind me—graduating at the top of my class, getting a job doing something I love, dating on my own terms. I like my new life. I don't want whatever's going on—whoever *knows*—to threaten that.

When Ivy pulls out of the grass in her minivan, I count to ten, then follow. It's not a simple drive to work. No, she stops at a little coffee hut first, and I consider pulling in behind her and ordering a quick cup for myself. But I don't want to lose her. Instead, I circle the block once, then trail her as she goes toward the outskirts of town, where a Walmart has opened alongside a strip mall. She goes into the shopping center first, and I slip from my car, keeping a safe distance as I skulk in behind her.

But she only buys diapers—a small package of them. Which makes me wonder if money's tight. I don't know much about babies, but I would think that—like most things—the larger the quantity, the cheaper the per-unit cost. When she goes to the checkout, fluorescent lighting illuminates her dark roots. She's in need of some time at the salon, another hint that maybe money's an issue. Maybe there's a financial goal here? Is she Hannah and looking for a payout to keep quiet?

Another angle to consider. Though what is she waiting for, if that's her game?

I slip back outside while she's still checking out and walk to my car, parked a few rows over from hers. The morning is damp, humid. The moisture is inescapable, and I huff out a breath. Louisiana is, for many reasons, claustrophobic.

Her last stop is the CPS office. She parks at the back of the lot, despite the fact that the sun is only now fully up, and walks in with her nose in her phone, not even glancing around. That wouldn't fly in New York. Was I once so trusting? Maybe it's okay in small-town life.

This might take a long time—hours, even—so I pop some Advil for my back, pull out my laptop, tap it to life, and get to work on the chapters my students have submitted. I've been avoiding them for obvious reasons, but their next rounds are due soon, and I owe them feedback. I work on one that seems to be an attempt to bring vampire romance back, adding a few suggestions here and there, recommending they make it fresh, not a repeat of what's already been done, and then I blow out a breath and force myself to open the file I've been avoiding.

Hannah's story.

Whoever "Hannah" really is.

Around me, the parking lot slowly fills up, but the chapters suck me in as I reread them. Hannah is either a good writer or the scenes are vivid because I already know the story. I leave comments about a few minor things—staying in a particular tense, removing filler words that aren't necessary. But then I get an idea.

What about adding a plotline about a friend Jocelyn confides in about her relationship with her teacher? That would help develop your character beyond her interaction with Mr. Sawyer.

I type the comment and my heart races faster as I reread it. I add, Let's call her Lizzie as a placeholder. Lizzie could appear as a friend . . . I taste blood as I bite down and continue, Later she could turn out to have a greater role in the story.

Not the sort of advice I give, usually. My writing students need to choose their own plotlines, develop their own characters. But this person isn't a normal student—they're messing with me. So I'll mess with them back. Let them know that *I know.* A smirk plays on my lips as I imagine them—whoever they are . . . Sam? Ivy? My own freaking mother?—reading the notes and realizing their game has just been taken up a notch.

A rap at the window jolts me from my thoughts. I look up, expecting to see Ivy staring down at me with surprise in her eyes. But instead, I see a face I'd hoped not to run into again.

Wendell Unger. *Chief* Wendell Unger.

Is he following me? He must be. I know this town is small, but twice in as many days?

I slap my laptop shut and creak down the window a bit. My heart thumps away in my chest, nerves telling me this can't be a coincidence. Why didn't I pay more attention to my rearview mirror? I'd been so focused on following, I didn't consider *being followed.* Does *he* know? Oh God, a thought smacks me in the face—and it's not the first time I've considered it. What if he's working with Sam? Some kind of multistate investigation. That happens, right? Though I doubt the detective in New York would be sleeping with the suspect . . .

"Good morning, Ms. Davis."

"Hello, Chief Unger."

"May I"—he gestures to the car—"inquire what you're doing camped out in a parking lot? Again?"

I point at the laptop. "Getting some work done while I wait on a friend. How about you?"

"I frequent the CPS office, unfortunately. Nature of the

job." He presses his lips together. "Why are you waitin' out here?"

My gaze drifts toward the front of the building. "Umm . . . I came to visit a friend, but she's out of the office. Figured I'd wait for her here so I'm not in the way inside."

"Mrs. Ivy Leighton?"

How the hell does he know? "Um, yes. Ivy." I try not to let him see that I'm rattled. Maybe in a town this small, there aren't many people who work at CPS. Maybe he knows we're about the same age, maybe—

"Don't look so surprised, Ms. Davis. You two were thick as thieves back in the day. Inseparable. It's a small town, not like your big city. We know who's friends with who around here."

I give him a smile that feels forced. "Of course. You have a very good memory." I'm ready to end this conversation. I don't want to answer any other questions, not without a lawyer present. But I forgot another thing about small towns— how chatty everyone is. And how everyone expects you to be chatty right back.

Chief Unger doesn't take the hint as I shift my laptop, look around anywhere but at him. Instead, he leans against the car, tosses his keys into the air, and catches them, like he's got all the time in the world. My stomach swims. Is he being friendly, or is he messing with me, trying to make me nervous on purpose?

"So, whatta ya do for work up in that big city, anyway?"

"I'm a teacher, a professor."

"That so? What subject?" He straightens, pulls a circular disc of chewing tobacco from his pocket, and opens it.

The pungent smell wafts to my nose, and I feel like I could gag. My stomach is shaky already. "English. Creative writing."

"Huh," he says, and his brow furrows like—like *something*. Like that piece of information is interesting. But English is a boring subject to most people; rarely does anyone find it *interesting* that I teach it. Most think of grammar rules or overly long books from the last century that are difficult to read.

"Well, best be heading out. Good to see you again." Chief Unger smacks a hand on the side of the car and crosses the parking lot back to his cruiser. I watch him go, but not before he glances back my way and squints, as though I said something interesting, something he's going to *remember*.

Before I can think it through, I'm turning the car on, shifting into drive, and heading back toward Mom's. *What the hell am I doing?* Stalking my ex–best friend. Taunting whoever this is via Microsoft Word comments. *Coming home* to Louisiana, where nothing good ever happened to me. Where, likely, nothing good ever will happen to me.

CHAPTER
12

I need to make a stop."

My eyes flash to my mother sitting in the passenger seat and back to the road. We just came from a doctor's appointment. "Sure. Where?"

"The church."

I frown. *Figures.* But what could she possibly need to do there at 6:30 in the evening? Daily mass was always 9 a.m. and 4 p.m., unless Saint Matthew's has changed things up, which I doubt. Lord knows the Catholic Church abhors change.

"What's to do there at this time of the evening?"

"Pray."

"Isn't mass done by now?"

"We don't need a ceremony to take time out of our day to talk to the Lord. You should try it sometime, might make you a better person."

I bite my tongue, rather than argue over which one of us is the shitty human. "Fine."

Ten minutes later, I pull up at the curb outside of Saint Matthew's and leave the engine running.

"Aren't you going to park and join me?" my mother asks.

"Not unless you need me to help you walk in. Praying is your thing. Not mine. I'd prefer to wait right here for you."

My mother juts her chin out, but opens the car door. "I don't need your help."

I wait a half hour, then another fifteen minutes more. When a full hour ticks by and there's still no sign of her coming out, I unbuckle my seat belt and turn the car off. She's probably taking her time to be spiteful, but she's also sick and frail. There's a tiny part of my heart that hasn't turned black when it comes to my mother, so I can't help but worry, even though I hate myself for doing it. Then again, this may just be her way of getting me to come inside.

The vestibule of Saint Matthew's hasn't changed one bit— church bulletin board with dozens of pinned posts, worn black pleather chairs that parents force their rowdy children to sit in when they grow too loud at Sunday service, holy water fonts on either side of the door leading to the nave. I peek inside and spot my mother sitting in a pew a few rows from the altar. A man sits next to her—a priest, I assume. I ponder turning around and going back to the car, waiting her out. But I need this day to be over with. So I take a page from my mother's book—lift my chin high with righteous indignation and walk in like my feet aren't burning with each step.

The priest spots me first, and my footsteps falter when I get a look at his face. *Father Preston*—the one Ivy told me she confessed *something* to years ago. This town might as well have been frozen the last two decades with the amount of change it's seen.

I look away, not wanting to meet his eyes. But when I glance to my left, a statue catches my attention. That was *not* here twenty years ago. The taste of bile rushes up from my stomach, yet somehow I keep putting one foot in front of the other.

Father Preston stands when I arrive at the pew they've been seated in. "Elizabeth. It's wonderful to see you."

I point back to the statue. "Is that new?"

"Saint Agnes? Why, yes it is." He smiles. "It's beautiful, isn't it?"

"When did you get it?"

"A parishioner donated it about a year ago, I think."

"What parishioner?"

His brows furrow. "It was an anonymous donation. Why do you ask?"

Another coincidence? How can one little town be filled with so many?

I look back at the statue, and cold seeps into my body. It's probably still ninety outside, and the church doesn't have air-conditioning, so it means one thing—a panic attack is coming. I need to get the hell out of here *quick*.

My mother still hasn't acknowledged me. Her head is bowed like she's full of shame. I thought this was the place you came to get rid of that stuff. "Mom . . ."

She turns. The change in her position lets me see there's something in her hand. I take a step closer, squint for a better look.

Drinking

Fornication

I close my eyes. *Her sin list.* No wonder it's taken so long.

Mom traces my line of sight and pulls the paper tight to her chest so I can't see it. Which makes me wonder—what else is on there? I should've read the entire thing when I had the chance earlier. Is she here to confess just *her* sins? Or does she feel the need to rat out everything she believes is a crime against the Lord, even if the sins don't belong to her?

———

"What can I get you?"

The bartender, a woman who looks barely old enough to

drink, slaps a napkin in front of me. She might be young, but she fills out the half shirt she's wearing pretty damn well. I guess that's more important in a place like this.

"I'll take a whiskey. Macallan Double Cask, if you have it."

Her lip twitches. "You're not from around here, are you?"

I shake my head. "Not anymore. I take it that means you don't have Macallan?"

"No, we don't."

"What type of whiskey do you have?"

"We got Hendrick's."

I don't bother to inform her that Hendrick's is *gin*, not whiskey. I'd drink rubbing alcohol at this point. "I'll take that. Thanks."

While Miss Half Shirt searches for the bottle, I take out my Amex and put it on the bar, then look around. This place was a boarded-up bar when I was a kid. I can't remember what it was called back then, but it definitely wasn't Liars Pub. It's a typical hole in the wall—dark so the patrons can't see the glasses aren't clean, wobbly wooden stools that need cushions, and a back room with two dartboards and a worn pool table. A guy with a mullet and a receding hairline leans over with a cue stick to take a shot. He catches my eye and proffers a leering smile. I turn away quickly, hoping he won't think my glancing around is an invitation.

I knock back my first drink within minutes of it being served. It burns as it slides down my throat, worms its way into my belly. I appreciate the occasional cocktail and wine with dinner, but rarely do I allow myself to get drunk. To-night, I plan on making an exception. It can't be more than a mile walk to Mom's. My rental car can stay in the parking lot overnight. Raising my hand, I call over the bartender.

"You want another?" she asks.

"Please."

A voice behind me catches me off guard. "Put hers on my tab, please, Willow."

I expect to find the mullet man when I turn, but I'm pleasantly surprised. Instead, there's a tall, handsome—albeit too young for me—man with a deliciously crooked smile. That smile widens, unveiling a set of cavernous dimples. *Oh my.*

"You are *definitely* not from around here," he drawls.

I swivel and face him for a better look. "Oh yeah? Why is that?"

"Because the girls from these parts drink one of three things: White Claws, High Noons, or Jack and Coke. And the third I keep away from because that means they're going to wind up sloppy drunk."

"I suppose the reason I don't drink any of those is because I'm a *woman*, not a girl."

Dimples looks me up and down. There's a sparkle in his eyes when they meet mine. "You sure are."

I chuckle. He's corny and over the top, but something about him appeals to me. It could be the confidence. There's nothing I'm drawn to more than a confident man. Which is why Sam isn't the first cop I've dated.

"What's your name?" I tilt my head. "Or should I just call you Dimples?"

"Name's Noah." He smiles, flashes those things like a weapon, and holds out a hand. "And you are?"

"Elizabeth." I put my hand in his, but instead of shaking, he lifts my knuckles to his lips and kisses just above them.

"Pleasure. Where you from, darlin'?" He waves his head. "Wait. Let me guess."

"This should be interesting . . ." I cross one leg over the other. Noah's eyes drop to follow before looking up unapologetically and wagging a finger at me.

"I bet you're from New York City."

"Indeed I am. What gave it away?"

"You just have that look about you."

"And what look is that?"

He grins. "Like you can eat a man alive."

"Considering you're standing here and just bought me a drink, I take it you enjoy being eaten alive?"

"I don't mind it." He leans in, putting his mouth next to my ear, and whispers, "But I'm a gentleman, so I'll always do the eatin' first."

The bartender interrupts, which I'm grateful for because this young'in has got me all hot and bothered. She places another drink in front of me and lifts her chin to Noah. "You want your usual?"

"Yes, please."

She raps her knuckles against the bar twice. "Coming right up."

Noah slides into the seat next to me and scoots it over a few inches until his knee is touching mine. "So what brings a city girl down to these parts?"

"I'm visiting family." I pick up my drink and take a healthy swig, watch the man next to me over the glass. "Tell me, how old are you, Noah?"

"Old enough."

"Old enough for what?"

He grins again. "Anything you want to do."

I chuckle. "I walked right into that one, didn't I?"

Over the next hour, Noah and I talk. Surprisingly, we have a lot in common—even though I did the math when he said the year he graduated high school and know he's ten years younger than me. Noah is a writer. He pens a sports column for the *Louisiana Post*, but he wants to write a novel someday. He has a degree in journalism from Tulane, runs half marathons, and is willing to travel for a good meal at a restaurant. He's read Tolstoy and Faulkner, but prefers to read Stephen King on a night when the wind is howling. And he's currently remodeling his house all by himself, rather than hiring people.

After my third drink, I'm relaxed enough to forget the reason I'm down here for the first time since crossing the state line. But my gut tells me the man next to me could make me forget *my name* for a while. So even though I rarely take up with a man under forty, I decide to make an exception. Noah excuses himself to go to the men's room, and I wait a few seconds, then hop down from the bar stool and follow.

I look around to see if anyone is watching before opening the door and slipping inside. Noah is facing the urinal. He doesn't turn until he hears the clank of the lock. When he does, his eyes go wide.

I grin. "You can finish up."

He chuckles and turns around. "Haven't even started yet. But suddenly I think it can wait. Whatcha doin' in the men's room, beautiful?"

"Seeing if you're worth going home with."

He raises a brow. "Is that so?"

I nod, and Noah takes two steps so we're nose to nose. He keeps his gaze locked to mine as he snakes a hand around my waist and pulls me flush against him. His other hand slips down to my ass, and he grabs a handful before bending and lifting me off my feet. My legs wrap around his waist like it's not the first time they've been there, and Noah's lips crash down on mine. He backs us up until I hit the door behind me with a loud thud, and our mouths open, tongues frantically colliding.

Noah presses against me, a steely erection straining through his pants already, and he rubs up and down. I'm wearing a dress, so I'm spread-eagle, and the friction sends a bolt of lightning straight down to my toes. *Definitely worth going home with.*

He tangles his fingers into my hair, fisting a clump. I gasp when he yanks my head back and his mouth goes to my neck. Noah sucks along my pulse line, and I'm already so turned on, I don't even care that I'm in this disgusting bathroom. I reach down between us and wrap my hand around his bulge, giving it a good, firm squeeze.

Noah groans. "You're killin' me, darlin', starting some-thing we aren't going to be able to finish for a while."

"Who says we can't finish it now? I want you. Please tell me you have a condom?"

"I do. But we can't do this here."

I start to undo his zipper. "Why not? Haven't you ever had sex in a public restroom?"

"No." He catches my gaze. "Have you?"

I look away without answering, but slip my hand into his underwear. His skin is so hot and smooth. I circle the crown with my thumb until I feel wetness.

Noah hisses and rocks his hips against me. "I'm gonna have to put you down to get the condom on."

"Fine. Just hurry."

Noah lowers me to my feet and reaches for his back pocket. He slips out a condom and places the wrapper between his teeth to tear it open. Once he's sheathed, I turn around and place my hands against the wall.

He doesn't have to be told what to do next. Noah's fingers slide beneath the edge of my panties. He strokes through my slickness and groans. "I haven't even touched you, and you're ready for me."

"So what are you waiting for, then?"

"Hot damn. I love New York women." Noah hikes up the back of my dress, wraps an arm around my stomach, and hoists me up to my toes. He uses his free hand to line himself up at my opening and surges forward, burying himself inside of me.

I gasp. There's a twinge of discomfort, but it's exactly what I needed. In fact, it's the best thing I've felt in ages. Noah's fin-gers press into my hips. "You good?"

My answer is to lean forward, pull almost all the way off him, and then slam back hard, taking him to the root again.

He groans. "I'll take that as a yes."

Everything happens at warp speed after that. Noah pumps

in and out of me hard and fast. It feels desperate and border-line angry, and I can't get enough of it. I move with him, meeting his every thrust, blow by blow. My insides are climbing, beginning to pulse on their own. When he slides a hand around and massages my swollen bud, I lose it. Orgasm rips through me with an intensity that makes me forget everything and anything. It's just what I was looking for.

After, we're still panting when I start to see the room around me clearly for the first time. It's dirty and it smells, and suddenly I need to get the hell out of here. I reach for the paper towels—the roll is sitting on the sink rather than in the dispenser a few feet away—and clean myself up before fixing my clothes. Barely two minutes have passed, and already I want this man inside me again.

Though not here next time.

"Would you like to take me home with you to have sex again?"

Noah smiles. "God, I really do love New York women. No bullshit, straight to the point."

"Have you been with a lot of other women from New York?"

His eyes sparkle. "Not a single one."

I chuckle. "Is that a yes?"

"That's a *fuck yes*. Let's get the hell out of here."

He starts to open the door, but I stop him. "Don't you need to use the bathroom?"

He winks. "It'll hold." Noah grabs my hand and guides me back to the bar, where he tosses a few twenties.

I'm so riled up, I don't even care that I let him pay the bill. I don't have enough cash on me anyway, and closing out the tab with a credit card would take far too long. After, he takes my hand again and practically drags me toward the door.

There are a lot more people here now than when I came in. A couple of guys say hello to Noah as we push through the crowd, but he cuts them off with a curt nod and keeps marching us to the exit. As we reach the door, it swings open. Noah puts his hand on my back and directs me out, not giving the patron coming in a chance to enter first.

The guy shakes his head. "Is there a fire somewhere, Sawyer?"

I freeze.

Noah doesn't notice I've stopped moving until his hand pulls because I'm still rooted in place. "What's the matter?" he asks.

"That guy just called you Sawyer?"

Noah shrugs. "Yeah. So? A lot of people do."

"Why?"

"Because it's my last name."

CHAPTER
13

It's almost four in the morning, and I'm staring at the ceiling, wondering what the hell is going on.

Because *something* surely is.

Those eyes. I have no idea how I didn't recognize them immediately. Noah Sawyer, his *son* . . . just happening upon me at a bar tonight? I chew my lip, roll over, gaze out the dirty, tobacco-stained window. A wiry tree climbs toward the sky, two birds perched there, chirping at each other. My vision goes out of focus as I stare. This is a small town. There are only a couple bars. Maybe . . .

Maybe it was a coincidence. The other men there knew him, called him by name. The bartender knew him, too, even his drink. So it's not like it was his first time there.

Of course, he walked up to *me*, bought me drinks, took a *real strong* interest.

Maybe he'd have done that for any half-attractive woman who was new in town. No doubt he's a flirt, with plenty of confidence, oodles of swagger. I swallow, stop myself from thinking of him like *that*—the way his lips fluttered over my ear, the look of excitement on his face when I walked into the men's room.

I slept with Noah Sawyer.

I was about to go home with Mr. Sawyer's son.

The son of the man I killed . . .

It's revolting to think that monster even had a child.

But what if Noah *knows*?

What if Noah is *Hannah*?

He said he was a writer . . .

I blow out a deep breath and roll off the side of the bed. I can't lie here and do this anymore. I'm still nowhere near ready to sleep after what almost happened earlier. It feels like I might be awake for days, I'm so wired. The drinks I had at the bar have long worn off. Finding out Noah's last name shocked me into instant sobriety.

My gaze finds my suitcase. My flight home is Saturday, but maybe I can get one tomorrow instead. Or today, rather, since it's long past midnight. I hate to leave my mother right now, but I need to be back at work next week anyway, and really, she doesn't want me here. Plus, I'm no use to her when I'm on edge, spiraling out of control. I'm paranoid, sure everyone's involved in whatever the hell is going on—Noah, Mom, the freaking priest, Ivy, even Chief Unger. If I stay here much longer, half the town will be suspects. I should get a list going. I could title it "People I Think Want to Ruin My Life."

I need coffee. Coffee will wake me up from this awful foggy haze I'm stuck in.

I walk out into the kitchen, and the smell hits me. Sour, mildew, *decay*—both of this house and of human life. *My mother is dying*. I swallow and lift the old silver percolator that my mom has used since I was a kid, and a rush of emotion hits me again. It seems to come in waves. I haven't cried yet. And I think it's because none of my feelings are pure. Sadness about my mother's health is mixed with resentment. Guilt for not being here is mingled with anger that she doesn't want me to be. It's exhausting, yet I can't sleep.

I scoop grinds into the old pot, fill it with water, look around as I wait for it to percolate. The floors have a layer of dirt on them, and the sink is stained with yellow scum.

Both need bleach and scrubbing. Maybe I can get someone in here to help Mom. She'd probably say it's a waste of money, that she doesn't *need* my help. Perhaps I could ask the church to say it's their doing, and give them the money for a cleaning company and an aide. I have a decent amount in my savings. Though . . . that would mean talking to Father Preston, wouldn't it? Random thoughts rattle around in my head as the smell of coffee floats through the kitchen.

A few minutes later, with my caffeine in hand, I go back to the tiny bedroom. I toss my suitcase on the bed, pull out a clean outfit, and begin folding shirts and pants, shoving everything inside. I'll take a quick shower, and then I can pack my toiletries and call the airline—

A thud stops me.

I let a shoe fall from my fingers and turn to look over my shoulder and listen. Silence.

"Mom?" I call.

Nothing.

I almost ignore it—probably she drank herself to sleep, and the bottle tumbled from her hand. But it was too loud of a clunk, bigger than a bottle.

"Mom?" This time, I walk into the hall so my voice carries. Again, there's no response. My heart begins to pound faster in my chest. "Hello?" I step hesitantly back toward the kitchen. I see her foot first. A white cotton sock with a hole in the heel, worn to nothing.

"Mom!" I'm on my knees beside her in the next second, touching her gray face, fingers feeling for a pulse. At first, there's nothing—just hot, fevered skin—*at least she's not ice-cold*—but then I find it. A slow, steady *thump, thump, thump.* Her eyes are shut; her mouth gapes open. Her hand twitches, at least a sign of life.

She . . . fell? I feel my forehead wrinkle in a frown. She's probably drunk. Of course she fell. Then I see the blood trickling from the back of her head. *Shit.*

I scramble back to the bedroom, search all over for my cell phone before finding it in my pocket, and dial 911.

I give the operator the address, tell her my mother fell, that she's unconscious and bleeding. The rest is a blur, but she makes me stay on the line while I wait fifteen long minutes, holding my mother's hand, afraid to move her—what if she has spinal cord damage? I remember a *Grey's Anatomy* where I swear they said *never* to move someone if you're not sure. After much too long, there's a knock at the door, then two people sweep in, both men. They ask questions in calm voices, and somehow I manage to match the tone with my responses, when inside, I'm anything but calm.

"My mother fell," I tell them, and I explain what little I know. That I got coffee, that I was packing, that I heard a *thud* . . . "God, what if I weren't here?" My eyes, wide with emotion, meet the gaze of the taller paramedic.

He says something like, "We'll take good care of her," totally ignoring my question as he locks the stretcher on wheels into place waist-high. "We're going to bring her to Memorial Hospital. Do you know the way?"

I shake my head. "I don't remember. I haven't lived here in a long time."

"You can follow us."

"Okay."

I get in the car, not having a clue what is happening. But there's one thing I know for sure. I can't leave town now.

———

"The medication she's taking can compromise her immune system. So when the infection set in, it really took hold." The doctor glances down at Mom and uses her pointer finger to push her glasses up her nose. "But the antibiotics we're giving her should work. We'll add a prophylactic antifungal therapy, just in case. She's weak, but we should be able to get her through this setback."

It's not lost on me that all of the staff have used *should* and not *will*—the medication *should* work, my mother *should* make it. I swallow. "Okay. Thank you."

The doctor leaves the room, and it's just Mom and me.

She's beneath a sheet, the head of her bed elevated. There's an IV taped to her hand, pumping clear liquids—*four* IV bags of them—into her body. The machines make a quiet chugging sound, keeping time with the monitor over her head.

Mom's not just in the hospital. She's in the *ICU*. A cold, creepy place, full of serious nurses who don't seem to smile. And of course, they shouldn't have to—they're literally keeping people alive. Keeping my *mom* alive, even though she's destined to die soon enough.

Six hours and twenty minutes later—I know, because I've been switching between staring at Mom and the clock on the wall—one of the serious nurses walks in. She presses her hand to my shoulder. "I don't think anything is going to change over the next twenty-four hours. The medications need to do their job, and we're giving her a sedative to keep her resting. Her vitals are stable. It's fine if you want to go home and rest."

"Okay. Thank you."

The nurse leaves, and I stand and stare down at my mother. I've obviously known she was critically ill since I walked in and took my first look at her—her skin color and sunken face told me before she confirmed it. Yet somehow it's not until this moment that it sinks in that it's going to be soon, *very soon*. If not this hospital admission, then the next or the one after that, but there won't be very much time between. I take my mother's hand and squeeze it. "Bye, Mom. I'll be back in a bit."

I'm lost in my head as I make my way out of the ICU, take the elevator down to the lobby, and walk through the automatic revolving front door. As I step out, a person is stepping in, but I don't even take note of them until I hear my name.

"Elizabeth?"

I look up and blink a few times. "Lucas?"

"I thought that was you." He smiles, swamps me in a hug that catches me off guard. "How the heck are you? It's been forever."

He shakes his head when he pulls back. "Damn, you look great."

I smile. "You do, too." And he really does. Lucas was lanky in high school, but now he's bulked up, grown into his looks, very manly looking. He used to fool around with Jocelyn, but I always had a little crush on him, too. He's wearing black scrubs, like a few people I saw in the ICU. "Do you work here?"

He nods. "I'm a PA. Are you visiting someone?"

"My mom."

He frowns. "I heard she was sick. You know how this town is—nothing's private. I'm sorry. Everything okay?"

I force a smile. "It will be."

"Good." He shakes his head, eyes sweeping over my face. "You really look amazing."

My belly warms. "Thank you."

"You live in New York, right? I always ask your mom how you're doing whenever I run into her. She brags about you being a professor."

"She does?"

He nods. "Are you married?"

"No. You?"

Lucas shakes his head. "I was engaged until about six months ago, but it didn't work out."

There's a short chirp, a beep of some kind. Lucas looks down and presses a button on a pager clipped to his scrub pants. He frowns and thumbs to the hospital. "I gotta run. How long are you in town for?"

"I'm not sure."

"Maybe we can get a drink, catch up. Let me get your number."

I hesitate. Not because I don't want to have a drink, but

because I'm suspicious of everyone lately. And Lucas was just mentioned in one of the chapters Hannah sent. Though that feels like one coincidence that is *actually* a coincidence. So I smile and nod. "Sure."

"I actually forgot my cell phone at home today. I didn't realize until I parked. So we'll have to do this old school." He pulls a leather satchel from his shoulder and unzips it, then tears off the corner of a piece of paper and hands me a pen. "Just like we did it back in the old days."

I jot down my number and hand it back with a smile.

"Thanks," he says. "I work three twelves—three days on, four off. Today is my last day on, but I'll check in on your mom this afternoon."

"I appreciate that."

"I'll call you?"

I smile. "Okay."

The hospital is only a twenty-minute drive from my mom's, but I yawn twice on the way there. Not having slept all night is catching up to me fast. I need at least a nap, and I should eat something, too, but probably after because I'm too tired to cook anything or go to a store. I pull into the driveway with big plans in my head, but it looks like they might have to wait, because there's another car there already. An unfamiliar pickup truck, red, a little rusty. Typical Louisiana. A man steps—no, *swaggers*—out of it, and I know immediately who it is, even before he shuts the door and I see his handsome face.

"Noah," I murmur. If I had any emotion left, I suspect I'd feel panicked. Angry. Suspicious. Instead, I feel like I might be a little drunk, though this time, alcohol has nothing to do with it. "What are you doing here?"

CHAPTER

14

You left this with the bartender." Noah holds up two fingers, a credit card scissored between them. "Willow called me," he says. "The bartender. I told her I'd try to return it to you."

I'd completely forgotten that I'd given my Amex to open a tab when I ordered my first drink at the bar last night. We'd left in such a hurry.

I step forward and take the card. "How did you know where I lived?"

"Wasn't too hard to figure out. You mentioned your mom was sick, so I asked around if anyone knew a local with the last name printed on your credit card." He shrugs. "It's a small town. Second person I asked goes to Saint Matthew's and knew exactly who I was talking about and where Theresa Davis lived."

I blow out a ragged breath. "Well, thank you for bringing it back."

"You believe in fate, Elizabeth?"

My eyes widen. *What is he asking me?* I shake my head. "Not really. I believe we all choose our paths in life."

"Then maybe you *chose* to leave that card behind, perhaps even subconsciously, so I'd come find you."

"I think it's more likely I'm getting forgetful in my old age."

Noah smiles, flashes those killer, boyish dimples. "Why'd you run out on me last night, darlin'?"

"I just . . . I had a little too much to drink. And when the fresh air hit me, it sobered me up. I realized I needed to quit while I was ahead."

"I thought we had a good time, had good chemistry."

"We did. But . . . you're too young for me."

"I'm twenty-seven, not seventeen. Besides, most women would put my being a youngblood in the pros column, not the cons."

Seventeen.

The age I was when . . .

I search Noah's face for signs that he's screwing with me. But I don't find anything sinister lurking. "It just wouldn't be a good idea to take things any further."

"Do you have a boyfriend back home?"

"No." I pause. I should cut off the conversation, go inside. But there's something about this man, even sober. And knowing who he is now, curiosity gets the best of me. "Do you have a girlfriend?"

"Not anymore. Broke up two months ago."

"Why?"

He shrugs. "Didn't want the same things."

"What does that mean?"

"She wanted a family . . . kids."

"And you don't want that right now?"

"I don't want that ever."

"Why not?"

"You ever get married or have any kids?"

I shake my head.

"Feel like telling me why *you* made that decision?"

I can't help it, I smile. "Got it."

Noah looks down, kicks his foot in the dirt in an *aww, shucks* way. "I like you, Elizabeth. Don't meet many women like you around here. I'd really like to take you out."

I pause. Something in the pit of my belly wants to say yes. Instead, I shake my head. "Not a good idea."

"Maybe. But some of the best times I've ever had started from bad ideas."

I chuckle. He has an answer for everything.

Noah looks up and catches my eyes. "Seriously, though, you seem like a woman who speaks her mind. And I don't hear you saying you don't *want* to go out with me. There's a difference between not *wanting* to do something and thinking it's a bad idea."

I didn't notice it last night, because the bar was so dark. But his eyes are the *exact* same color as his father's—deep mossy green with specks of gold. There's a lot I can't remember from twenty years ago, but a person remembers the face of a person they're about to kill. The only difference is Noah's eyes have a light that shines from them, a sparkle that reflects the sun. Mr. Sawyer's were cold and flat, even when he was still breathing. Same as last night, I find myself very drawn to this man.

"How long you in town for?" he asks when I still haven't responded.

I thumb toward the front door. "I'm not sure anymore. I was planning on leaving today. But then my mom fell. She's in the hospital now."

"I heard about her health. The woman who told me where you live mentioned your mom was sick with cancer."

I nod. "Her prognosis isn't good."

He nods. "I know how hard that can be. My mom died not too long ago. Heart disease. It was tough to watch."

"I'm sorry." And I am . . . but he's also just opened a door . . . "Do you still have your dad?"

Noah looks away. "He died when I was just a kid."

I wait, hoping he'll say more. But he doesn't. Instead, he swings his keys around and tosses them in the air, catching them with a jingle as they come down. *Must be a Southern thing*. "Welp, I guess I should be going. I really would love to take you out, but I won't push, especially when you're going through so much."

I nod. "Thank you again for returning my card."

"Anytime. And if you ever feel like company—just a friendship, a shoulder to cry on if things with your mom get tough—you call me." He winks. "I wrote my cell on the signature strip on the back of your credit card."

I smile. "Thanks, Noah."

He steps forward and kisses my forehead. It's sweet and feels innocent enough.

"Take care, Elizabeth. I wish you well."

I watch him walk away, but as he does, an overwhelming sense of fear that I'm about to lose something I need hits me. "Wait!" I yell as he's pulling his truck door closed.

He unfolds from the driver's seat and gives me his full attention.

"Why don't you come inside for a little while?"

———

"Is this you?" Noah picks up a framed photo and turns it to me. I'm in my communion dress, hands steepled like the good Christian my mother always wanted.

"It is."

"Are you religious?"

"No."

He looks at me expectantly. After a minute, he grins. "Aren't you going to ask if I am?"

"Nope. That's your business."

He smiles and sets down the photo. "You see, that's what makes you different from the ladies around here. You think it's okay to keep some things private."

"Of course it is."

He shakes his head. "The women I've dated want to know every thought going through my head."

"Sounds like they're insecure."

Noah shrugs. "Maybe." He looks around the room. "So is this where you grew up? This house?"

"It is."

"It's nice."

"It's a shithole."

He laughs. "See? There you go again. No bullshit. You just tell it like it is."

"Would you rather I bullshit you?"

"Not at all. I appreciate a woman who is straight with me."

I tilt my head. "So does that mean you're being straight with me, Noah?"

His brows draw together. "About what?"

"Everything. Anything."

His eyes jump back and forth between mine. "I haven't told you one lie since we met."

Again, he looks sincere. But did he select his words carefully? He hasn't *told me a lie*—but are there things he's failed to tell me? Omissions? Like he knows who I am? That he sat down next to me on purpose? That he is a student of mine . . .

I make use of the attention he's giving me, keeping our gazes locked. "What made you approach me last night?"

"You were the prettiest girl in the room."

"*Woman*, not *girl*, Noah."

His eyes do a quick sweep over my body, and he grins. "Right. All woman. That's for shit-sure." He steps closer. My heart races, but I stand my ground. Noah brushes hair from my shoulder. "You're really beautiful."

Something about his voice, the Southern drawl I haven't heard in ages, makes butterflies flutter in my belly—some a little lower, too. "Thank you."

He leans in and takes a deep inhale. "Smell damn good, too."

"It must be the hospital."

He grins, undeterred, and brushes his nose along the pulse

line in my neck. "Couldn't stop thinking about you last night when I got home." He groans. "What happened in that bathroom was something else."

My eyes shut, my head lolls back, giving him better access. Hot breath tickles my skin. Noah's mouth moves to my ear. "Can I kiss you again, Elizabeth? Touch you again?"

I want to say no, but I also want to forget—forget my mom is dying, forget about Hannah Greer, forget about Louisiana. Plus, I really want to feel his body press up against mine again. Though, with my life spinning so out of control lately, I need to be the one to take the lead. Without saying anything, I put my palm to his chest, nudge him back not-too-gently. He takes one, two, three steps backward. When the backs of his knees hit the couch, I give him a good push, and he falls down onto it. Then I climb on his lap, straddle his hips, and seal my mouth over his.

I'm momentarily thrown by how soft his lips are now. But then Noah's tongue dips inside, his fingers dig into my hair, and he winds a clump of it around his fist and holds me tight once again. Soft goes out the window after that. I started this, and I'm on top, but somehow it feels like he's kissing me and not the other way around, like he's topping from the bottom. And . . . I like it. I like how aggressive he is, how tight his grip is. My eyes roll into the back of my head when he pushes up and grinds a steely erection against me through his jeans. One of his big hands grips my hip and starts to move me back and forth. It feels so damn good, the friction hitting the perfect spot . . . But then a cell phone rings. I try to ignore it, dive further into the kiss to block it out—but Noah pulls back. "Should you get that? It could be the hospital."

I blink a few times. *Shit*. He's right. And what the hell am I doing anyway? I climb off him and look around for where the sound is coming from. The kitchen. My purse.

"Hello?"

"Is this Elizabeth Davis?"

"Yes?"

"This is Kate Stern. I'm a nurse at Memorial Hospital."

"What happened?"

"Your mother's stats have dropped. We might need to intubate. The notes show you weren't sure if your mother had a living will or an advance directive."

I shake my head. "I was going to look for one when I got home. But I didn't get a chance yet."

"Can you do that now and call me back?"

"Of course."

"Thank you."

I swipe the phone and head to my mother's bedroom—to the file cabinet she used to keep in her closet. I don't even know if it's there anymore. A man's voice startles me—I'd completely forgotten Noah was even here.

"What happened?" He stands. "Is everything okay?"

I keep walking without stopping. "No. I'm sorry. You should go. I need to get back to the hospital."

CHAPTER
15

The temperature in this hospital room seems to have dropped a couple more degrees. My fingers are cold, my toes frozen inside my shoes. Or maybe I'm in shock, staring across the room at my mother. I want to call her *lifeless*, but as that may literally be the truth soon, I can't bring myself to think it. Rather, she's motionless—eyes closed tight, head at a slightly awkward angle, a tube protruding from between her lips. Next to the bed, a machine breathes for her, loud mechanical inhales and exhales mixed with beeps. The screen is lit up, white, blue, green, red—numbers I can't make sense of.

I couldn't find any paperwork detailing what kind of medical care she wanted, no DNR or advance directive, not even a will. By the time I arrived, they'd already put the breathing tube in.

The nurse who's been here all day comes by. She stops in the doorway. "Hi, Ms. Davis. I just wanted to let you know, I'll be leaving soon. The night nurse will be Michael, and he'll be by to check in with you shortly." She smiles. "You're in good hands with him."

"Okay, thank you."

Is it really late enough to be night already? I guess so. Outside the small window, it's grown dark. It feels like an hour ago I was pouring coffee and packing a bag, planning on saying goodbye to Mom and disappearing back to New York, knowing that in a month or two or three, I'd get a call telling me she was gone.

I hadn't let myself think about that part. About how I'd feel—would I cry then? I swallow bitter hospital-cafeteria coffee and gaze at her, skin and bones beneath the white sheet and teal-green blanket printed with the hospital logo. She wasn't a good mom. In fact, she was pretty shitty. Mostly because of the alcohol—at least that's what I want to think. It's easier if I have something to blame it on. It wasn't that she didn't care to come home or make sure I had dinner— it was the vodka. Addiction brings out the ugly in people. It hits me that I should probably make sure the nurse knows she's a drinker. Will she have withdrawals, even here in the hospital, sedated with a breathing tube down her throat?

I don't know.

I stare down at her. I have some good memories, even if I have to search way back to find them. Before the alcohol became her priority, before men became more important than me, back when . . .

A memory flits by. Mom in a yellow dress. We were in bayou country, thick with cypress trees, sluggish marshes, and the smell of seafood. I don't remember too much, just us walking down a wooden dock, the planks hot beneath my feet. She picked me up, carried me on her hip, twirled us around while we laughed. It's one of my last memories of feeling safe, loved. The memory fades, and I'm left wondering if maybe I dreamed it up. Maybe my imagination filled in gaps where I had no positive memories. If she wakes up, I think I'll ask her if we took that trip.

There's nothing to do now but wait, see if the antibiotics work, if the breathing machine can take some of the load so she can rest and grow stronger. My gaze skims the bags hanging from the IV pole yet again. There are six now—they added something called norepinephrine to keep her pressure up. She's getting blood, too, pumped into another line they put in her.

I sigh, resigning myself to one fact: I can't leave Louisiana.

I was fooling myself to think I could. Like it or not, this is where I'm supposed to be.

Maybe for more than one reason. This and . . . The IV bags blur as my mind wanders to the *other* reason. There are too many unanswered questions. About Noah and his father. I reach for my phone and send my department chair a quick email telling her I have a family emergency, that my mom is sick. I'm going to need a few more days off, maybe a week.

Hours pass, and I close my eyes, take a deep breath in, and exhale, trying to silence my swirling thoughts. And despite it all, Noah cuts through again. I invited him in. Kissed him again. Might have even—

"Ms. Davis?"

My whole body jolts.

"Oh, I'm sorry. Were you . . ." I look up to find a new doctor in a white coat. She's short, with blunt-cut hair framed around her tiny face, looking at me with concern. "Are you okay, ma'am?"

"Sorry, yes, I'm fine."

"Would you like me to ask the nurse to bring in bedding? That chair converts." She gestures to a stiff blue chair sitting under the tiny window.

"No. But thank you." My gaze shifts to my mother, then back to the doctor. "How is she?"

"She's stabilized for the time being. Her stats have come up since we started the antibiotics and put in the breathing tube. We'll keep her sedated overnight. Hopefully, tomorrow we'll see more improvement. I know it looks scary right now, but she's getting everything she needs."

"Okay." I nod. "Thank you."

I stay another hour, but when I yawn for the third time, I decide to call it a day. I can't remember the last time I slept.

Before I go, I check in with the nurses' station and let them know I'll be back tomorrow, make sure they have my number handy.

Outside, the air is damp, heavy. But at least the claustrophobia of the small ICU room fades. The sky glows with a smattering of stars, and I focus on breathing as I walk out to my rental car. My phone buzzes as soon as I start it up, and I look down and find a text.

> **Sam:** Hey. Are you back from your trip to Louisiana?
> Get together this weekend?

I swipe it away, put my phone down, and start the car. Life is complicated enough at the moment.

When I reach the house, I take a shower and grab my laptop before climbing into bed. I need to check my email to see if my department chair has responded. Maryellen often takes a few days, so if she hasn't, I'll call her in the morning to make sure she has enough time to find a professor to fill in while I'm out. But the email at the top of my inbox is the old one from Hannah Greer, and I can't help myself. I hit reply.

> Hannah,
>
> Your story has definitely caught my attention. I'd like to schedule a Zoom to discuss what might come next. Please let me know a date and time that is good for you.
>
> Thank you,
> Professor Davis

After I hit send, my finger hovers over the last chapter she submitted. I consider rereading it and looking for something—*anything*—I might have missed that could give me a clue who the hell is doing this to me. But today has been rough enough, and I wind up slamming the laptop shut. I'm not letting myself reread anything right now. Though maybe tomorrow it's time I speak to the only other person on this planet who *should* know what happened twenty years ago.

The next day, I don't wait for hours in the parking lot. I pull up, park, sip my third coffee of the day, and within minutes, Ivy's walking toward my rental car. She strides purposefully, like she spotted me through the window and knows why I'm here. The sun beats down overhead, and I can see beads of sweat forming on her brow.

"What are you doing here?" she snaps after she climbs into the passenger seat. I hand her a coffee, which she rolls her eyes at. "You call me out of the blue after twenty years, then show up at my office and offer me a coffee, like we sit around and chitchat every day over a cup of Folgers?"

"Hello to you, too. Does that mean you don't want it?"

She sighs. "I can't drink coffee after two p.m. or I won't sleep. Plus, it's like a hundred degrees out."

"Fine. I'll drink it." I drop it into the cup holder.

"Why are you here, Elizabeth?"

"You know why."

"No, I don't. I've given it a lot of thought, and it's *just a coincidence*, and you're paranoid. Now I don't want to think about it anymore."

I turn and glare at her. Last time we spoke, she seemed pretty convinced, what with the Saint Agnes pendant. But now I see the resolve in her eyes as she looks forward, refusing to meet my gaze. She doesn't want it to be real, and so she's decided it isn't. As long as she sticks her head in the sand and continues her merry little life in the middle of nowhere Louisiana, she'll be fine. Or so she's convinced herself.

"Okay . . ." I reach into the back seat for my bag, yank

out my laptop, click a few buttons, and pull up the chapters. "Read these."

"I don't want to read this stupid—"

"If you're so sure it's just a coincidence, you have nothing to lose. Read them, Ivy."

With an even more exaggerated sigh than the last, she takes the computer, adjusts the angle of the screen, and squints, like she needs glasses. *God, we're getting old.* I pluck the readers off the top of my head and shove them at her.

"Thanks," she mutters and slips them on, peering at the screen.

I sip my coffee, waiting and watching. I know what comes next. I know what she'll say.

"Oh my God." Her voice comes out tiny, strained. "You were serious."

"Of *course* I was serious!"

"This is . . ." Her hand goes to her chest. After another moment, she closes the laptop quickly, like she can't read any more. "Lucas? The kneeling? The pendant? But who could know, Lizzie, *who?*"

My old name. A nickname no one uses anymore. It unsettles me more than I care to admit. "I don't know," I say.

"Why now? It's been *twenty years.*"

Again, I shake my head. "I don't know."

Silence. Then Ivy turns my way, her hand clasping my arm. "You've been seeing that guy, right? His son? Noah."

I fight the urge to roll my eyes. *Small towns.*

"No, we just met at Liars Pub, the place on Main Street."

"Is it him?"

Of course I've been kicking that very question around since we walked out of the bar. As crazy of a coincidence as it is that we would meet, my gut thinks that's all it was. "I don't think so, but I don't know for sure."

"Well, we *need* to know."

"What would you like me to do, ask him? *Hey. Are you pretending to be my student and sending me a twisted story because I killed your father?*"

Ivy's eyes dart around the parking lot. "*Shhh.* Keep your voice down."

No one's near the car, but she's right. Lord knows, Chief Unger seemed to have materialized out of thin air. I lower to a whisper. "I don't think it's him."

"Well, can you go back to the bar? Maybe get him drunk and start him talking?" Her voice fades off. She gnaws on her lip, deep in thought. "Even if it's not him, maybe he knows something we don't. He had to know his father better than anyone still alive." Her eyes roam my face. "You're still as pretty as you were back then. He's a man, a single one from what I understand." Her eyes meet mine. "Get close to him. Do whatever it takes. We have to figure out who this is. We *have* to."

I study her, surprised by her cunning. I wouldn't have thought Ivy, of all people—small-town Ivy, who got married soon after high school and never left Louisiana—would suggest such a thing.

But I do know one thing.

She's right.

I nod. "I'll work on it. I will."

Ivy's shoulders relax. "I need to get back. I have a foster parent coming for a checkpoint meeting."

"All right. I'll call you."

Ivy pushes open the car door, swings her feet, and is about to get out. I touch her shoulder. "Ivy, wait."

She turns.

"It's good to see you," I say. "And I'm sorry I accused you."

She smiles sadly. "It's good to see you, too, Lizzie. You really do look amazing."

"So do you."

She snort-laughs. "You're full of shit. But thank you for lying."

I smile. "I'll let you know if I find out anything."

Twenty minutes later, I slow my car and turn into the parking lot of Liars Pub. I park the car, shut it off, and scan until my eyes find what I'm looking for.

A red pickup. *Noah's* red pickup.

CHAPTER
16

I glance up at the tattered vinyl sign hanging over the door as I reach for the handle. "Ladies drink half price and free hot wings."

I suppose it explains why the parking lot is so packed, compared to last time I was here.

Three steps inside the bar, my eyes lock on Noah. He's on the other side of the room, but he looks up, spots me, and a slow smile spreads across his face. He's talking to a blond girl wearing a yellow sundress—well, she's talking to him—but she seems to have lost his attention as his eyes follow my every step. I wonder if she's the one—the one who wants the white picket fence and a yard full of kids.

I make my way to the bar, ignoring men whose eyes rake up and down my body, definitely ignoring the guy in the trucker hat who drawls, "Damn, is it hot in here, or is that just you?"

Noah's waiting by the time I push the rest of the way through.

There must be a speaker overhead, because in this corner of the room, the music is deafening. Noah leans to my ear and yells over Luke Combs. "You have no idea how happy I am to see you."

I sense eyes still watching me. Glancing over to where

Noah just came from, I find Little Miss Sundress looks irritated. To her credit, when our gazes meet, she stands taller, doesn't look away. *Good for you.* I ignore her anyway.

"I think someone else might not be so thrilled I'm here."

Noah's brows pucker. I lift my chin in the direction of the woman, who is still staring.

He waves her off. "That's Ginny. We're just friends."

I'm not sure Ginny got the memo on that. "She's very pretty."

"Doesn't hold a candle to you."

The bartender walks over, a different woman from last time. Same half shirt, though. Must be the uniform. "You need something, Noah?"

He looks to me. "You want Hendrick's again?"

I shake my head. "I'll just take a water."

He grins, then turns back to the bartender, holding up his Miller Lite. "Another one of these and a bottle of water, please, Kiki."

"You got it."

Noah reaches out, tugs at a piece of hair that's fallen in my face. "If you didn't come for the alcohol, then you came for something else?"

I'd driven here with the intention of chatting him up, seeing what I could get out of him. But this close, information isn't what I feel like taking anymore. There's real chemistry here. It lights up my body, makes me feel like a sparkler on the Fourth of July.

I tilt my head. "Maybe I came for the free hot wings."

His lip twitches. "Would you like me to order you some?"

"No thanks. I'm not hungry."

Noah's playful dimples make an appearance. He reaches forward, puts a hand on my hip, and my skin tingles beneath his touch. I remember how those fingers dug in not long ago, how good they felt on my bare skin.

"Is this where you spend all your free time?" I ask.

"Not usually. I prefer the Big Devil Bayou on the north side of town. Do you know it? I fish off the old dock."

"I do. Though I'm surprised that dock is still standing. I haven't been there in decades, and it was rotting back then."

Noah sips his beer. "I replaced the decking a few years back. Not too many know I did it, so I usually have the place to myself. I go there to calm my mind."

"Why aren't you there now?"

He grins. "Because I met you here, and I was hoping I'd run into you again."

I feel heat rise within me. He's an irresistible temptation I can't ignore.

Suddenly, the music blaring through the shitty speakers cuts mid-song and a woman's voice comes overhead. "Hey, everyone. We're about to get started. Our first brave soul for the evening is Tonya Woodsman. She's going to be singing 'Before He Cheats.' Let's give her a warm welcome."

The bar erupts in applause, a bunch of whistles and hoots and hollers. Unfortunately, the only thing I hate more than country music is *karaoke* country music. Though a few seconds later, the woman takes the mic and starts to belt out something about bleach blondes, and she's actually pretty good. Her deep, raspy voice sounds better than the stuff that was playing a few minutes ago. Noah and I watch her for a moment. Halfway through the song, he leans over and says something, but it's so damn loud in here now, I have to cup my ear.

"What?"

He yells louder. "I asked how your mom is doing."

"Oh." I shake my head with a frown. "Not great. They had to put her on a ventilator."

We go back and forth for a few minutes, trying to have a conversation. But more than half the time we have to repeat ourselves. Eventually, Noah yells, "How about we get out of here, so we don't have to scream? Maybe go to my place?"

He reads the wariness on my face without me having to

say anything and leans to my ear again. "I promise I'll be on my best behavior. I won't try anything, if that's not what you want. We can just talk, without having to yell." He pulls back and winks. "Unless you decide otherwise. I really like it when you make the moves. It's sexy as fuck."

The first time we met, we had sex, and I almost left with him. The second time we were alone, I was on top of him ten minutes after we went inside the house. What are the chances we're going to *just talk*? Though I do need to get closer . . .

"How about we go for ice cream instead?" I ask. "Or for a walk?"

Noah shrugs. "If that's what you want. But I would love to show you the work I'm doing on my house. I'm renovating it top to bottom. Taking me forever, but I'm doing it all myself. I make furniture as a hobby. This is my first real construction project."

He sounds sincere, but it's not actually *him* I don't trust. It's me. I've been making some dumb decisions lately, present company included. I'm still debating, getting ready to decline the invitation, when he sweetens the offer.

"It's not far. Only about two miles away. It was my parents' house for thirty years, so I'm trying to update it and make it my own."

My parents' house.

I know where Mr. Sawyer lived. Drove past it enough times with Jocelyn back in the day. But I've never been inside. Maybe it holds the answers to all the questions I have. How can I say no?

I take a deep breath. "I'll follow you in my car."

Noah smiles like he's just won a prize. "Excellent."

The five-minute drive is nerve-racking. I consider calling Ivy on the way, telling her I'm about to go into *his* house. But her husband would probably ask who was on the phone, and then there would be a digital footprint connecting us since I don't have my prepaid with me. I can't be that sloppy, not now. Not after all these years.

My palms are a sweaty mess as we turn down Glenn Oak Drive. It's a wide road, with bald cypress trees lining both sides of the paved blacktop. Ghostly gray tendrils of Spanish moss drape from one side of the road to the other, creating the feeling of going through a tunnel. It's pretty during the day, eerie as hell at night. Especially when it's leading to a place I'm dreading stepping into almost as much as I can't wait.

We pull into the driveway, Noah's red pickup first, me behind him. I look up at the familiar house and white-knuckle the steering wheel. It looks exactly the same as I remember.

Calm down, Elizabeth. He's not in there.

He's dead.

He's fucking dead.

Noah walks to my car and opens the door, extends a hand to help me out. I take a deep breath before unfolding.

"Don't look at the outside," he says. "That'll be the last thing I get to."

Once I'm standing, he doesn't let go of my hand. Instead, he laces our fingers together for the walk to the front door. I'm *not* a hand-holder. But I don't pull away because there's a fifty-fifty chance I'll pass out before we get to the door. My breaths are coming in short, shallow spurts, and I'm light-headed and nauseous.

Noah creaks open the rickety door, reaches inside, and flicks on the lights. He extends a hand for me to walk in ahead of him.

"Ladies first . . ."

I manage to put one foot in front of the other. I'm not sure what I expected—dark, gloomy rooms packed with musty furniture covered by sheets, cobwebs hanging all over—but it's nothing like I'd imagined. The first room we enter is bright and airy, with high ceilings, walls painted creamy off-white, and wide-plank oak flooring. A sweeping staircase is off to one side, and there's even a big, rustic-looking chandelier hanging in the center.

"It used to have eight-foot ceilings, but I opened up the first and second floor to make it one. Probably going to regret it when the August air-conditioning bills start rolling in, but I like the way it makes me feel when I enter."

"It's really beautiful."

He points up to the ceiling, to a giant skylight I hadn't noticed. "During the day, I get a ton of sun, so I don't need to turn on any lights at least." Noah puts his hand on the small of my back and guides me to the next rooms. There's a big kitchen with a new double island, a laundry room, formal dining room, and two bedrooms. Every room is in a different phase of construction. Upstairs, he shows me two more bedrooms, one of which is the only room not under construction so far. It's where he sleeps, but it has only a basic frame holding a mattress because he put all the other furniture in storage.

Noah continues with the tour, opening the last door on the left and flipping the light switch. "This is the only other room I haven't started. It was my father's office."

Floor-to-ceiling bookshelves line three of the walls. I walk over to the nearest one and run my finger along some of the old, leather-bound spines.

"He was a collector. My mother always said if anyone breaks in, let them take her jewelry, just leave the books. Apparently, they're worth more."

I scan the shelves, freezing when I come to an area of framed photos. My heart might even stop beating for a few seconds when I see the eyes. They're cold, distant, even though he's looking straight at the camera. Noah walks over, stands close behind me. He lifts his chin and gestures to the middle frame. "I was three in that photo."

I hadn't even noticed the little boy holding up a fish, too stuck on the evil monster standing next to him.

"Maybe you knew my father," he says. "Damon Sawyer? He taught English at the high school."

I shake my head. "No."

"You sure? Mr. Sawyer? It's not a very big school. The kids usually know all the teachers, even the ones they don't have."

I feel him watching me now. It takes everything I have to keep my composure. It was stupid to say I didn't know him. *Of course* I'd know him. Everyone knows everyone in this Podunk town, especially a teacher who *died*. But self-preservation answered before I could think it through, as if saying I'd never heard the name would make it true. But I'm stuck now, so I need to go with it. I shake my head again. "The name isn't familiar."

"What year did you graduate?"

I swallow, trying to think of a way around this. "Two thousand and five."

Noah reaches to the shelf, picks up a frame that's sitting face down. He turns it over and hands it to me. A giant close-up of Mr. Sawyer's face stares at me. For a moment, I think I might vomit.

"Are you *sure* he doesn't look familiar? Two thousand and five is the year he died . . ."

CHAPTER

17

I tilt my head and squint, do my best to feign confusion. "Did you say Mr. Sawyer? I thought your last name was Meyer?" It's the closest to Sawyer I can come up with under pressure. It's a big, fat lie, of course, but from the uncertainty in his gaze, he can't tell for sure. That also means he doesn't necessarily *believe* me . . .

He's about to step back, step away from me and distance himself, which is a sign of mistrust. I act without thinking. Again.

"I hate to admit this, make the math even easier to figure out my age, but high school was like twenty years ago. I don't even remember the names of teachers I *did* have." I close the little space between us, grab his forearm, yank his body against mine. His chest is hard as a rock, and I trail my fingertips from his defined pecs to the ridge of his hip, and lower.

He hisses when I dip under his shirt and scrape my nails along his smooth skin.

"I can think of better things to do than stroll down memory lane," I whisper. "How about you?"

The smile comes back to his face. I bet I could get him to agree his last name *really is* Meyer, given a few more minutes.

Sex has always been my way to forget, and clearly I'm not alone. The conversation we were just having about his father is about to become a distant memory for Noah.

But this isn't only about distracting him now. My own body trembles with real desire.

I sweep my other arm around his neck and pull him down for a kiss. He doesn't resist. Just the opposite. His tongue dips inside, taking the lead like the other day at Mom's house. Noah groans as his hand wraps around my back, and he clutches me tighter to him.

For a moment, we pull back and just breathe, heat building between us, our foreheads pressed together. Our eyes meet for a moment, those eerily familiar eyes . . . and I lean in, take his bottom lip between my teeth, and bite down hard.

"I like that," he growls. "When you do that. When you"— I lower my mouth, nip at his collarbone, bite his neck—"take control." He gasps.

I pull back. "That's good. Because that's what I need right now." I smile and reach for the bulge between his legs, tracing the shape, teasing. Even through his jeans, I can feel how hard he is. Noah's teeth clench, and his eyes light up. *Mr. Sawyer who?*

He steps forward, reaches for me, but I smack his hand away and shove him hard. He wasn't expecting it, so he doesn't brace himself, and his back hits the wall with a loud *thump*. The impact knocks one of the photos from the shelf, and it falls to the floor, dragging my attention with it. The close-up framed photo of Mr. Sawyer is staring back at me. My pounding heart screeches to a halt, and I take a step back, hand covering my chest as I work to breathe.

"Are you okay, Elizabeth?"

I look away and shake my head. "It's just . . . I'm sorry. We're moving too fast again."

"I was just following your lead . . ."

"I know you were. And I'm sorry. I don't mean to play hot and cold with you."

Noah rakes a hand through his hair and blows out a deep breath. "It's fine. I understand. How about we sit down? Just relax. Want a beer?"

I nod, and he disappears into the kitchen. He comes back a moment later with a smile and passes me a bottle of beer. But my body feels tight now, anxious, like a snake coiled to strike. I just don't know what or who to strike *at*.

"So, darlin'. Um . . ." He gulps the beer, gives me a kind smile, and I start to think I should have just kept things going. Talking is dangerous when I'm not in the right frame of mind. "Why'd you move up north, anyway?" he asks.

I stare too hard at the label on my beer. It's Shiner Bock, the golden sticker peeling at the corner. "Family problems. What else?" I take a sip and wince at the taste. I don't really like beer, and right now I could use something stronger than this stuff.

"Yeah. I understand that." He sighs heavily. I wait for him to go on, elaborate on exactly *how* he understands, but he doesn't, and I take a long moment to just look at him. Even now, at this moment, when I'm questioning my own sanity for being here, there's something about Noah I like. His easy way of going about things, his calm demeanor—I can feel it. Like it's seeping into me, making me calmer, too. I no longer feel like I want to bolt, escape him as fast as I can. I feel a pull toward him—physically and otherwise. But I need to keep focus, remember the conversation I had with Ivy. I'm here to get close to this man and get to the truth. Maybe I can still turn this night around.

"Did your mom ever remarry?" I ask.

He snorts before taking another swig of beer. "Nope. My mother, God rest her soul, was devoted to my father. She never got over him dying."

"That . . . that must've been hard."

Noah goes quiet for a long time. Eventually, he nods and asks, "Your parents still together?"

I look away, considering. "No. My father left when I was young. It was just me and my mom growing up. She's an alcoholic." I pause, looking at him while he's busy staring at his own beer bottle. He seems reflective, like maybe I hit on something he's familiar with, so I keep talking. "I don't really remember my dad. He just took off one day. And Mom—I'd get home from school, and she'd already be passed out. Those were the good nights. Because if she was passed out, I wasn't left alone all night while she went with the new 'uncle' of the week."

I never talk about this stuff. It's been bottled up tight for so many years that I didn't think the rusty cap would ever come off. And yet the words come too easily from my mouth. Like now that the top has been twisted off, now that someone's finally listening, the memories can't rush out fast enough.

"Well . . . that must have been hard, too," Noah says when the silence has stretched too long. He shifts uncomfortably. "I had one good parent, at least."

I blink, wait for more. It doesn't come.

"Which one?" I ask, my voice soft. Like I care. And maybe, oddly, I do a little.

Noah doesn't answer. Just slaps a hand to his thigh and rises to his feet. "Gotta hit the head." He leaves the room, and I let out a breath held high in my chest. My gaze moves around, locking on the large, wooden desk that sits beneath the only window. Before I consider my actions, I'm at the desk, yanking out one drawer after another, searching for . . . I don't know.

Anything.

A smoking gun, perhaps?

I have to be quiet, have to be fast.

"Elizabeth?" Noah's voice interrupts. He's a few feet away, coming down the hall already. "You want another beer?" I slide the last drawer shut and mentally search for an excuse to be standing here because I don't have time to move. In a panic, I yank my phone from my pocket, press it to my ear, and nod along like someone's talking to me.

"I understand," I say as he steps into the office. He stops, stares at me, eyes full of concern.

The hospital? he mouths. I nod and turn away, focused on the make-believe conversation while I stare out the window.

Before I pretend to disconnect, I give myself a second to consider the whole evening. Noah doesn't seem to be questioning why I'm standing at the desk, doesn't seem to know I just rifled through it. But it's yet another too-close-for-comfort moment, and I think it's best I leave—in a hurry, not leaving room for questions. Or room to wind up in another lip-lock, which I desperately *want* to do and think is an awful idea. Especially *here*, in Mr. Sawyer's *house* . . .

"I have to go," I say. "I'm sorry."

"Is your mom okay?"

I shake my head. "She's not doing well."

Noah frowns. It seems genuine. "I'm sorry. Do you want me to take you to the hospital? Maybe you shouldn't drive when you're so worried."

God, he really is sweet. I've done nothing but play hot and cold with this man, and yet here he is concerned, offering to drive me. I force a smile. "I'll be okay. But thank you."

"I'll walk you out."

At my car, Noah cups my cheek. "I know how hard it is to lose your mother. Call me if you need anything, okay? I mean it."

I nod. "Good night, Noah."

A mile up the road, instead of taking the right turn for the hospital, I make the left turn home. Mentally, I berate myself— for almost getting caught, for *enjoying* him. As insane as it is, my body is still on fire for the man. Even if his eyes do look just like Mr. Sawyer's . . . God, what the hell is wrong with me that I'm attracted to him, knowing they're related?

As soon as I'm inside the front door of Mom's house, the stench of stale liquor and sickness hits my nose, and I realize I've forgotten my purse in the car. This may be a small town, but I've been living in New York City, and there, you don't leave anything anywhere if it matters to you. So I walk back out the door, through the country-night darkness, and lean from the driver's side to grab my purse from the passenger's seat. As I'm climbing back out, a car whooshes by on the road behind me. I look up just in time to catch the taillights. The taillights of a *red pickup*.

CHAPTER

18

"I'm fine all by myself." Mom swats my hand away.

I push the walker in front of her again. "The doctor said you need to use it. You might be out of the woods for now, but it's going to take some time to get your strength back."

She reaches for it like she's going to take it, then lifts and flings it across the hospital room. *Guess he misjudged your strength.* Whatever. The one thing my mother taught me that's been valuable in my life is you can't help people who don't want to be helped. So instead of hovering as she makes her way to the bathroom, I decide to pack up her stuff. It's been a long six days since she was admitted, four since she woke up.

The nurse comes in as I'm zipping the duffel. She looks around and smiles. "Mrs. Davis make an early escape?"

"She's in the bathroom. Wouldn't let me help her, of course."

"She's an independent woman with a beautiful soul."

I have to turn away so the nice nurse won't see me rolling my eyes. My mother swings open the bathroom door.

"Elizabeth, you better . . ." She stops short when she realizes someone else is in the room. God forbid anyone see how she treats her own flesh and blood.

The nurse rushes over and grabs Mom's elbow. "Mrs. Davis, you shouldn't be walking unattended."

Of course, my mother doesn't tell *her* where to stick it. She even plays into the role of a dying woman. She hunches her back and shuffles her steps like she didn't just have the strength to toss a piece of medical equipment across the room.

The nurse helps Mom into bed and tucks her in. "I just started working on your discharge paperwork," she says. "We should have you out of here within an hour."

"Take your time, dear." Mom pats the nurse's hand. "I know how busy you are. I'm just grateful for all you've done."

As soon as the woman leaves the room, my mother's face changes. It contorts back to the miserable one reserved just for me. I'll never understand what I've done to deserve so much hatred. Then again, I suppose, my being born was enough of a burden on her.

"Did you even bring me clean underwear? I can't be going into God's house without my privates covered."

"You almost died a few days ago. You were on life support. Don't you think maybe you should just go home and rest?"

"The Lord doesn't rest. Besides, it's Sunday. Where else would I go after my life has been spared but to thank our maker? I'm walking out of here on my own. It's a miracle."

"Or," I mumble under my breath, "it's antibiotics."

"I *heard that*."

Forty-five minutes later, we're in my car and on our way. My mother looks over as I merge onto the highway. "It's disrespectful to wear dirty sneakers to church."

"Your shoes don't look dirty."

Her eyes narrow. "I meant *yours*. Do you have a change of shoes in this fancy rental car somewhere?"

I smile and keep my eyes forward, focusing on the road in front of me. "Not planning on going in, Mother. I'll take you, if that's what you really want. And I'll happily help you inside. But after that, I'll be waiting in the car."

Mom purses her lips. Though at least she keeps quiet the rest of the drive. I arrive at Saint Matthew's fifteen minutes before mass starts. Father Preston is already at the door, all smiles and handshakes, greeting the early congregants as they arrive. I pull to the curb and shift the car into park.

"Would you like me to help you out, or are you just going to smack my hand away again?"

Mom ignores me and reaches for the door handle. Considering she was almost dead only a week ago, she really has a good amount of pep in her step when she wants to. She disappears inside the church. I sit watching the locals gather, dressed in their Sunday best. After a few minutes, I grow bored and start to fiddle with my phone—at least until a family crossing the street catches my attention.

Ivy. A child holds each of her hands—boy with a collared dress shirt on one side, girl in a blue dress on the other. Seven or eight years old, at best. I know there must be one younger, too, because she bought diapers that time I saw her, but there is no baby today. The man next to her must be her husband. He's wearing a suit, but I can still tell the shirt underneath is too tight. His potbelly is testing the limits of some bulging buttons. Church could be dangerous today—a parishioner might lose an eye. Behind them trails a third child, a teenage boy looking down at whatever gaming device is in his hands. He doesn't even look up as they cross the street, same as every Gen Z with a cell phone on the streets of Manhattan.

Father Preston's face lights up as they approach.

Looks trustworthy, doesn't he?

A man who will lull you into telling him anything. My mother. Ivy.

I tap my fingernails on the steering wheel as I watch. *But what does he do with it?*

I'm still tossing that question around when Ivy and her family disappear inside. Right behind them is a man I didn't even notice coming. *Chief Unger.* Dressed in his uniform. He nods at the priest and walks on in. A few minutes later, a man I don't expect turns up.

Noah.

He's shoulder to shoulder with Little Miss Sundress from the other night. Her blond hair is pulled back, and the sundress is pink today, but it's definitely her. Noah says something and she laughs, grabbing his bicep as they cross the street. *Minnie?* Was that her name? No, Ginny. Definitely Ginny.

"She's just a friend," he said.

They reach the door, and Noah's hand goes to the small of her back in a familiar way. Looks like more than friendship to me.

Another few minutes go by. Father Preston waits for a family jogging to the door before he reaches up, releases the mechanism holding the door open, and begins to shut it. As he does, he looks around once more for stragglers. But his eyes catch mine. He nods and waits. When I don't offer anything in return, he frowns and disappears inside.

I stare at the closed door for a long time. The entire cast of characters is at church today, isn't it? My mother, Ivy, Father Preston, Chief Unger, Noah. There's a niggle, reminding me there's another person, too—one who might not be a suspect, but her presence irks me in a different way. Noah's companion. *We're just friends.*

I run my tongue along my bottom lip, remembering the way I did that to Noah last night, right before sinking my teeth in. He liked it, said I was different from the women from these parts. I can't help but wonder if Little Miss Sundress does things like that for him.

My mind bounces around among all the people I've seen in the last ten minutes . . . so many questions, so few answers.

What does Father Preston know?

Did I start Noah's engine running and Little Miss Sundress got the ride?

Why is Chief Unger so many places that I am?

How does he always appear without me seeing him approach?

Will Ivy's husband's buttons give way? And who watches the child still in diapers when they all come here?

Curiosity gets the best of me, and before I can think it through, I'm turning off the ignition, getting out of the car, and opening the door to the church.

Inside, I slip into the empty back row. My eyes scan the pews one by one.

Noah sits the closest to me. Eight rows from the rear, last seat from the aisle, Blondie sitting dutifully beside him. I briefly wonder again if she might be his ex, the one who wanted marriage and kids, even though he said she was just a friend. She looks like the type. Noah's arm is stretched out along the back of the pew behind her, but his hand isn't touching her shoulder.

One row up, diagonally across from Noah, is Ivy and her family. Her little girl is sitting next to her, picking her nose. Ivy notices and pushes her hand away. The older boy's head is down—probably sneaking to play his game, shooting people and blowing up cars in church. Bulging Buttons and the other boy are at the end of the row. Her husband's eyes look closed, though I'm pretty sure he's not praying, but falling asleep. Can't say I blame the poor guy.

My eyes ping-pong between Noah's row and Ivy's. Do they know each other? Have they met? They're sitting less than ten feet apart. If *he's* Hannah, he must have plans for her, too.

Chief Unger sits closer to the front, one row behind my mother.

What's he up to? I've run into him a little too often. Could he be colluding with the authorities in New York?

I scan the rest of the church. As my eyes cross from one aisle to the next, the little hairs on the back of my neck rise as the sensation of being watched comes over me. I look up and realize *I am* being watched—by Father Preston. Our eyes meet, and he smiles and continues preaching.

A few minutes later, everyone stands for a prayer. The

good father walks to his pulpit and opens a Bible. He says something about forgiveness and marriage. It's not until I hear the word *harlot* that he snags my attention again.

"'I will not punish your daughters when they play the harlot, nor your brides when they commit adultery; for the men themselves go aside with the harlots . . .'"

I blink a few times. *Is this really in the Bible?*

I hear bits and pieces of what he's saying—it's almost like certain words are spoken more clearly than others. "Murmur, murmur, murmur—*sexual deviants*. Blah blah blah—*infidelity*."

And . . . is he looking at Ivy right now? Preaching directly to her? Or am I imagining it?

Maybe I'm losing my mind. Being in this place is enough to make me question my sanity. But when everyone drops to their knees for the Eucharistic prayer, I can't do it. I look at Ivy. She's kneeling, just like the rest of them. My eyes slant to the big, *new* statue on the other side of the church. *Saint Agnes.* The patron saint of *virgins* and *victims of sex abuse*. I can't take it anymore. My head spins. It feels like my throat is closing, and I'm pretty sure another panic attack is on its way. I stand, suddenly in desperate need of fresh air. But as I rush out of the pew, I trip over my own feet and land with a loud *umph*.

A few heads turn—including Noah's.

But I ignore them all, climb to my feet, make a beeline for the door.

Outside, I bend over, hands on knees, and gulp a few deep breaths. Once I'm capable of walking, I lock myself into the safety of my rental car. I need to go home. Today, if possible. Being here is too much. Maybe distance will bring me clarity, at least soothe my paranoia.

Mass seems to take forever to let out after that, but in reality it's probably only fifteen or twenty minutes more. Mom walks to the car. I can't tell if she's acting for the benefit of her flock, or she's just tired, but she doesn't look very sturdy on her feet now. So I get out and take her arm. Surprisingly, she doesn't shoo me away this time. Though maybe she wants me to look the part of doting daughter. Whatever. I'm just glad to help her in whatever little way I can.

I'm closing her car door when Noah jogs over, sans Miss Sundress.

"Hey," he says.

I walk around the car, not slowing my pace to chat.

He brushes a wayward hair from his face. "I'm glad you're still in town."

"Not for long," I say and reach for the driver's-side door. "I'm heading home to pack now."

"You're going back to New York?"

"My mother is out of the hospital. I need to get back to work."

"Can I have your number, at least?"

I smile sadly. "I don't think so."

"Are you coming back?"

My eyes slant to my mother inside the car and return to his without saying anything.

He looks at me for a long time. "I really enjoyed meeting you, Elizabeth."

Did you?

He looks sincere. But what the hell do I know anymore?

I blow out a heavy breath and climb into the car. "Take care, Noah."

As I pull away, I glance in the rearview mirror. Noah's still standing there. Just watching.

CHAPTER
19

I thought returning home would be a relief—that stepping off the plane at JFK, taking the trains home, and walking through the doors to my building would put me at ease. I would breathe again without the humid air of Louisiana. I missed being able to walk in a store and be anonymous instead of running into people I grew up with, people I suspect of *something* . . .

Instead, as I head to the university, that prickle on my neck won't go away, not even after two days. I duck around a corner, then glance through the window front of a café, looking to see who's following me. Of course, there's no one—or rather *everyone*, an assortment of people in all sizes and shapes, headed to the library, to a class, to meet someone. No one is looking at me, though. No one following. At least, no one I see. *I'm being ridiculous.*

I huff out a breath and pull my sweater closed. It's an uncharacteristically chilly morning for the third week in June. I clutch my second cup of coffee, trying to relax enough to avoid squeezing it so tightly it bursts. I didn't sleep well last night. Only a few catnaps where I fell asleep for fifteen or twenty minutes, then lay awake for hours, staring at a dead plant on my windowsill, a gift from Sam the first time he came over. The symbolism isn't lost on me.

As if on cue, my phone buzzes in my pocket, and I slip it out to find Sam's name. I haven't answered his last few messages. I know I need to have a conversation with him, end things politely. He's been kind to me, and I owe him that much. But my head isn't in the right place. It's an effort just to focus on reaching my office, getting to my first class on time. The bustle of campus usually invigorates me, but today—today it's too many people.

Finally, I reach my office. My calendar stares at me from the wall, and I realize tomorrow, I'll be getting more chapters. My stomach roils at that—or maybe it's all the coffee without any food.

I sit down at my desk, then bolt back up to my feet. Someone's been sitting here. My chair is adjusted all wrong. I force myself back down, tentative, feeling the different position of the armrests, the depth of the chair. Whoever sat here is *bigger* than me, taller. My gaze drifts over my desk, but nothing appears out of place.

Was someone going through my things? I imagine Sam or a student or . . .

I swallow more coffee and adjust the height of my chair, eyes darting around the room searching for anything else that's changed. Nothing seems out of order, so I slide open one wooden drawer, then another, and another. My hand pauses on the cool metal of the handle, trying to *think* . . . Is there anything someone might have found?

No, of course not. I have no connection to my old life anymore. No pictures, no datebook with private notations, not even a scribbled-down telephone number lying around. My only connection is the story. Hannah Greer. But that's all digital now, locked away on a server.

It leaves me uneasy, though, and as I gather my things to go to the lecture hall to teach, my mind drifts to Jocelyn. Jocelyn, who wasn't in Louisiana and who I can't find so much as a mention of online. Maybe it's time I find her? She's the missing piece of this puzzle.

A few students are already seated as I enter the classroom and get settled at the front. I pull out my notes for today's lecture. Thankfully, I've taught this class a million times and can do it without any prep. I take my cell out to switch it into silent mode, and Sam's last message appears in preview.

Sam: Get together tonight?

I sigh. Then a thought hits me. Maybe it's time I ask Sam to help me find Jocelyn? Would that be using him? *Maybe. Probably. Yes, yes, it would be.* But these days, I'm not above anything. I nibble on my bottom lip as I debate doing something I know is shitty, not to mention risky. The last of my students file in, and I need to get started, so I force myself to make a decision and text back before silencing my phone.

Elizabeth: Sure, sounds good.

———

The evening starts with wine. As if I didn't already feel like a shitty person, Sam's gone all out, gotten a fancy bottle he says is the *reserve* blend, three burners are going on the stove, and he handed me flowers when he answered the door. The wine is fruity and thick, and I take a long draw, letting it roll over my tongue.

"How's your mom?"

I look up from where I'm studying my glass at the kitchen island. He uses tongs, tosses wild field greens, pours olive oil and vinegar and a seasoning—God, this man turns cooking into an art. I appreciate it, even if I don't have any desire to do it myself.

"Um, she's . . . okay." I try to remember if I told him she was in the hospital. That she's *dying*. Did I text him that? Mention it? Probably not.

He turns his back and moves to the stove to turn the pork chops. I open my mouth, almost tell him. But I don't. It's opening a can of worms, a can full of emotions and heaviness, and that's better left shut tight where I don't have to think about it. "It was good to see her," I finish with, because that's what's expected when you go home and see your mother.

"And Louisiana? How was that?" He turns, hands on hips. My gaze traces the strong, handsome lines of his face, and I can't help but compare him to Noah, even though there's a twenty year age gap. They're both self-assured, borderline cocky.

"Fine. Humid. Churchy."

Sam's gaze is heavy. He nods slowly, like he's trying to figure out what I'm up to. Or maybe it's just my paranoia.

"It's nice to be back." I force a smile, know he'll take that as me saying it's nice to be back *here* with *him*. And that's exactly what happens. His lips curl up, and he leans in, kisses me. I let it linger, manage a smile back. But inside, I feel like shit. He's a really nice guy.

We drink more wine, polish off the bottle.

After dinner, we fall into his bed and don't come up for air until 1 a.m. Sam seems satisfied, sated even, and I'm glad for that, at least. I feel pretty darn relaxed, too, and I think I might even sleep tonight. But first, there's something I need to do . . .

I crawl over and prop my head on a fist, leaning on Sam's chest. His heart is still pounding beneath his rib cage.

"I have a favor to ask," I say.

"Hmm?" he responds sleepily.

"When I was in Louisiana, I couldn't find one of my friends. She was one of my best friends in high school. With my other friend, Ivy, we were like the three musketeers. But

Ivy hasn't been able to get ahold of her, either. I thought she moved down south, maybe to Florida. I'm sort of worried. I tried to look her up online, but I couldn't find anything."

"Maybe she got married? Changed her name?"

"Maybe, but . . ." I sit up, frown. "Shouldn't there be a record of that?"

Sam searches my gaze, nods. "Yes, there should be."

"Do you think maybe you can look her up in that system of yours?"

"Sure. What's her name?"

I stare at him. Even in the dim light, I can make out his features, and I watch carefully as I say, "Jocelyn Burton."

Mostly, I can't imagine he has anything to do with any of this anymore. And he doesn't make a weird face or look shocked. He just thinks it over for a moment and shrugs.

"Sure, I can run her for you. Anything else you have? Birth date or city she was born in?"

"I can write it all down for you in the morning."

"Sounds good. I'll look into it first thing. Don't want you to worry." His hand smooths over my head, through my hair. "I'll do whatever I can."

"Thanks," I say. But I feel like an even bigger piece of shit because of how sweet he is.

We settle beneath the covers, and before long, his breathing takes on that steady, even rhythm of sleep. I expect to pass out, too. But I don't. It's like every other night lately. I'm staring at the ceiling, wondering who I can trust, if anyone. My mind wanders to tomorrow, to the next chapters that are due. Will Hannah submit more of her story? She still hasn't answered my email. And if she does, what secrets will her story tell next?

CHAPTER

20

Chapter 3—Hannah's Novel

Jocelyn's heart raced as she walked through the empty halls. Today was the first time Mr. Sawyer had told her to come so late. Normally, they met after school, when activities were still going on and students were milling around. But now it was six in the evening, and the second floor was so empty that her footsteps echoed, reverberating off the walls. The extra few hours of waiting had seemed to drag on forever. It reminded Jocelyn of a line she'd once read in a book: *Sometimes the anticipation is more exciting than the event.* Wasn't that the truth of most things in high school? First kiss, junior prom, Christmas—all letdowns. Yet Jocelyn's time with Mr. Sawyer was different, likely because she couldn't ever *anticipate* what he would have her do. As soon as she did, he changed things. They'd been meeting for almost a month now. During their last session, *he'd* read to *her* for the first time—poetry. He said he'd never shared it with anyone else. His voice had been low and raspy as he spoke. *So damn sexy.* She didn't understand a lot of what he'd written—Jocelyn hoped one day she'd be smart enough that she would—but she thought his words were beautiful nonetheless.

As she entered room 206 and walked to the desk where

she normally sat, she immediately noticed Mr. Sawyer's
desk had been moved. It wasn't smack in the middle at
the front anymore, but relocated to the far left corner.
She plopped her backpack down on the floor and slid into
the plastic chair.

"You moved your desk?"

Mr. Sawyer ignored her question, strolled to the
back of the room, and shut the door. The *sch-lenk* sound
of the lock clanking closed made Jocelyn feel like her
insides were vibrating. She loved being alone with him,
loved having all his attention. Yet . . . there went her
palms, sweating already. It was only a matter of time
before her throat grew tight.

"Is your essay for today ready?"

Mr. Sawyer always made her write about her screwed-up
life. But this week's assignment had been more difficult than others because it really hit home. She'd been
tasked to write about her loneliness.

Jocelyn wiped her palms on her jeans and straightened her spine. "Yes."

"Very well, then." He walked back behind his desk
and pointed to the floor right next to him. "Here. On
your knees. Eyes down."

It was the first time Jocelyn wouldn't be sitting
ten feet away, and the thought of being so close to
Mr. Sawyer both thrilled her and freaked her out. Though
by now she knew better than to hesitate when he instructed her to do something. So Jocelyn pulled her yellow spiral notebook with the butterfly from her backpack
and scurried to the front. She felt Mr. Sawyer's eyes on
her as she walked, yet she didn't dare lift her gaze.

Jocelyn knelt, shifted her weight from side to side
trying to get comfortable, though her knobby knees were
too bony for that. She took a deep breath, preparing to
start, but her inhale brought a smell that gave her pause.
Masculinity. Woodsy—maybe cedar, mixed with leather and
something else she wasn't familiar with. There was also
the slightest hint of coffee in the concoction. She'd

never really noticed a man's cologne before, but she
liked the way it made her feel. Though it made her wonder what Mr. Sawyer might be smelling this close to *her*.
The washing machine at home was broken again, so Jocelyn
hadn't washed her jeans after her shift at McDonald's
yesterday. Chances were pretty good that she smelled like
three-day-old burnt oil and french fries. Or worse, considering it was hot today and the near-empty stick she'd
rubbed under her armpits after gym class had more plastic
than deodorant.

"Is there a problem, Miss Burton?"

Jocelyn shook her head. Her eyes traced the first
line of her paper, but when she took another deep breath
to begin reading, that smell hit her again. "You smell
really good," she whispered.

There was a long pause. As she waited for a response—
something . . . anything—Jocelyn worried the compliment
might have upset Mr. Sawyer. But when he eventually
spoke, she heard the smile in his voice, even if she
didn't look up to see it. "I'm pleased that you noticed.
You may begin."

She cleared her throat. "'Loneliness isn't the ab-
sence of company. It's a haunting void you feel inside,
even in a crowded room . . .'" Over the next ten minutes, Jocelyn read eight pages—describing a night her
mother was at work and she was home alone. She remi-
nisced about a stormy night, how the wind had moaned a
low pitch that rose and fell in unpredictable patterns,
making her shake with uncertainty. She'd taken the gun
her mom kept in her nightstand and tucked it under her
pillow, she was so afraid. Tears streamed down her face
as she read about the time she'd visited the beach with
her friend's family, how she'd snuck out when they were
all sleeping and stood on the rocks at the edge of the
jetty, wondering if anyone would notice if she fell in
and the giant waves swallowed her. It was gut-wrenching
to say the words aloud, but reading what she'd written

was never the worst part. The worst was the time *after* she finished, the hour she had to look down. Because all of the feelings that had bubbled to the surface got stuck. Jocelyn wished she could look out the window, watch a finch or a blue jay, let her mind wander and find some peace. But she didn't want to disappoint Mr. Sawyer. Plus, at some point, when he was ready, Mr. Sawyer would praise her—and that would make her feel better.

So she waited. And waited. Until eventually the shuffling of papers, the sound of the pen's tip scratching along the pages of the notebook he wrote in, came to a stop, and Mr. Sawyer reached out. He cupped Jocelyn's chin and lifted until their eyes met.

"Are you enjoying our sessions, Miss Burton?"

She nodded. "I don't feel lonely when I'm with you."

Mr. Sawyer's lips curved to a smile. "Excellent. And have you spent time lately with the boy I sometimes see you with in the hall?"

"Lucas?"

The smile on her teacher's face wilted. "Yes, him."

She shook her head. "No, I haven't seen Lucas."

Mr. Sawyer's eyes narrowed, and his lips tightened. No words were necessary. He wasn't sure he believed her.

"I haven't." Jocelyn swallowed. "I swear."

Mr. Sawyer searched her eyes, but there was nothing to find because she wasn't hiding anything. She'd blown Lucas off recently. They used to spend time together after school, sometimes make out behind the chicken coop on the side of his parents' house, but now she mostly spent her free time with Mr. Sawyer or working on one of his assignments.

He tilted his head. "Has a boy ever touched you, Jocelyn?"

The crimson bloom of her cheeks answered for her.

"Point," Mr. Sawyer said sternly. "Show me where you've been touched."

Jocelyn thought about lying, but the way his eyes

were searing into her, she was certain he'd be able to tell. She took a deep breath, held it, and pointed to her breasts.

"Anywhere else?" he asked.

She shook her head.

Mr. Sawyer's eyes darkened. "Are you ready for more discipline?"

There was no hesitation on Jocelyn's part this time. She nodded enthusiastically. "Yes. I'm ready."

"You realize that if anyone was ever to find out about our sessions, I wouldn't be able to help you anymore and you would lose your chance at a scholarship, right?"

"I won't tell anyone."

Mr. Sawyer's thumb rubbed his bottom lip for a long time. Eventually, he picked up his pen and scribbled an address on his notepad. Tearing the strip of paper away, he held it out to Jocelyn.

"Thursday. Six p.m."

She went to take it, but he didn't let go. Their eyes met.

"Boys will use you. They won't ever really want you because they won't see the potential in you like I do. All they'll see is a poor girl with dirty, used clothes, and a loser for a mother." He stroked her hair softly, then fingered the split ends at the bottom. "A girl who doesn't even cut her hair. You're lucky I'm helping you."

CHAPTER
21

I haven't slept more than three hours a night in the five days since I returned from Louisiana. I sit in the subway seat, face dropped into my hands, and consider my options: yoga, meditation, massive amounts of wine? None of it has worked yet. It's like this warped reality I can't escape. Exhaustion, pulling at me from one moment to the next, distracting my every attempt at getting back to living my life, but as soon as I crawl beneath the covers, I'm awake.

Wide awake. Staring at the ceiling, my chest tight, breaths coming short and fast. I start to think about the chapters . . . and what comes *at the end* of the story. Hannah didn't take my bait and add a friend named Lizzie, but we both know she'll appear on the page sooner or later, don't we?

As I raise my head, checking to see which stop we're at, I catch a man's gaze lingering on me. He's tall with a beard. He looks away, caught. I reach for my bag, hands shaking like I'm withdrawing from something. Withdrawing from *sleep*, from my body's inability to shut off, even for a few hours. I stand and move swiftly through the car, tucking myself into a different seat, behind a group of teenagers. I peer around them, trying to catch sight of the man, but he's gone.

I exhale.

Not following me, then.

I take a long look at every other person near me, but
they're all busy—staring at phones, reading books, listening
to music. No one's paying me any mind, yet I'm on high alert,
and I can't be any other way.

As soon as I reach campus—glancing behind me, watching
for the man, for anyone else who seems to be trailing me—
I head straight for the health clinic. Since I'm a professor, they
put me ahead of the half dozen students waiting to be seen,
and I'm in a room in ten minutes.

"Ms. Davis?" A young woman enters, glancing up from
a clipboard. She looks like another student, but her ID badge
reads Kendra Young, Nurse Practitioner.

I open my mouth—almost correct her to *Professor
Davis*—then purse it shut. It doesn't matter what she calls me.
What matters is that Kendra Young likes me enough to write
a prescription for something that will let me sleep, let me silence these swirling thoughts, even if only briefly. So I forget
the honorific and smile back at her, summoning all my inner
strength to seem normal, like a well-adjusted woman who just
needs a little help during a difficult time in her life.

"Yes, that's me," I manage.

"How can I help you today?" Kendra pulls up a rolling
stool, crosses her legs, looks at me with an open gaze, a warm
smile.

My shoulders relax a little. She's good at her job, at least
the people-skills part. I think through my carefully crafted
story, one that's not *too far* from the truth.

"My mother. She's . . . dying. Slowly."

"Oh, I'm so sorry." Kendra leans in, a concerned look on
her face.

"I'm just so . . . anxious. I'm having trouble sleeping. She's
in Louisiana, and I was there to see her recently, but I had to
come back to teach classes." I ramble on, talking fast, letting
tears well in my eyes, tears that surprise even me. "Anyway, I
was hoping you might be able to give me something that will

help me sleep. I think if I could get some rest, I could keep it together."

"Oh, of course. Let me just give you a quick exam." She touches a hand to my elbow, takes blood pressure, listens to my heart, my lungs, asks me some routine questions about other medications I take. When I leave, it's to head to the nearest pharmacy to pick up some Ambien I desperately need.

The pharmacy is located next to Mr. Hank's nursing home. As soon as I have the pills safely in my purse, I'm a lot calmer, so I go next door for a visit. New York, as big as it is, is a lot like a small town, too—everything crammed together.

Mr. Hank is like comfort food to me. Seeing him boosts my mood because it reminds me that there's *someone* in my life I've always been able to depend on. I find him where I usually do, in the communal TV room. But unlike my usual visits, there's a woman in a wheelchair sitting next to him, holding his hand.

"Hi, Mr. Hank." I smile at him, glancing over at the woman.

"Elizabeth! When did you get here?"

"Just now. I was running an errand nearby and couldn't pass up popping in. I hope I'm not interrupting." I'm not sure if the woman's another patient or a visitor, but she looks at me and narrows her eyes.

"Have you been fooling around with my Charlie?"

"No, ma'am." I smile. "Charlie and I are old friends." I shift my gaze to my ex-landlord. "Aren't we, Mr. Hank?"

"Sure, sure." He pats the woman's hand. "Elizabeth lives here in my building, right across the hall. I keep my eye on her. Young girls in the city can never be too careful."

It's so odd how he can remember my name and where my apartment was, but not realize he's been living in this nursing home for nearly five years now. I nod and look over at the woman, wondering if she's going to think what he just said is strange.

She's still looking at me suspiciously but gives a stiff nod and brushes back her gray strands. A staff member approaches and bends to speak to her. "How about we go get you a muffin, Ms. Parsons? You didn't eat breakfast this morning."

The woman frowns and sighs, but doesn't argue. Once she's out of earshot, I drag a chair next to Mr. Hank. "Who was that? Do you have a new special lady friend?"

"Nah." He grins, waves me off as if she's nobody. "But when a pretty girl wants to hold your hand at my age, you go along with whatever bullshit you have to." He winks, and it makes me laugh—actually laugh—a refreshing moment after these past weeks. It makes me happy, too, that he's mostly lucid. It's a reminder that there's been good in my life. "So what's going on, missy? You look tired. Are you having trouble sleeping again?"

Did I tell him that recently, or is he referring to when I first moved to New York twenty years ago? Or maybe he thinks the trouble I had sleeping back then was last week because he's got his years confused again. I'm not sure, but Mr. Hank is one of the few people who knows the truth about how and where I grew up. Well, not the *full* truth—not about Mr. Sawyer, but I told him about my family life at least. Alcoholism is one of the things that first bonded us. His wife died of cirrhosis of the liver a year after I moved in. "I was away," I say. "I went to see my mother."

His bushy brows shoot up. "You went to Louisiana?"

I take a deep breath in and blow it out. "I did."

"How'd that go?"

"Not great. My mother is dying."

He reaches over and covers my hand with his, gives it a squeeze. "The drink finally get her?"

I shake my head. "Cancer. Pancreatic."

"I'm sorry."

"Thank you."

"How long are the doctors saying?"

"Not too long. A month or two."

He nods. "You gonna go see her again?"

"I don't know what I'm doing. I have a few more weeks of the summer session to finish teaching. I guess I'll see how things are then." I sigh and shrug, anxious to change the subject already, even though I'm the one who brought it up. So I lean and bump shoulders with him. "But tell me about you. You're not gonna replace me as your best girl with that Ms. Parsons, are you?"

"Never." He winks. "You're stuck with me for life."

For *that*, I'm truly grateful. Mr. Hank and I talk for another hour. About nothing important—the horses that ran today, the new patient who moved into the room next to his, about how he's hoping it doesn't snow tomorrow. I don't remind him it's the end of June and not January. Mostly he's with it, and I feel lucky to have had a good visit today. Toward the end, a nurse comes by to tell him it's almost time for lunch. He introduces me to her, calling me Molly instead of Elizabeth. Molly was his wife's name.

"I should get going, but I'll come back soon. And I'll bring donuts next time."

He points to me. "Chocolate."

I smile. "Anything else would be criminal." I give him a hug goodbye.

When I pull back, he clutches my arm for a second. "She loves you, even if she doesn't say it and isn't good at showing it."

"Who?"

"Your mother."

I assume he means because *all* mothers are supposed to love their daughters, but then he adds, "She told me."

"My mother told you she loves me?"

He nods. "Never mentioned it because I knew how much you struggled to move on after you left."

I don't usually correct him, but my response slips out. "But you've never spoken to my mother."

"Except that once, when you were sick in the hospital for a few days."

My heart deflates. For a moment there, I thought maybe he'd *actually* spoken to my mother. But he's just confused again, because I've never been in the hospital in New York, and my mother has never once said she loved me. Not even to me. I try not to let it get me down, but it feels like a punch in the gut.

He cups my cheek. "I love you, Molly. Don't be sad."

I press a kiss to his forehead. "And I love you, too. And how can I be sad when I have you in my life?"

I've no sooner exited the floor and stepped back onto the elevator when my phone vibrates with a text.

Sam: Dinner tonight?

I sigh. The only plan I have for the evening is to take one of the sleeping pills in my purse and crash, forgetting the last month ever happened. My fingers hover over the keypad, about to text back, when it vibrates a second time.

Sam: I got some information on your friend Jocelyn.

My eyes go wide.
So much for sleeping tonight. I can't type back fast enough.

Elizabeth: Dinner sounds great!

CHAPTER

22

"You okay, babe?"

I feel like I'm about to burst. I've been here almost a half hour now, and Sam still hasn't mentioned anything about Jocelyn. I'm trying to be patient, not let on how desperate I am to get the information, but it's not easy when you're running on caffeine and adrenaline.

I force a smile. "I'm fine. Why do you ask?"

Sam studies my face. I really wish he wouldn't play detective with me. He shrugs. "You look tired. Stressed."

Great. Now the shitstorm going on inside of my body is spilling over to the outside. "My neck's bothering me again," I lie. "Woke me up a few times the last couple of nights."

He turns the burner down to simmer, walks around to the side of the island I'm sitting at, and puts his big hands on my shoulders. "You should've said something. You know I have magic fingers."

Sam's fingers are, in fact, pretty magical. He kneads into my neck muscles, and my head immediately drops a few inches. It feels like it's just been disconnected from a tension rod. I can't help it, I groan.

He presses his thumbs in deeper. "Feels good?"

"Yeah," I breathe out. "Thanks."

After a while, I start to think maybe the tension in my

neck *was* the problem. Because it feels like I could curl up into a ball and go to sleep right now. But then Sam opens his mouth again . . .

"So, I found three people with your friend's name in the state of Florida."

My head jerks upright, and I brush his hands from my shoulders. "Oh?"

Sam kisses the top of my head. "Need to stir my sauce." He walks back around to the other side of the island and starts fiddling with the knobs on the stove, as if I'm not holding my breath, waiting for the rest of what he has to say. Of course he doesn't know what's at stake. But when he opens the drawer where he keeps the spices and starts rummaging, I can't wait any longer.

"And? What were you able to find out about the three people?"

He pulls out a jar of oregano, twists the cap, shakes some flakes into the sauce he's making. "Two of them are easy enough to rule out. You said you and your friend went to high school together, so I'm assuming she's mid- to late thirties?"

I nod. "We're the same age."

"That's what I figured. One of the three is only sixteen, and one is in her late eighties."

"And the third?"

Sam turns and meets my gaze. "She's in prison."

My eyes grow wide. "Prison? For what?"

"Manslaughter."

It feels like my heart is trying to pound through the wall of my chest. "She killed someone?"

He nods. "Drunk driving, five years ago. Blew a stop sign. Hit an old man."

I'd thought maybe Jocelyn had gotten married, or even died. *Prison* had never entered my brain. Though it makes sense, doesn't it? Drinking. Being reckless. No doubt she's struggled with both since what happened. Jocelyn hadn't had it easy from the start. That's why she let a forty-year-old man take advantage of her. I digest this new information, swallow it down. But then a new crop of questions bubbles from my gut. Could it still be her? From prison? They have computers and internet access there, right? At least that's what it seems, though granted, my education on the subject comes from *Law & Order* reruns.

Sam walks over to the leather bag he carries back and forth to work. He unzips, pulls out a piece of paper, and slides it across the counter to me. "This is her mug shot."

I blink a few times, disappointment and relief hitting in equal measure. "That's . . . that's not Jocelyn."

"Are you sure? You said you haven't seen her since high school, right? I had to check the age listed twice myself after seeing the picture. She looks more like late fifties than late thirties. But hard living can do that to you."

I shake my head. "People change, but their skin color doesn't. That's definitely *not* Jocelyn."

"Oh. Well, I guess that's good."

Except . . . if she's not in Florida, then where the hell is she?

"Is it possible that whatever database you searched can't find her because she got married and goes by her married name?"

Sam shrugs. "Anything's possible. But not likely. I ran the name straight and as an alias. So it should be everyone. Maybe your friend isn't in Florida anymore. Does she have family back in Louisiana you could ask? If you know a parent or sibling's name, I could probably get you contact information on them. What town did you say you were from again?"

I didn't. And I've already shared too much, so I intend to keep it that way. "Would her name have come up in your search if she was dead?"

"It should. All deaths are reported to Social Security, and their records feed into the national database I pulled from. It's pretty accurate. The only time I've seen it wrong is when"—Sam catches my eyes—"someone doesn't want to be found."

———————

"You want to watch a movie?" Sam tosses a hand towel onto the kitchen counter. We've just finished cleaning up after dinner. "Or maybe I could work on the knots in your neck some more. I still have that oil you like in my nightstand."

A massage offer from a man is never *just* an offer for a massage. And the air feels too thick in this apartment for heavy breathing tonight. What I need to do is go home and take one of the sleeping pills I picked up but haven't yet taken out of the white pharmacy bag. It's time.

"I'm actually going to sleep at my place tonight. I have to work on some papers."

"Can't you do that here?" Sam glances over at the chair I put my stuff on when I came in. My laptop is sticking out of the top of my tote bag.

I try to soothe his bent feelings by pushing up against him. It hits me that I did the same thing to Noah only a week ago—used sex to worm my way out of a tight corner. I'm not proud of myself, but I also don't stop. "It's impossible to focus when you're around."

"I'll go in the other room."

"That won't help. I need to go home."

He pouts. "Fine. Whatever. I'll call you an Uber."

I shake my head. "I'll take the subway."

"Can you at least give me this one? You don't see the shit I see happening on the trains at night."

I sigh. "Fine. I'll Uber. But I'll call my own."

He shakes his head, purses his lips. I manage to make a quick escape after that—a chaste kiss, a promise to text tomorrow that I probably won't keep. The moment I step out onto the street, I feel much less constricted. That thought shifts my mind to Noah. There's a much greater chance that Noah is the one sending me the chapters than Sam, yet I don't feel suffocated around Noah. I wonder why that is. I cancel the Uber Sam watched me order and head to the subway station. It's a four-block walk, and when I arrive I realize I don't remember a single step of it. I can't recall any of the buildings I passed, the faces of fellow pedestrians, or stopping at any crosswalks. Sam was right. I'd be safer as a passenger than on my own. Though I'm here at the station now, so I might as well keep going. A few steps into my descent down into the subway, my cell phone buzzes. I stop on the stairs since service under the city can be spotty. It's an unknown number, but I swipe to answer anyway.

"Hello?"

The line is quiet. I climb back up the stairs to the street level, thinking maybe it's the connection.

"Hello?"

A cab horn blares, and some sort of a siren screams in the distance. I cover the ear without a cell phone pressed to it, trying to drown out the sounds of Manhattan. I'm pretty certain I can hear someone breathing. It's the second time that's happened in the last few days.

"Hello? Is someone there?"

I squeeze my cell tighter to my head, push a finger into my other ear. There's definitely someone there. I can hear the faint sound of inhales and exhales. And as ridiculous as it sounds, my gut tells me the breathing is *Noah's*. But why do I think that? Does his breathing have a unique pattern? I don't remember noticing it when we were together. I've spent way more time with Sam and couldn't tell you if he has a particular way of breathing.

I must be losing my mind, because it hits me that I didn't give Noah my number. *Sleep. I need some freaking sleep.* I swipe my phone off, look around to see if anyone is watching, and jog back down the stairs into the subway. The quicker I get to my apartment, the quicker I can pop a pill and conk out. Things will be clearer when I'm rested.

Luckily, the rest of the trip home is uneventful, at least until I shut my door and my phone buzzes again. This time, though, it's a text, not a call. The person isn't saved in my contacts, because no name comes up, only "Unknown" and a phone number—one with a Louisiana area code.

My pulse picks up as I click to open the message.

Unknown: Hey. It's Lucas. Sorry it took me so long to reach out, but I lost your number. I've been searching for it since the day we saw each other at the hospital. Finally found it tonight. I must've put it in my lunch bag for safekeeping and somehow it stuck to the ice pack and I didn't notice. It's apparently been in my freezer for a week. Never thought to look there. I've been kicking myself in the ass for losing it. I really wanted to see you again. Any chance you're still in town?

I let out a lungful of air, debate not responding. But Lucas is harmless, and the thought of him discovering my phone number in the freezer is actually pretty funny.

Elizabeth: Hey, Lucas. I'm already back in New York.

I watch the little dots jump around on my screen, happy for the distraction. I always liked Lucas.

Unknown: Damn. You think you'll be back in town anytime soon?

Elizabeth: I'm not sure.

A frowning emoji appears before his next message.

Unknown: That's too bad. Let me know if anything changes and you get back down. I really enjoyed seeing you. I always hated that we lost touch during senior year.

There's *a lot* I hate about that year . . .

I nibble on my lip, thinking. Jocelyn used to fool around with Lucas. Maybe he knows where she is; maybe they kept in contact. Though I hate the thought of talking to anyone from my little town about her, and for some stupid reason I still don't want to leave a digital footprint of me asking about Jocelyn. Which is absolutely ridiculous at this point, considering I've asked an *NYPD detective* for help, yet I decide against making waves with anyone connected to Minton Parish. Instead, I respond truthfully.

Elizabeth: I do, too. You were always a good friend to me, Lucas.

He responds right away.

Unknown: Doesn't have to be past tense. Give me a call if you find yourself back in town. I'd love to see you.

Elizabeth: Take care of yourself, Lucas.

Unknown: You, too, Elizabeth.

I sigh and look around my apartment. I usually don't go to sleep until eleven, but the pharmacy bag on my kitchen counter is calling my name. I tear it open, twist the cap off the bottle, and swallow two Ambien without any water. I'm determined to sleep tonight, so much so that I plug my cell into the living room charger, rather than taking it into the bedroom and using the one on my nightstand like I normally do. The last thing I need is another call from the breather to wake me and keep me up all night.

Ten minutes later, I climb into bed and wait for the medicine to kick in. My mind races with so many thoughts. *Does Noah know who I am? Who donated that Saint Agnes statue? How long does my mother have left? I need to break things off with Sam.* But the question my mind keeps coming back to tonight is, *Where the hell is Jocelyn?*

CHAPTER

23

I roll over and grasp the bottle of pills. Last night, I slept for eight straight hours. And tonight, part of me wants nothing more than to down another Ambien (or three) and get another good night's sleep. But the moment I twist the lid off, I think of my mother. Her problems with addiction. It means I'm primed for the same problems, and the last thing I want is to become dependent on medication. I don't even know if Ambien is habit-forming, but I'm not taking any chances.

Anything can grow addictive, can't it? *Anything*. Even people.

I sit back up, scrub a hand over my face. A glance at my phone tells me it's not even eight yet. I'm just so tired. Maybe I'll watch some TV. I set my phone back on the nightstand, but as I plug it into the charger, the screen flashes with an incoming call—an unknown number. Again.

I shouldn't answer. I should let it go to voicemail. But I can't *not* answer. I can't sit here, adding *Who was that?* to my list of unanswered questions. So I snatch it up, hit the green button.

"Hello?"

No response. Just . . . inhales, exhales.

My chest tightens. "Hello?" I snap. "I can hear you breathing, you know!"

Again, I immediately think it's Noah. And again I remind myself he doesn't have my number. And why would he call and just breathe at me? Unless . . . unless he's the one sending the chapters. And his goal is to scare me. To haunt me. *Revenge.*

I hang up. There's no need to feed into whatever it is this person hopes to achieve—no matter *who* it might be. Instead, I scroll through my contacts until I get to my mother. My finger hovers over the call button as I think back to the conversation we had just before I walked out her front door.

I'll call you in a few days to see how you're feeling, Mom.
How about I call you when I feel like talking instead?

Of course she hasn't called. I'm pretty sure she never will. I've tried not to think about her, not to worry about her. She doesn't deserve my concern, much less my thoughts. Yet . . . I feel compelled to make sure she's okay. I'm sure a psychiatrist would have a lot to say about the reasons why. I shake my head at myself, but press the green call button anyway.

"Hello? Elizabeth?" Her voice is creaky, breathless. She sounds awful, like she's at death's door. I ignore the pang of guilt I feel that I'm not there with her.

"Mom? Are you okay?"

"I'm dying. Of course I'm not okay." She coughs, moving the phone away, but I can still hear it, hoarse and rattling. When she comes back to the phone, she clears her throat. "Why are you calling?"

I let a beat of silence permeate the air. *Why, indeed?* "I just wanted to check on you."

"Been to church yet?" she asks. "I live a good Christian life, and my sins are numerous. You live a heathen's life, and your sins—"

"I have to go, Mom. But I love you." I hang up and stare down at the phone, thinking of all the stories I've heard about when a parent is dying, and in those final moments, parents and children who have been at odds find a way of reconciling their differences. I don't think she and I will ever get to that point. She'll go to the grave swearing she knows best, even though she drank and smoked herself to death.

A knock coming from the other room—fast and harsh—jolts me from my thoughts. Someone's at my door. Sam, maybe? But would he just show up? I never texted him back today, so probably not. I huff a sigh, climb from bed, and clutch my phone like a weapon while I peek through the peephole. But it's only Mrs. Patterson, my next-door neighbor.

I crack the door open. I'm not dressed for company. "Hello?"

"Here, dear, I keep getting your mail." She passes it to me through the crack, gives me a quick smile, then totters away with her cane.

"Thank you."

I climb back into bed, more unsettled than ever. An hour later, I'm still staring at the ceiling, this time thinking of Jocelyn. She had to have ended up *somewhere*. If she were still in Florida, she should've shown up in the searches Sam did. I need him to go wider—check the entire United States. After yet another hour passes and my brain is still swimming in the same old pool of dead ends, I finally give up and get back out of bed.

I have papers to grade, grades that still need to be entered into the university's system, and a few dumb, mandatory human resources videos I'm supposed to watch. So I grab my laptop, take a seat at the kitchen table, and try to make myself useful. But before I can log into the university's grading system, I notice an email from Hannah Greer. It wasn't there earlier.

My heart races, blood goes hot with nerves pulsing through my body. I swallow and click. There's no message, no content to the email. She's clearly ignoring my request to speak with her over Zoom. The only things the email contains are attachments.

And those are labeled Chapter 4 and Chapter 5.

CHAPTER

24

Chapter 4—Hannah's Novel

Jocelyn pulled up to the address. She stared at the building, then back down at the numbers, wiping her sweaty palms against her skirt. The place wasn't quite what she expected. Instead of somewhere nice, or maybe even Mr. Sawyer's house, it was a motel that looked like it had gone out of business. Except the red neon Vacancy sign blinked steadily, so—it was still open? She fidgeted, looking around the bumpy parking lot self-consciously. No sign of Mr. Sawyer.

Eventually, his car pulled in. She looked at her ratty bicycle, parked next to her, wishing her mother's car hadn't died this morning. Jocelyn stood just outside the small office, trying to look relaxed and calm, when she was anything but. The sight of him sent excitement through her. He was a good-looking man—older, smarter, more worldly than she'd ever be. And yet he was here to meet *her.*

"Hi!" she called, waving to him. But then she quickly put her hand down, feeling like an idiot for greeting him like such a teenager.

"What are you doing?" He approached quickly, took her elbow and yanked her around the side of the motel.

"You can't be seen just standing out here like that. They'll assume you're turning tricks."

"What?" She looked up, eyes wide. "Turning what?"

"They'll assume you're a whore. Look at you, how you're dressed." He glared down at her, anger in his voice.

Jocelyn stole a glance down at her short skirt, the V-neck blouse she'd stolen from her mother's closet. She was trying to look nice for Mr. Sawyer, thought he'd like it. It was . . . mature, she'd thought. Maybe she'd judged wrong, though.

"I'm sorry," she mumbled. "I just wanted to look nice for you."

The admission sat between them, crackling with tension.

Eventually, he sighed. "Go hide that bicycle in the woods at the back of the parking lot. Stay there for a while. Come back in half an hour, after it gets dark. We can't be seen going in together. Room 212. I'll leave the door open."

Jocelyn stared at him, slack-jawed. Hide in the woods? Surely he was joking. But the way his eyes narrowed, he was serious as could be. She pressed her lips together, nodded, and started the long walk across the cracked pavement. The brush at the edge of the woods was damp, and within minutes, her shoes were soaked through. It wasn't a cold day, but she shivered nonetheless, finding a stump to sit on as the world grew dark around her.

Jocelyn didn't like the dark. Bad things could happen to you in the dark, especially out here. A twig snapped somewhere beyond her, and she turned quickly, staring out into the darkness.

It must nearly be time. Stupidly, she'd forgotten to check her watch when the sun went down—not that she could see it now, anyway. She waited another five, ten minutes, then got to her feet and hurried back toward the motel. Hopefully, it wasn't too soon. She didn't want to give him yet another reason to be angry.

But when she cracked open the door to 212 and stepped in, he didn't tell her to leave. No, he sat at the desk against the wall in the corner of the room. She shut the door behind her quietly and took a few steps in, but froze when she saw what he was wearing.

His underwear. White boxer briefs. Heat crept up her cheeks, and she couldn't help but stare. The underwear left little to the imagination. And he was fit. A man, definitely not a boy.

Her heart pounded in her chest as she took in the room—dimly lit, a bed, Mr. Sawyer nearly naked. She was nervous, but she wasn't *scared* exactly, more anxious and maybe excited. She licked her lips, curious to see what came next.

"Remove your clothing. Everything but your bra and panties. Then kneel here." He pointed to a spot near his feet.

She hesitated only a moment, then hastily peeled off the blouse, shimmied out of the skirt, pulled down the tights. The cheap motel carpet felt rough beneath her knees, but she knelt, breathless, awaiting his next command.

"Put your hands together like you're saying your prayers. Bow your head."

Trembling now, she did as she was told. Her skin tingled with anticipation. Was he going to touch her? Kiss her? Mr. Sawyer shifted in his chair, and she couldn't help it—she snuck a peek up. A bulge appeared beneath his boxer briefs. *A big bulge*, she thought, taking a shaky breath. It fascinated her, maybe frightened her some, too.

She huddled there, hot despite the fact that the room was cold and she had no clothes on. She shivered with eagerness as she waited. What would come next? Would he want to have sex? She was a virgin, but most of the girls her age weren't anymore. Ivy had already had sex with two different boys. Whatever Mr. Sawyer wanted to do, she would do it. Jocelyn wanted to make him happy, after all. Because she liked him, thought he was handsome and fascinating, but also because he could change things for her—make her life better, take her away from this shitty town.

Finally, after what felt like an hour, he moved. He stood and strode out of her line of vision. This was it. Something was going to happen now. She quaked internally, waiting for his touch, his fingers on her back, her shoulder, anywhere—but it didn't come. Instead, she heard noises behind her—clothes shifting. Perhaps he was preparing the bed? But a moment later, he was back. Crouching in front of her. Fully dressed.

What had she done wrong? Tears sprang to her eyes. If he was dressed, that meant . . . that meant he didn't want her. He'd sat there, judging her nearly naked, and his response was to *get dressed*. She wasn't attractive enough, of course.

He reached toward her, cupped her cheek. His warm, big hand on her skin felt like a relief, and she leaned into him.

"You're a good girl." He moved closer, pressed his lips to her forehead. Then he pulled away and tossed her clothes at her. "Get dressed."

She hurried to do so, swiping angrily at the stray tears descending her cheeks. She wanted to turn, to ask what she'd done wrong, but she was also afraid to.

"Jocelyn?"

"Yes?" she squeaked. She stood hunched, looking down at the ground, her clothes on but askew.

"Look at me."

She raised her gaze just in time to see the back of his hand come up and slap across her face. Her head turned from the force of it. "Don't dress like a whore next time," he bit out. "Same time next week. Wait in the woods."

CHAPTER

25

I barely make it to the bathroom before my dinner is coming up.

Slumped over the porcelain toilet, knees pressed to the cold tile, I'm heaving. I reach for toilet paper to wipe my face, but more races up my throat. I've never been so violently ill before. It came on with no warning, no queasy belly or overwhelming nausea.

I remember that hotel room Hannah described. Insipid beige walls, heavy, moss-colored curtains that hide what goes on inside, the musty odor from years of neglect. The way the dim lighting couldn't seem to catch on anything to reflect, and the worn, cheap carpet that was damp from more than just blood.

I'd only been inside that room once. *That night*. The night Jocelyn called crying and told me she needed help. Yet the images in my head are so vivid from the descriptions in the chapter I just read, and the picture Jocelyn had painted in my mind when she'd finally come clean and told me what had been going on for months.

I flush the toilet, drag my body up to the sink, splash some cool water on my face, and rinse my mouth. A face I barely recognize reflects back at me from the mirror. I look terrible, gaunt, with hollowed cheeks, dark circles ringing my glassy eyes.

This bathroom is too small, tightening around me, so I go out to the living room, open a window to let in some fresh air, and pace back and forth across the Persian rug I couldn't afford but bought anyway, because I wanted a real one—unlike the knockoff in my mother's living room.

I can't live like this anymore, in a state of limbo, waiting to be exposed. I just want whatever this unknown person has planned for me to be done with. Turn me in, if that's the ultimate endgame. At least then I could formulate a plan and figure out next steps. But this waiting, not knowing, being left to my own devices to imagine a dozen different scenarios of what *might* be going on, leaves me feeling helpless. Without control. And I *need* control. Otherwise, I have nothing.

I keep walking. Ten feet. Back and forth, the length of the rug underfoot, each journey only five steps before I turn around. Maybe if I keep moving, keep pushing, my mind will eventually follow along. Because right now it's stuck. Stuck on that room. Stuck on *where the hell* Jocelyn is.

My head hurts. I try to conjure up a picture of her that night when I found her, but it's fuzzy—like I've been drinking and have to squint to make out her features, only squinting makes her face blurrier. Yet I can see that damn motel room clear as day. The same thing happens when I try to visualize Mr. Sawyer. He's a blur, too, though I saw a picture not long ago at Noah's. My brain is probably trying to protect me, considering what happened the last time I saw the two of them together, but I desperately *crave* seeing their faces.

A thought hits. It halts my pacing. I *can* see their faces. In my yearbook. It's buried in one of the boxes on the top shelf of my closet, along with other shit I don't need but couldn't bring myself to toss out when I moved. Like the Bible my mother gave me when I was a little girl.

I rush into my bedroom, grab the chair from my desk in the corner, and climb up to reach the boxes. I'm not sure which one the yearbook is in, and there isn't a pretty way to take just one box down. They're crammed in tight, a house of cards that will fall apart when I pull the first one. So I don't bother to attempt to be neat. I pry one box out and lean back out of the way as the two on top fall. The last I take with me when I climb down.

My heart pounds as I tear into the first dusty box, the sound of blood frantically swishing through my ears. Inside are things I don't need—old photos, a tattered baby blanket, a purple stuffed elephant that I don't recognize at all. I dig my way to the bottom, but there's no yearbook. So I grab the next box. But it's not in there, either. I'm just about to give up on the third box, which is filled with old sweaters, when I lift the last one, and my heart stops. There's a flash of the old orange-and-black school colors.

Minton Parish High School
2004–2005 Yearbook

I feel myself shaking as I lift it out. It's just a book filled with pictures, for God's sake. *Get ahold of yourself already, Elizabeth.* But berating myself does nothing to make me calmer. So I dive in. The teachers' section is first, so I thumb through the alphabetical, now-dated-looking photos, until I get to names that start with an *S*. As soon as I turn the page, my eyes meet *his*.

Or *Noah's*.

Because their deep green irises are identical—same shape, same color, same tiny golden flecks surrounding the pupils. I hate the man, loathe him with everything I have. He took so much from me. From Jocelyn. It's twenty years later, and I still can't escape him. Yet—and on some level, I know this is incredibly fucked up—I can't help but notice how attractive he is. Or *was*. Square jaw, incredible bone structure, lips that women pay good money for these days. There's something so undeniably masculine in his features. I stare down, feeling so much turmoil in my thoughts. Anger builds within me, and I flip the page with so much fury that it rips in half.

Oh well. I toss the paper aside without checking to see if his photo is ruined and move on to the student section. The senior class photos are a decent size. Three rows of three, nine faces to a page. I only need to thumb to the second page to find the names that start with *B*. But Jocelyn's photo is missing. I check the names—Ballard, Bloom, Byson. No Jocelyn Burton. I scan the page a second time, reading all the names, and then flip back to the *A*s in case her photo is out of order. Finding nothing, I do the same with the *C*s. Could she have been absent during picture day? Toward the bottom of the page that ends with Daniel Cullen, there's a gray box where there should be a student's photo—Monique Carter. The words *Camera Shy* are printed diagonally across it. Underneath, the same information is typed as appears under the squares that aren't missing photos.

Monique Carter
Nicknames: Moni, MC
Sports and Activities: Yearbook Club—Senior,
Soccer—Freshman, Photography Club—Junior and Senior
Favorite Quote: "The sky is full of stars. There's room for us all to shine."

Even if Jocelyn had missed picture day like Monique, she should still have her information under an empty square, right? Maybe she's listed on the wrong page or something. I thumb back to the beginning of the senior photos and scan each face, one by one. A few pages after the one Jocelyn should be on, I'm caught off guard when I run into my own face.

God, how young I looked. Such an innocent smile. Those pictures were taken mid–school year. It makes my chest hurt to think how I had no damn idea what was coming. How *not* innocent I would be at the end. I stare for a long time, not even realizing I'm crying until a fat tear drips down onto the yearbook. It lands on my photo, right in the middle of my cheek. *Fitting.*

I wipe wetness from my face, clear my eyes enough to look below the photo and read what's typed underneath. I can't remember what I listed as my favorite quote. Though I never make it that far down, because my world unravels at the second line.

Elizabeth Davis
Nickname: Jocelyn

CHAPTER
26

Chapter 5—Hannah's Novel

Lucas's arm draped over her shoulder as Jocelyn laughed at something he said while they walked through the parking lot. It felt good. The attention, the warmth, the kindness. She'd felt so lost lately.

Chatter behind them drew her attention, and Jocelyn glanced back—a couple of juniors were shoving each other playfully. Her gaze returned to Lucas's new car, a slate gray hatchback with an engine that clanked. It barely held together, but he'd picked her up, saved her from the mile walk this morning in the hot sun. And it was fun, riding shotgun with the windows down, blasting the music on the radio, feeling free. While other kids' parents dropped them at the front door to the school, she usually arrived flushed, overheated from the Louisiana humidity.

"So, what are you doing after school?" Lucas asked.

Jocelyn kept step with him, and for a moment, it almost felt like they were a thing. A couple. An *item*.

"Oh, I have—uh, plans," she began, trying to think of a lie that was better than *I'm meeting Mr. Sawyer at a motel* . . .

"God, he's such a dick."

Jocelyn jerked her head up to see who Lucas meant.

A car—a familiar one, a dark blue sedan far newer than the one they'd ridden to school in—was parking in a spot twenty feet in front of them. As the man pulled forward, shifted into park, she could feel the weight of his glare through the window. When they passed behind the car, she looked sideways, meeting Mr. Sawyer's eyes in the rearview mirror.

Her stomach swam with sudden nerves. He didn't look happy to see her. To see *them*. She realized, with a jolt, it was Lucas—he didn't like Lucas. And hadn't she promised to steer clear?

"He gave me a D last semester," Lucas said. "I had a B average until I missed the last test. He gave me a zero because I left in the middle of the day, and he thought I was trying to avoid his exam. I had the freaking flu."

But Jocelyn had stopped listening. She stepped sideways, out of Lucas's grasp, and looked back once more—though Mr. Sawyer had disappeared. Probably inside, to his classroom, a classroom she wouldn't see him in today because of yet another stupid school assembly.

"I think he's a really good teacher," Jocelyn murmured as they entered the school.

Lucas stopped, squinted at her. "Huh? Mr. *Sawyer*?"

"I gotta go." She turned on her heel and hurried away, ignoring Lucas as he called after her to wait up, that he hadn't meant to make her mad. Part of her wanted to stop, tell him it wasn't his fault, that he hadn't done anything wrong—but she couldn't. She couldn't be seen with him at all.

Jocelyn spent the rest of the day picking nervously at her jeans, until a tiny hole formed at the knee. *Great*, her last pair that was more or less in one piece. She forced her hands under her butt, sitting on them, watching the clock tick by. Soon it would be time for the assembly. She'd find him, apologize, make sure he understood Lucas's arm around her had meant nothing.

But when the time finally came, with hundreds of students flooding the halls, filing into the gym, Mr. Sawyer was nowhere to be found. He wasn't seated near the other teachers in the corner. He wasn't stationed at the doors, where a couple of adults always took up post to make sure kids didn't sneak out. He was just . . . not there.

She bit her lip until it bled, then wiped blood away hurriedly on the back of her hand. She should have known better. Should have thought it through. Isn't this what he was talking about, learning discipline? Knowing how to control herself, how to do what she was supposed to? She berated herself through the whole assembly, through-out the rest of the day. But at least she'd see him that night. It was, after all, Thursday—*their night*.

Jocelyn's face went hot, remembering what Mr. Sawyer looked like, how chiseled his body was. She imagined touching it. Imagined *him* touching *her*. Maybe they'd go all the way tonight.

Was she ready?

For him, she was. Not for some teenage boy like Lucas, but for a man, a real man? One who could take care of her? Totally. Of course she was. She *had* thought everything through enough to wear jeans instead of a short skirt. Shoes instead of kitten heels. Mr. Sawyer wouldn't be upset with her this time.

After school, she walked home, found her mother's keys, and took the car, which had finally gotten a new battery. This time, she parked in the back, where she couldn't be seen so easily. Without being told, she got out, trudged into the woods, and found a spot where she could sit and wait, watching room 212. She could have waited in the car—that would've been less scary than sitting in the dark. But Mr. Sawyer had told her what to do, and she didn't want to upset him, not when he might already be upset about Lucas. As the sky grew darker, her eagerness increased, until she nearly trembled.

Soon night fell, and still, no Mr. Sawyer.

She waited another hour, but there was no sign of him. She waited one more hour, nearly falling asleep on

the log she sat on. Maybe she'd missed him? Maybe she
had dozed off for a few seconds, and now he was waiting
for her? She stood and went to room 212, listened by the
door before knocking.

But no one answered.

There was no noise.

With a sinking feeling, she realized he wasn't coming.

The following day there was no fifth-period assembly,
which meant Mr. Sawyer's class was on. Jocelyn hadn't
seen him yet, even though she'd passed by his room between every single period. He normally stood in the
hallway before classes. Was he avoiding her? Or was she
overthinking it? He couldn't be *that* mad at her for walking with Lucas, right? She'd wanted to call him the night
before, even looked up the phone number at his house. But
she knew that crossed a line.

She slipped into her usual third-row seat across from
Ivy, practically shaking with nerves, hoping he'd meet
her eyes, maybe slip her a note. Anything. Something.

But he didn't. Mr. Sawyer stood at the front of the
class, and when the bell rang, he began lecturing about
their reading assignment. His eyes were hard, narrowed.

"Pay attention," he said at one point, rapping his
knuckles on his desk. Everyone sat a little straighter.
She looked up, wondering if he was talking to her—
she had been lost in her thoughts—but he looked everywhere *but* at her.

At this point, she couldn't deny it any longer:
she'd made him mad.

She let out an unsteady breath, trying to pay attention. But inside, she was falling apart. Had she ruined
everything?

Jocelyn waited until class ended, fussed with her
backpack until every other student had filed out. Then,
quietly, hands clutched in front of her, she approached
him. "Mr. Sawyer?"

"What?" He didn't look at her. His words were cold, rigid. He straightened a stack of papers on his desk, tucked them into his satchel.

She lowered her voice to a whisper. She wasn't supposed to say this out loud, especially not *here*, at school. "You didn't come last night."

He snorted. "I presumed you had other plans."

Silence stretched between them. Outside, there was the clang of lockers slamming shut, the squeak of sneakers over the shiny hallway floor. But in the room, it felt like the whole universe revolved around just the two of them. And that universe was about to dissolve, disappear, before she'd even gotten to understand it.

"Wh-what?" she managed. Then she realized. "Lucas is only a friend—"

Mr. Sawyer looked right at her then, raising a palm in a clear signal to stop. "Listen, you can associate with whoever you want. But if you're going to be a whore, I can't waste my time on you."

The words hit Jocelyn like a sucker punch to the gut. Tears sprang to her eyes, hot and burning. "I—I won't see him anymore. I swear."

"We've had this conversation once already." Mr. Sawyer brushed by her, and she nearly smacked into the wall.

"Wait—"

He huffed a sigh, came to a stop. "What, Jocelyn?"

"I won't see him anymore. Really. You're the only person I want to see, the only person that matters."

He turned ever so slightly, giving her a searching look. Overhead, the bell rang, signaling the next period starting, and Mr. Sawyer looked deep into her eyes before shaking his head and exhaling. He yanked his wallet out and pressed bills into her hand.

"Tomorrow night. Last chance. But you'll have to get the room. The kid in the office is a former student of mine. He recognized me, and I can't be seen getting a room again. I told him I was having work done at my house, but I can't be getting the key all the time."

Jocelyn accepted the money, eyes wide. "But I'm not eighteen yet."

"They don't care. They don't ask for ID at that shithole. Room 212. Got it?"

She swallowed. "Okay."

"And don't use your real name."

She opened and closed her mouth, searching for words. She felt relieved he was talking to her, still wanted to meet with her—but also, she was getting the room? The idea of going in the lobby, of being *found out*—a cold sweat broke over her, just thinking about it. "What name should I use?"

"Jocelyn Burton."

"Okay. Why that name?"

Mr. Sawyer lifted his bag onto his shoulder. "It was my mother's name, her maiden name was Burton." He looked away, strolled to the classroom door, then paused to turn back. "And, Jocelyn, there will be punishment." He gave her a long look. "Don't come if you don't want it."

CHAPTER

27

I'm starting to look like my mother.

The thought stabs at my heart. I grab the concealer I've just put on and apply a second, thicker layer under my heavy-lidded eyes. It cakes into the fine lines, emphasizing instead of hiding the creases. I should've iced the swelling before attempting makeup, but I didn't have the energy when I dragged myself out of bed after another sleepless night. It's been almost three days since I've slept anything more than a fifteen-minute catnap. Every time I shut my eyes and start to drift off, memories flood back. Bits and pieces. Flashes of moments. Like me kneeling in front of Mr. Sawyer in *that* room and him backhanding me across the face. Hard. Not even the sleeping pills have helped. Lord knows I've taken a handful over the last forty-eight hours.

I just can't wrap my mind around so much. I've written everything down in a notebook—trying to gather all the puzzle pieces before I can attempt to solve it. The memories. The clues I've missed. All of which make sense now—how Jocelyn didn't come up in a search, why my recollection of the details in that motel room were so vivid, Lucas telling me he hated how we'd lost touch in senior year. Yet *nothing* makes sense.

Except maybe my dating habits for the last twenty years—

why I never wanted a man for more than sex, why I couldn't bring myself to have a relationship with even the nicest guy. I'd always been proud of my independence, never stopped to think *why* it was so important to me. Now I question whether I was being strong and independent or if I was *afraid*—afraid to trust a man.

My cell rings from the other room, and I toss the makeup onto the bathroom counter and rush to grab it. I'm waiting for a call.

"Hello?"

"Hi. May I speak to Elizabeth Davis, please?"

"This is she."

"This is Emma from Dr. Sterling's office. I'm returning your call."

"Yes, hi. Thank you." I'm not sure what to say next, because I have no idea who this doctor is to me. *If* she's even someone to me. I pick up the appointment card lying on the counter, the one I found in the bottom of the box with the yearbook. A date is scribbled in blue ink, the year nearly two decades ago. The edges are tattered and worn, like it spent time in a wallet. For all I know, the card belongs to someone else. My name isn't written on it, just a date and time and an office address here in the city.

"Did you . . . need to make an appointment?" the woman says after I'm quiet for too long.

"Oh. Yes, please."

"Can you confirm the last four numbers of your Social Security number for me? I just want to make sure I have the right patient."

"Sure. It's five, four, six, four."

"Great, thank you." I hear some clacking on a keyboard, and then . . . "Has any of your information changed since the last time you were here?"

"I'm not sure."

"What's your address and telephone number?"

I rattle off my information from twenty years ago and hold my breath, waiting.

"Great. Let me check what we have for the next available appointment."

She found me. I am a patient.

My heart races. *I've been to a psychiatrist.* And I don't remember.

"How is next Thursday at two?"

I can't possibly wait that long. I'll die of sleep deprivation. Is that even possible? Do people die of lack of sleep? It certainly feels like I could. "Is there any way I can come in sooner?"

"Are you in crisis?"

If this isn't a crisis, I'm not sure what is. "Yes. I can't sleep. Can't eat . . ."

"Okay. How about tomorrow morning? I can add you to the schedule before Dr. Sterling's day starts. She's busy at the moment, but I know she won't have a problem with that."

I breathe out a sigh of relief. "That would be great. Thank you. The sooner the better."

The following morning, I arrive at the address on the card at six thirty. The building is nondescript, typical of many skyscrapers here in the city. I can't swear I've been here before. It doesn't jostle anything inside of me. Not a feeling. Not a memory. Since I'm early, I walk to a coffee shop a few doors down and grab a double espresso. I slept a little last night—two hours in one shot. But my body is dragging, even if my mind is spinning a million miles an hour.

At 6:50, I ride the elevator up to the eleventh floor and find suite 1111. Still, nothing rings a bell. But when I open the door and see the small waiting room, I'm certain I've been here. The woman at the window smiles warmly.

"Hi. Elizabeth?"

I nod.

She passes a clipboard with some papers through the small opening in the glass. "If you could, please fill these out. It's been a while since we've seen you."

"Of course." I take a seat, fill in the blanks on the forms— insurance carrier, current medications, hospital admissions. But between each question, my eyes dart around the office— I'm trying to remember something, *anything*, just being here even. I'm on the last question when the door to my left opens.

"Elizabeth?"

I turn, and my heart stops. *I remember her.* A younger version, but I've definitely met this woman. A memory flashes in my head.

A locked room.

Me banging on the door.

A hospital?

A mental ward?

Was I locked in a mental ward?

The doctor lowers her voice. "Elizabeth? Are you okay?"

I swallow and stand. "Sorry, yes."

It doesn't look like she believes me. Why would she? I'm full of shit. I'm a fucking train wreck. But she smiles warmly and nods toward where she just came from. "Come on back."

I follow her down the hall to an office. It's familiar, but I'm not sure if it's because I've been in here before or because it looks like something you might see in a movie. There's a long beige couch with a navy-and-beige armchair across from it. Shelves are lined with books, and a coffee table displays magazines fanned out. A box of tissues waits on the end table.

Dr. Sterling walks to the lone chair, motions to the couch. "Have a seat. Make yourself comfy."

I sit, but I'm anything but comfortable. My eyes keep scanning the room, searching for something to spark another memory. The doctor gives me time to do whatever it is I need to do before she sits, crosses her legs, and begins.

"So, it's been a while." She smiles.

"How long?"

She picks up a file from the table next to her and opens it, lifts a few papers. "It looks like almost nineteen years. We had our older charts digitized a decade ago before destroying them, so I was able to review your records."

"Do you remember me?"

"I do."

I meet her eyes. "I don't remember you. Well, I do. Your face is familiar. But I don't remember being a patient."

To her credit, the doctor's face remains impassive. She's good, been at this a long time.

"Is having difficulty with your memory a new problem?"

I take a deep breath and exhale, nod my head. "Have I ever been to this office? Been in this room?"

"Once. To be fair, it might look different. The office has been redecorated a few times since then."

The image of the locked hospital room flashes in my head again. "Was this office the only place we met?"

Dr. Sterling's face grows concerned. But she quickly slips her poker-faced mask back on. "We initially met when you were hospitalized."

"Hospitalized for what?"

The doctor hesitates. Rightly so. I might be suffering from some sort of mental breakdown, but I haven't lost my common sense. I sound unhinged. Any decent psychiatrist would take one look at me—at the bags under my eyes, at the bruised bottom lip I've chewed to a pulp, at the erratic way I'm acting— and deem me fragile, want to take it slow. But I can't take the wait anymore. I *need to know* what the hell happened to me, and I need to know now. So I sit up straight, attempt to look a little normal, and try to convince her I'm stronger than I am.

"I'm a full-time English professor at Pace University. I've

been there for twelve years now. I haven't called in sick or missed a day of work until recently, when my mom was hospitalized. I date. I go to the gym. I don't do drugs or drink more than socially. I swear, up until recently, I thought I was completely normal. I might appear a little scary right now, but that's because I haven't been able to sleep for days, since random memories started coming back, things I've never been aware of, at least not in nearly two decades. I *need* to know what happened to me. The unknown is eating me alive."

Dr. Sterling looks into my eyes. I can see the wheels in her head turning as she mulls over what to do. Eventually, she nods and opens her folder again. "You were brought to Creedmoor by a neighbor." She flips a few pages and traces her fingers across typed words. "A Mr. Hank. Do you remember him?"

My heart races. *Oh my God*—what Mr. Hank said the other day about me being in the hospital, about how he'd spoken to my mother and she'd told him she *loved* me. That might be true? I swallow a lump in my throat to respond. "Yes. He's my old landlord, who's also a good friend. But why did he bring me in?"

"You suffered a break of some sort. I was your treating physician. You hadn't slept or eaten in a week, and your neighbor was concerned for your well-being. When you arrived, you told us you were someone other than who you are."

I swallow. "Jocelyn Burton?"

Dr. Sterling scans some more pages in her folder. Stops with her finger in the middle of some handwritten notes. "Yes, that was it."

"What else did I say?"

"Not too much. You didn't want to talk. Your neighbor told us that the week before there had been an altercation at your apartment."

"What kind of an altercation?"

"It was never clear what exactly had occurred. Your neighbor heard yelling and found you in the hallway, screaming at a man. He chased him away with a baseball bat."

I shake my head. *God*. I don't remember that, either.

Dr. Sterling continues. "We gave you some benzodiazepines to help you sleep. The hospital kept you on a psychiatric hold for a few days. But once we determined you weren't a threat to yourself or others, we had no legal basis to keep you. You came to one follow-up appointment here at the office, but didn't continue treatment after that."

"Did I tell you anything at the appointment?"

"You shared that you'd once had a relationship with an older man. And that he . . . used to make you kneel. Apparently, the night your neighbor intervened, you'd had a date who tried to make you . . . pleasure him from that position, and you got upset. It triggered you."

An instant headache forms, and I rub at my temple. *I told someone about Mr. Sawyer?* "Did I say anything else about the older man?"

Dr. Sterling shakes her head. "I got the feeling there was more to that relationship than you cared to discuss. But you didn't want to talk about it, or anything related to growing up in Louisiana, or your time in Florida before moving to New York."

"My . . . time in Florida?"

She nods. "You said you'd spent a few weeks there before coming to the city."

Jesus. A period of my life is blacked out. I guess that's why I thought Jocelyn went to Florida. I suppose she did . . . I take a minute, trying to absorb everything—all the new pieces of the puzzle.

After a while, Dr. Sterling sets the file on her lap back on the table and leans forward. "Has something specific happened recently that brought you in today? Or have your memory issues just gotten worse?"

I'm torn on how to answer. I don't want to reveal too

much, but I also need to understand what's going on in my head. Vague is best here. "Recently I was reminded of something bad that happened to a friend of mine two decades ago. At least I *thought* it happened to her. Except now . . . I'm not sure the friend exists. She *never* existed. I'm pretty sure it happened . . . to me."

Dr. Sterling nods. "Our brains are very protective of us. After a trauma, we can sometimes suppress memories, or even create false ones. It's called dissociative amnesia."

She tries to get me to talk more about the traumatic event, but I keep redirecting and asking questions about what she's called dissociative amnesia. *Will everything come back at some point? Is there a way to speed that up? Does having it once mean it could happen again?* By the time the soft buzzer on the clock on the table between us goes off, I'm drained. Not that I wasn't before, but now it feels like I might not be able to get off this couch.

Dr. Sterling stops the alarm and lifts her notepad. "I know this was a lot to take in this morning. How are you feeling right now?"

"Like I wish I was a polar bear and could go into hibernation for a few months."

She smiles. "I'd love to set up another appointment. I think we could work through some of the issues we've touched upon today."

"Can I think about it?"

She nods and stands. "Of course."

I extend my hand. "Thank you for making time to see me."

"I will always see a patient in crisis. But I hope this isn't goodbye, Elizabeth. I really do think I can help."

I smile politely. I'm sure she could. The problem is, who would she help . . . Elizabeth or Jocelyn?

CHAPTER

28

The days start to blur, one after another—climbing out of bed after a restless night, chugging coffee to garner enough energy to shower, slathering on layers of makeup to hide the dark circles under my eyes. Wash. Rinse. Repeat. Even if I'm in shambles on the inside, I have to force a few bites of food—I've lost eight pounds and counting—have to make my way to work and answer emails, teach classes, grade papers.

I may not know what's real and what's not, but I will *not* lose my job. At least today is a Tuesday, which means basic English all day. I can do that in my sleep. Three classes in a giant lecture hall, all freshmen ignoring me while I teach the basics of composition. I blow out a breath, adjust my glasses, drink my fourth coffee of the morning, and stare out my office window. I watch the campus below, the students walking to and fro. One stops, looks down at his phone, then up at the building I'm in—right at me, actually. I go still, suck in a breath. Is he looking for me?

Of course not. He's about nineteen. Lost. Like they all are freshman year.

I catch the time on the clock hanging on my wall and realize I'm going to be late for my last class if I don't get a move on. So I grab my notes, a pen, and my laptop and hurry out of my office. I try to focus on the lesson I'll be teaching today as I head toward the lecture hall, think about how I can make the fundamentals of editing interesting in some way. But my mind drifts, circles back to the same place it's gone for days.

I'm Jocelyn.

The words echo in my head, take my breath away.

He did those things to me.

I gulp. Come to a stop. Press the palm of my hand against the cold brick wall and just breathe.

No, it happened to her, *to Jocelyn—*

Who is me.

Dr. Sterling made that much clear.

"Professor?" A student's voice breaks through, a young woman's. "Are you okay?"

I look up to see a vaguely familiar face. Gabby something-or-other. She's in my class, the one I'm probably late to now.

"Fine, thank you."

Today, right now, I am not Jocelyn. I am Elizabeth Davis. Only Elizabeth Davis.

I straighten, beckon for her to proceed before me into the lecture hall. The room, loud with laughter and talking, goes quiet as I enter. I attach my laptop to the dock, pull up the lecture, and begin speaking. Luckily, I know this material by heart. After twenty minutes, I'm feeling a little lightheaded, so I make a last-minute deviation, calling up the assignment I'd planned to give for homework. "So today, we're going to break into groups and come up with the edits needed for this draft paper."

This is not how this class normally goes—with eighty or so students, it's too big for group work. But I need a break, need eyes to be anywhere but on me. It will be chaotic, and few will actually accomplish anything because they'll all take out their phones or whisper about what they're doing next weekend, but the class seems happy for a change of pace.

I sit on the edge of a table at the front and just breathe as they work. My gaze lingers on a young couple sitting together.

I've seen them before they enter my class. They walk the halls laughing, shoulder to shoulder, touching, flirting.

It makes me think of Jocelyn and Lucas.

They used to fool around, didn't they?

But *there is no Jocelyn.*

Which surely means *I* used to fool around with Lucas.

Were we a thing? I can almost see it in my head, the way I'd smile around him, would light up. I cared about him at one time, felt safe when I was with him.

I think back to Louisiana, to seeing him at the hospital, the way my whole body warmed, how I'd felt *something* toward him, even if I couldn't remember the history.

My body hums with the knowledge that I've kissed him. That I don't even recall it.

Soon enough, the bell rings, class ends, and I rush out as fast as the students. Normally, I stop by my office, hang around in case any students need to speak to me, but not today. I go directly home, get into bed, prop my pillows against the headboard, and dig back into reading about dissociative identity disorder. People with the illness can experience different types of amnesia. Some can *depersonalize*, literally split their personality in two. They can see themselves objectively as someone else.

Me, as Jocelyn.

But it doesn't make sense. That's basically multiple personality disorder, right? I google it and learn that the term is outdated; it's not how doctors view a person now. I chew my lip, hitting the back button, scanning the internet for anything and everything.

What it comes down to is that I'm not crazy. I'm *successful.* I finished college and graduate school, have held various jobs down for twenty years now. I have an apartment, pay my rent on time. I go to the store, buy food, and exercise. I have relationships. They're not perfect relationships. I'm not . . . *perfect.* God knows. But the way these articles describe a person . . .

I'm not sure I can reconcile it with me.

It's just unbelievable.

And exhausting.

At some point, I fall asleep. I'm jolted awake by the stutter of my phone over the nightstand. I grab for it, but I've missed the call. I groan, toss the phone back where it came from, and fall back into bed. Finally, I was sleeping, and without any pills for once. Irritation runs hot through me, but a second later, the phone vibrates again.

This time, I sit up, push my laptop away from the edge of the bed so I don't dump it on the ground, and reach for the phone.

Lucas.

My stomach flutters, remembering my earlier thoughts. That it wasn't Jocelyn, it was *me.*

"Hello?" I answer, just before it flips over to voicemail.

"Elizabeth?" Lucas sounds tired. I peer at the bedside clock—1 a.m., my time. Does that make it midnight for him? When I don't immediately answer, he continues, "Are you there?"

"Yeah, I'm sorry. I was asleep." I clear my throat. "What's going on? Why are you calling so late?"

There's a long pause, and suddenly, I know what he's going to say before the words come out.

"I'm so sorry, Elizabeth. It's your mother. She's gone."

CHAPTER

29

Where are all the dead people?

I've never been down here before, in the basement of Chapman and Sons Funeral Home, but I bet this is where they are. The ones waiting—for embalming, for hair and makeup, for their loved ones to come and cry over them. And the ones waiting on the other end—bodies done being displayed and the only thing left is cremation or burial.

All of the wakes are held on the main level, two rooms back-to-back. Sometimes they make it into one, if the person was popular. Lord knows I've come here enough times. It's the only place of its kind in Minton Parish. My grandmother's wake was here—she didn't need the two rooms made into one. And Ivy's dad—he did need the two rooms. When I was younger, my mother used to make me come here with her whenever people from church died. We'd both put on dresses and pretend we were good Christians.

A thought hits, makes my blood run cold. Was Mr. Sawyer's wake in two rooms? Did all the town come to pay respect to a man who didn't deserve respect? I hadn't stuck around long enough to find out. That fucker probably packed the place.

My musings are interrupted by a voice. "Ms. Davis?"

I stand, practically jumping from my seat.

The man extends his hand with a solemn face. "I'm Kenny Chapman. I'm very sorry for your loss."

"Thank you."

He motions down the hall. "Right this way. I'm sorry to have kept you waiting so long."

"It's fine."

He opens one of the closed doors to reveal an office. There's a desk with chairs, some catalogs, tissue boxes carefully positioned on my side. An archway to my right leads to a bigger room, one full of caskets—display pieces like we're shopping for blouses at Macy's. It makes me wonder, do they come in sizes? Are there clearance options? Name brands and generic?

Kenny Chapman tucks his chair in and opens a folder. "So your mother already made most of the arrangements."

I blink a few times. "Excuse me?"

He offers a practiced smile. "It's common. Parents often want to take the burden from their children, save them from having to make choices during a difficult time." He slides a piece of paper across the desk to me. "These are the things she picked out. I can still show you them, if you'd like."

A lump forms in my throat, thinking of my mother coming here by herself—sick, knowing she was dying, picking out her own casket. I swallow, pushing down the shitty feeling that has threatened to rear its ugly head ever since my phone rang last night. *If I keep moving, the guilt can't catch up with me.*

I lean forward, look down at a full page of typed-up line items. It must be fifteen rows long, each with a price tag at the end:

Base service fee: $2,295

Embalming: $895

Hearse: $350

Full day viewing—two sessions, *double room*

Of course my mother thinks she needs the double room. I stop reading and scan down to the bottom line. The total is more than $9,000. I point to it. "Did she pay this already, too?"

Mr. Chapman frowns. "No, I'm sorry. She didn't. We do offer a prepayment option that locks in the rate, but your mother didn't opt for it."

For some absurd reason, that makes me smile. It's just . . . so *Mom*.

He reaches behind him to the credenza, grabs a board with all different types of wood displayed. "Your mother chose the glossy red oak—it's a beautiful piece—with the premium white satin liner."

"It's very nice."

"Would you like me to show you a full-sized glossy red oak casket? We have one on display in the other room. Since the bill wasn't prepaid, there isn't a formal contract and you can still replace anything that isn't to your satisfaction."

I shake my head. "No. But thank you. Whatever she picked is fine. I want her to have what she wanted."

Kenny Chapman nods with a smile. "Wonderful. Then there's just the matter of payment."

"Do you take Visa?"

"We do."

I dig into my purse, pull out my wallet, and hold the card across the desk. "Here you go. Is there anything else we need to discuss?"

"When would you like the service to be held?"

"I don't know. As soon you can do it, I guess."

He slides the invoice back to his side of the desk, takes a convenient credit card machine from a drawer. "We'll need tomorrow to prep. How would Friday work? Two to five and seven to nine for viewing hours?"

"Okay."

"And nine a.m. for mass at Saint Matthew's on Saturday, followed by a short ceremony at the crematory?"

"Sure."

"Would you prefer to make the arrangements with Saint Matthew's or have us handle that?"

"You, please."

"Of course. There's a two-hundred-and-fifty-dollar preparation fee."

I purse my lips. I don't know why, especially since the bill is over $9,000 already, but adding another fee to make a phone call just irks me. "Maybe you could use the *non*-premium white satin liner, and we can call it even?"

Kenny Chapman looks appalled. I don't care.

He clears his throat. "We'll absorb the fee as a courtesy."

I don't think it will break him. I force a smile. "Thank you."

He swipes my card, slides a receipt over for me to sign. I scribble my name and stand. "Is there anything I need to do?"

"We'll need clothing. Her favorite dress or outfit, perhaps?"

"Anything else?"

He shakes his head. "I don't think so. We'll make sure the church includes the viewing times in their weekly bulletin that goes out tomorrow so their parishioners are aware of your mom's passing."

"Great. So drop off clothes tomorrow and then just come at two p.m. on Friday?"

"You and whatever family members you'd like to invite can come at one for a private viewing. We want to make sure you're happy with the way she looks."

I lift my purse to my shoulder. "It'll just be me."

He nods, steps around his desk, and extends a hand. "Again, I'm very sorry for your loss."

Out front, I gulp fresh air. How the heck does that guy spend all day in that place? It smells weird, and my chest feels scratchy, like I'm breaking out in a rash. Though outside isn't much better; it's thick and soupy. By the time I walk the twenty

steps to my parked rental car, my skin is damp with a sheen
of sweat. God, I hate how sticky this time of the year gets in
Louisiana. Actually, I dislike this place year-round. I've been
here less than eight hours, and I'm already itching to leave.
Maybe I should do it—put this crappy rental car in drive and
head north. Don't stop until I hit Manhattan. But there are
things I'm hoping this trip will accomplish, aside from burying
my mother. Like rattling my memory, filling in the rest of the
missing pieces.

As if on cue following that thought, my phone buzzes
from somewhere in my bag. I start the ignition to get the air
going before digging it out. Lucas's name is displayed on the
screen, an incoming text. *He* is definitely a puzzle piece, so I
swipe to read.

Lucas: Hey. Heard you're in town.

How the heck did he know already? Another text follows
before I can respond.

Lucas: You went to the Grind for coffee. New owner
since we were kids. Higher prices. Still gossip central.

A memory comes back. I'm not sure if it was repressed, or
I just had no reason to think about it until now. But it makes
me smile.

Elizabeth: Do you still pour an inch of sugar into your
coffee cup before filling it?

Lucas: LOL I don't. I take it black now. Diabetes runs in
the family. Do you still drink yours until it's ice-cold, yet
you despise iced coffee?

My smile widens.

Elizabeth: I do.

Lucas: I just wanted to reach out and say I'm sorry about the way I broke the news to you the other night. I should've given you a minute, let you wake up first.

Elizabeth: It's fine. I appreciated that you called instead of a stranger from the hospital.

Lucas: If there's anything I can do, just let me know. I work three twelves, so after eight tonight, I'll be off for four days. If you want a shoulder to cry on, ear to bend, drinking buddy . . .

The drinking part sounds like a good idea, though I'm not sure I can wait until eight o'clock tonight. Today already feels like it's been a week long, and it isn't even five in the afternoon. But Lucas might be able to unlock some more memories . . .

Elizabeth: Thank you. I appreciate that. It's been a long day, so I'll probably go to bed early tonight, and I have some errands to run tomorrow, but maybe we can get together at some point after the services are over? They're going to be Friday.

Lucas: I'd like that a lot.

A warm feeling spreads through me.

Elizabeth: Okay, great. I'll text you.

The door to the funeral parlor opens. Kenny Chapman walks out and looks around. Mine is the only car in the parking lot. He lifts a hand to shield his eyes from the sun, gets a look at me, and waves. I guess I'd better go or he'll be add-

ing a twenty-five-dollar parking surcharge to my bill. I put
the car in drive and head home. Well, not home—but to my
mother's house. I'm not looking forward to going inside. Actually, I'm dreading it. But I can't stall forever. Though I can
make a stop, pick up a bottle of wine to take the edge off
when I get there, maybe two bottles. I should probably pick
up some food, too, but I'm not hungry. The liquor store is
on Main Street, the two-block-long strip of stores that cover
basic small-town necessities—Laundromat, grocery store,
bank, barbershop . . . It's also diagonally across from Liars
Pub. I glance over at the cars in the parking lot on my way in.
None look familiar. No red pickup tonight. But as I walk out,
two bottles in hand and my head still spinning, I remember
something Noah mentioned to me in that bar the last time
we were there—the place he goes when he needs to clear his
mind. Big Devil Bayou.

I return to my car and toss the wine I've just bought inside. Maybe the bayou can clear my mind, too. Or better yet,
maybe I'll find someone there who can make me forget my
life for a while . . .

CHAPTER
30

The air feels even thicker out here.

I park along the edge of the brush, walk the path I somehow still remember to get down to the beat-up old dock. Damp soil and decaying leaves yield an earthy scent unique to the bayou. The spongy ground squelches with each step as I push Spanish moss hanging from gnarled cypress trees out of my way. Thick roots snake out to make the short trek in heels even more daunting than it needs to be, while cicadas and mosquitos buzz all around, creating a low hum. It's interrupted by the occasional croak of a frog or chirp of a bird, but it's otherwise eerily quiet. Yet there's still something beautiful about this place—the way the late-afternoon light filters in through a canopy of bending trees and their damp trunks seem to glow. Though none of it holds a candle to the sight of the man wearing a white T-shirt and backward baseball cap holding a fishing pole while sitting at the end of the pier.

Noah must sense he's being watched. He sits up a little straighter, turns, and glances over his shoulder. His slow, confident smile curves up when he sees me, and what is otherwise an awful day feels a little brighter. There's a glimmer of hope, a promise of *something*. I'm not sure what, but something besides thinking about my mother.

I walk down the long pier to the end and take the seat next to him—without hesitating, without asking.

"Hey." He doesn't hide the surprise in his voice, though according to Lucas, it's public knowledge that I'm in town. "You're here."

"I am."

I wait for him to say something—to ask why I'm back or say what everyone says when someone important to you dies: *I'm sorry*. It's a pressure building under my skin, and I just want to get it over with.

But Noah just sips his beer and extends the half-full bottle to me to take a swig. "Been boring around here without you," he says. There's a hint of a smile, his dimples making their presence known. "Glad you're back."

All I can do is stare at him. Stare into his *father's* eyes. Oddly, it doesn't make me want to turn and run, even knowing it was *me*, that *I am Jocelyn*. Instead, as I accept the beer from his hand, Noah's eyes zone in on my lips. I take a long pull, and the hungry look on his face makes me feel something very different from the way I've felt the last twenty-odd hours. I'm probably deranged for feeling it, knowing what I now know I've done—I swallow—with his *father*. But I don't care.

My hand clenches the beer bottle, and I imagine gripping Noah's hair in my hands, pulling tight enough to make him hiss in pain, in pleasure. I envision my nails scraping down his skin, the palm of my hand covering his mouth, being in control, on top this time. I salivate, practically able to hear the loud crack of my hand connecting with his skin. *Hard*. Fantasy lets me escape the world that is reality, the reason I'm here.

For a few precious seconds, I pretend *Noah* is the reason I'm here. He may as well be.

"How did you know where to find me?" he asks.

"When we were at the bar before, you told me where you

go to clear your head. Mine needs some clearing today, too. Hope you don't mind I crashed your party."

Noah takes the beer back, takes another long swallow, and we both stare out at the murky water. I can understand why this is a place that can clear his mind. There's a unique stillness out here that you can't find anywhere else—*especially* not in New York City. After a long bout of silence, I look over and catch Noah's eyes once again.

"What was it like to lose a parent?"

He blinks at me, seeming startled by the question. For a second, I think he's going to refuse to answer it, maybe reel in his line and head back to his truck. But instead he chugs what's left in the bottle, then reaches for another and cracks it open, staring into space for a while before sighing. "Shitty. Even if you don't always get along, it's like you've lost something you'll never get back."

"You didn't get along with your parents?"

He shrugs. "Not my father. I was only a kid, but we butted heads. He . . ." Noah hesitates, shakes his head.

There's something there, the way he's unsure about continuing. It makes my heart rate pick up, anxiety pulse in my head. My mouth goes dry, even in this peaceful place. "What?" I ask, prodding him. "He what?"

He shakes his head. "Nothing. Everyone adored him here in town. But people are complicated, you know?"

Boy, do I ever.

"Sure," I say, "I get that." The layers of feelings around my mother threaten to rush forward, but I grab the new bottle of beer from Noah's hand and slug back a healthy amount even though hops taste like dirt to me. "How was he complicated?"

Noah looks at me. A muscle in his cheek feathers, like there are words on the tip of his tongue, and he's not sure he wants to let them out. But he searches my face, and maybe he sees that I truly need to know. He nods. "He did some things to the family that weren't right."

I stay quiet, waiting for more, but Noah doesn't elaborate. Though it's not hard to believe Damon Sawyer could do wrong to his own family. An underage girl, a grimy motel room . . . If a man would do that, I can imagine he could hurt just about anyone. My blood pressure ticks up a notch.

"Mom would forgive him," Noah says suddenly. "She was an angel and forgave to a fault, but I—I didn't find it so easy." He purses his lips, stares out at the bobber attached to the line on his fishing pole, and stays quiet for a long time before continuing. "My sister died when I was three. She was four years older. It was an accident, but I blamed him."

My eyes flare wide. "What happened?"

"She fell at the park, from the top of the jungle gym. Broke her neck. She died instantly. My dad was supposed to be watching her."

My hand covers my heart. "I'm sorry."

"Thank you." He nods. "Anyway, there are other things, too. Like I said, it's complicated. But first I lost my sister, and then a few years later I lost my mother and father on the same day."

"What do you mean? I thought your mom died last year."

"Technically. But the truth is, when my dad died, he took my mother with him. She was never the same. She fell into a deep depression, spent most days staring out the window or sleeping in bed. I lost a mother and a father all at once."

"That's terrible."

Noah meets my eyes. "It is. Because my mother was an amazing woman. She didn't deserve to spend the rest of her life so drugged up she couldn't boil water herself."

I stare at him, wanting to press, wanting to ask for more details. But there's pain in Noah's eyes, and I think maybe he's never talked to anyone about this. Maybe, in his own way, he's as affected by his father as I am.

"How did your dad die?"

I can't believe I just asked that, just blurted out the insane question. But now that it's out there, I hold my breath, waiting for the answer.

Noah looks up, meets my eyes with an intense stare. "He was killed."

I don't react. Don't move. Don't so much as breathe. I can't sort out if that's accusation in his gaze or if it's pain. If it's *both*.

"Robbery gone wrong," he adds, and the pressure lets off. I can exhale.

The peaceful water and swaying cypress trees all around me suddenly feel very claustrophobic. And my line of thinking is as erratic as my surroundings. I've bounced from wanting to dominate this man to making him talk about his dead father and dead sister. Something inside me twists, writhes, and in the moment, it feels utterly wrong to be here, talking about this with him.

"I have to go." My announcement is abrupt, but I don't care. I climb to my feet.

"Wait." Noah scrambles to stand, too, reaches out, touches my arm. "Please don't go. Or—or we can both go. We can go to my place. I want to . . ." He lowers his voice a notch. "Help make you forget."

Forget what? For a heart-stopping moment, I think he means his father—that he wants to help me forget *him*. But then he says, "Your mom. I heard. I'm really sorry."

Like simmering water coming to an angry boil, my insides clench, threatening to erupt with sudden rage. He acted like he didn't know. He sat here beside me, cool as a freaking cucumber, letting me ask him about *his* father, *his* family, letting me think he hadn't heard the news, that he was pleased to see me back in town—but really, he knew. I yank away from him, turn to go.

"Elizabeth." His voice is a bark, an order.

It makes me go still. Takes me back to a dim motel room, the rough carpet beneath my knees—

Noah's arms wrap around me, crush me against him, holding me tight.

I should scream at him. Should knee him in the balls and stalk out of here.

Instead, I melt.

I breathe.

And I give in and let a man comfort me for the first time in twenty years.

CHAPTER
31

"Y ou look good." I smile. It's sad that it's probably the first time I've given my mother a compliment in . . . Well, maybe it's the first one ever. And she's lying in a casket for it. Dead. Even sadder is that it might also be the first time our conversation doesn't end in an argument. Unexpected tears fill my eyes, and I sniffle them back.

It feels like I should say a prayer. She'd like that. I probably wouldn't have given that to her when she was alive, but somehow it feels okay to do now. Maybe it's because I'm doing it on my terms; I'm not being forced. My eyes drop to the floor in front of the casket. There's a kneeler, a cushioned block of wood to rest your knees. But hell will freeze over before I'm ever in that position again. *Sorry, Mom.* I bow my head, close my eyes, and whisper the Hail Mary.

A few moments later, there's a light knock at the door. Kenny Chapman steps into the viewing room.

"How is everything?" he asks. "Is there anything you'd like changed before visiting hours begin?"

"No. They did a really good job on her hair and makeup. She looks pretty. At peace."

"Excellent." He nods. "An early guest has arrived, as well as a florist with a delivery, but we still have a couple of minutes, so I'll let you have this time with your mother alone."

I look over at Mom, take a deep breath, and shake my head. "It's okay. You can let them in. I'm done."

"Very well."

A florist carries in a big white cross made of roses. I'm still standing at the casket, watching them set it up, when Father Preston walks up and joins me. *Where did Kenny Chapman go? Is it too late to change my mind and say I'd rather be alone?*

"I'm very sorry for your loss, Elizabeth. Your mother was a wonderful woman, a devout member of Saint Matthew's."

I nod, manage to mumble a thank-you. I'm going to need to get better at this if I'm going to survive today.

Father Preston turns and faces me head-on. "I came by to visit Theresa the other morning. We had a long talk, and I promised her I would speak to you."

"About what?"

"Your mother would really like you to attend confession."

I feel my heart skip a beat. "Why? What did she tell you?"

"She expressed concern about your relationship with Christ. Many times when people veer away from their faith, it's because our bond with God is broken by our sins. Confession allows us to seek true forgiveness and repair that connection." He searches my face. "Everyone sins. Big or small. Even I go to confession, Elizabeth."

"Really? And what do you have to confess?"

"That's between me and the Lord."

"Then why is it that I have to tell my sins to *you*?"

A few people wander into the back of the room. I recognize one as Mom's neighbor. "Excuse me. I should greet people."

Father Preston reaches out, rests a hand on my arm, stopping me. "There is no sin that can't be forgiven when you're truly ready to repent, Elizabeth."

I frown and shake my head. "I wouldn't be so sure of that."

The next few hours are a blur. A sea of people come and

go—Mom really did need the double room. People from church, neighbors . . . It seems like most of the town is here at some point. The polite smile glued on my face is starting to hurt, so I'm grateful when someone walks in that I don't have to pretend for. Ivy. And she's alone. I excuse myself from yet another stranger telling me what a wonderful woman my mother was and head straight for my old best friend.

Ivy smiles sadly. "I'm sorry about your mom, Elizabeth."

"Thanks." I nod toward the door leading to the hall. "Do you think we can talk?"

"Sure."

Kenny Chapman and a dowdy woman in a black suit are manning the front entrance, opening the door for people as they come and go. So I steer us in the opposite direction, to the ladies' room. Luckily, it's empty.

"How are you holding up?" Ivy asks.

"Are we talking about my mother dying or the chapters?"

"Both."

"My mother dying, I'll get through. The other thing, I'm not so sure . . ." I shake my head. "It's been difficult."

"So you've received more?"

I nod. "Five chapters so far."

"And everything in them is accurate?"

"Down to room number 212."

The color drains from Ivy's face. "Oh my God. Who can it be and what do they want?"

Her reaction makes me 99.9 percent sure she isn't behind this. But I need more than that. I need to be absolutely certain. I lean in, lock eyes with her. "Is it you, Ivy? I need to know."

"What?" Her face twists. "Of course not. Why do you keep asking me that? Why the hell would I dredge up the past? I have as much to lose as you, if not more. My husband thinks I'm a good person." She pauses for a few seconds, her mouth opening and shutting, then opening and shutting again, as if she has something to say but isn't sure if she should.

"What?" I urge. "Tell me."

Ivy meets my eyes, then takes a big breath in and out. "Before I tell you something, I need to know if you believe I'm not the one doing this to you, not haunting you by sending the chapters."

We stare each other down for a few moments. She was and still is the best friend I've ever had. Twenty years may have gone by, but I'm almost certain she's telling the truth. I nod. "I believe you."

She lets out another big breath. "Okay. Good."

"Now what do you need to tell me?"

Ivy swallows and looks down. "I was always a little jealous of you."

"Jealous of me? For what?"

"You were so pretty and smart, and I was just so . . . ordinary."

"That's not true, Ivy. You—"

She holds a hand up, stopping me. "I don't want to debate it. Whether it's true or not isn't the issue. It was how I *perceived* us years ago. I loved you with all my heart, but maybe a part of me would've rather been you than me. That's the only explanation I can come up with, even after all these years."

"Explanation for what? I'm not following you."

Ivy's eyes meet mine once again. "I slept with Mr. Sawyer, too."

My eyes bulge. "*What?*"

She starts to ramble, her words coming fast. "You were acting weird, and you wouldn't tell me why, and one day I saw you riding your bicycle toward the outskirts of town when you'd told me you had to stay in and help your mom, so I followed you. You went to the motel to meet him." She shakes her head. "I was jealous that a handsome man who was so much older was interested in you, so I wanted to see if I could make him interested in *me*."

I clutch my chest. "Oh my God. Ivy, how could you never tell me?"

"I was embarrassed and ashamed, and it didn't last that long. I only met him at the motel a few times, and after we finally . . . did it, he smacked me and told me I made noises like a whore. I never went back."

Tears fill my eyes. "How could you have ever thought I was smarter than you, when you had the sense to not go back? I kept going, Ivy."

She pulls me into a hug. "I know. And I'm so sorry I didn't talk to you about it. I swear, I had no idea you were being abused, too, until Sawyer died and you told me what had been going on. I just thought I made noises like a whore. To this day, I'm silent when my husband and I have sex."

Jesus Christ. That man screwed up so many people. Ivy holds me for a long time before pulling back. She grasps both of my shoulders and looks into my eyes. "I'm so, so sorry I didn't save you, Elizabeth."

"Nothing that happened is your fault. You don't need to apologize. I'm sorry you got sucked into things."

She sniffles back tears. "I could've saved you, and I didn't."

I shake my head. "If there's one thing I've learned in my screwed-up life, it's that we can only save ourselves."

Ivy pulls a paper towel from the dispenser and wipes her nose. "It's a good thing your mama isn't breathing anymore. Because if she heard you say that, she'd be calling the priest for an exorcism while screaming that only *God* can save us."

Only Ivy could make me laugh during my mother's wake—after telling me she's kept a monumental secret from me for twenty years. "You got that right."

She smiles. "I have to get going. My daughter fell asleep in the car on the way here, so I left my husband with her in the parking lot."

"Wait. Just give me another minute." I swallow. There are things I still need to know. "I need to ask you a few questions,

and some of them might not make any sense, but your answers
are really important."

"Okay. What?"

"Were you there that night?"

"What night? The night he . . . ?"

I nod. "The night Sawyer died."

"Of course. You called me upset, and I came to the hotel,
helped you make it look like a robbery."

"Were we the only two people in the room? You and me?"

Her eyes dart around the empty bathroom, even though
anyone coming in would've had to pass us. "Yes, except for
him."

"Mr. Sawyer?"

She nods.

I'm relieved to know what I remember about Ivy's involve-
ment wasn't made-up. It's difficult to know what's real or not
after finding out the truth about Jocelyn. I can't trust my own
memory.

"Was I . . . close to Lucas?"

Ivy's brows furrow. "You were until—well, you started
to pull away from both of us toward the end of senior year. I
didn't know why until I found out about you and Mr. Sawyer.
But you really liked Lucas before that, and he seemed pretty
into you, too. You used to fool around. Why are you asking
me this?"

I really don't want to get into the issues I've been experi-
encing. So I avert my eyes. "It was a long time ago, and some
things are fuzzy. What about Mr. Sawyer's daughter? Did you
know he had a little girl who died while he was supposed to
be watching her?"

Ivy blinks. "No. When did that happen?"

I'm relieved it isn't common knowledge and another thing
I've somehow blocked out. I've been questioning that since I
got home from the bayou the other night. Minton Parish is a
small town; everyone would've been talking about a little girl

dying. But Ivy and I were still in middle school at the time, so I guess we didn't put it together with Mr. Sawyer the teacher when we got to high school.

"She died four years before him," I tell her.

"What happened?"

I shrug. "An accident . . . supposedly."

The bathroom door opens. A woman I vaguely recognize walks in. I think she belongs to my mother's church. She smiles at me sadly and makes her way into a stall. Her presence effectively brings an end to my private conversation with Ivy. It's just as well. The less we say out loud, the better.

Ivy pulls me into a hug again and whispers, "I'm here for you, if you need anything, Elizabeth."

"Thank you."

She nods toward the door. "Your mom is at peace now. I hope you can find some, too."

"Thank you for coming."

Hours later, I think the entire town and part of the neighboring one has finally come by. My mind keeps circling back to what Ivy told me today, analyzing whether it changes anything in this game of Clue I keep playing in my head. I don't think it does. But I'm physically and mentally exhausted, so drained that I might have a shot at sleeping tonight. There're ten minutes left in the last session, and the number of people in the room is finally starting to dwindle. I'm watching a woman wipe tears and genuflect in front of the casket when a hand on my shoulder startles me. Though I quickly settle. I have no idea how, but I know who it is before I turn.

Noah smiles, flashes a dimple. "Hey."

I smile back. For the first time today, the gesture isn't borne from a sense of duty. I actually feel happy to see him. "I didn't expect you to come."

"I wanted to pay my respects." He looks into my eyes. "I also thought maybe you could use a friend."

I tilt my head. "Is that what we are? Friends, Noah?"

"I can be anything you want me to be." His eyes drop to my lips. "The night we met was pretty damn great and has me hoping maybe you'll want me to be a little more than friendly. Though you'll have to stop running out on me for that to happen."

My insides flutter like a schoolgirl's. "I bet not too many women run away from you."

He winks. "Doesn't matter. There's only one I'm trying to catch."

A man I've never met interrupts to offer his condolences, and then a couple swoops in to tell me how lucky I was to have a mom like mine. Noah steps back, makes room for strangers. Because it's nearing the end of the viewing hours, I wind up getting pulled from one person to the next. But even as a line forms to say goodbye, I never lose sight of Noah. And I know he never takes his eyes off me, because I *feel* them.

When a lull finally happens, he makes his way back to the front of the room, where I'm standing. "I'm gonna head out. But I'll be home all night if you want to come by."

"Come by for . . . ?"

Noah leans in and kisses my cheek, moves his mouth to my ear. "For whatever you want. Ball is always in your court, Elizabeth. Always."

CHAPTER

32

The drive to my mother's house is silent. Usually, I turn on a podcast or music to occupy my mind. But tonight, only the slow patter of rain on the windows and the squeak of the windshield wipers keep me company. Today was a lot to digest—too many voices, too many people, and all of them telling me how perfect my mother was, how lovely, *such a good mom*. I grind my teeth just thinking about it. And then Father Preston, telling me I should tell him my *sins* . . .

I wish I knew what my mother told him.

When I pull into the driveway and cut the engine, I'm not ready to leave the car. This place hasn't been my home in a long time, if it ever was at all. It was always hers.

I survey the peeling paint, the door that hangs wonky in the frame, long-dead flowers in cracked terra-cotta pots. I blow out a breath, manage to put the key into the ignition to restart the engine. I don't want to be here. Not now. I don't think too hard as I back out of the driveway, pull onto the road, and start driving toward town.

Maybe I'll go to the bar again. Noah won't be there. He said he was heading home. Perhaps a drink with a stranger. We don't even need to exchange names. We could go to a hotel, have meaningless sex to help me clear my mind for a little while.

But then I remember the only hotel in town is a place I'm not stepping foot into.

I take the turn that leads to downtown, but before I hit the main street, a face pulses through my mind. A smile. A promise. *Dimples.*

But then . . . another face flashes—not *his*, but his father's.

I grip the steering wheel until my knuckles turn white and force my thoughts back to Noah—how he showed up tonight, how he somehow charms me even when I'm feeling uncharmable. *He* can make me forget.

I turn the steering wheel and make a sharp right at the last second. No longer headed for the bar and a drink and a stranger, instead headed for Noah.

His house is dark, silent. I glance at the clock—9:40. Not *too* late. He did say he'd be home. But maybe he went to the bar instead, or maybe—maybe he went to sleep? I slip out of the car, unbothered by the idea of waking him. At the front door, I knock lightly, then almost immediately try opening it, and it whispers as it swings wide. Never in a million years would I have let myself into a man's house before today, not even Sam's. But my adrenaline is pumping, and I justify my actions by telling myself Noah left it open for me.

I step in, listening for him—for any sound at all.

But there's nothing.

I remove my shoes and pad silently through the downstairs of his dark home. No one is down here, so I continue over a rug, up the stairs, until I reach the hallway leading to his bedroom. A shallow stream of light slices across the floor. I inch up, lean forward until I can see him. He's sleeping in bed, head resting on a thick pillow, the comforter pulled up over his hips, but his chest is bare, abs showing. Their definition is apparent, even in this gray half-light. I stand there for too long, just watching him, tracing the outline of his jaw, his straight nose, with my gaze.

The way Mr. Sawyer watched me.

A rush of emotions hits—anger, vulnerability, sadness, hatred, and last, though not least, *desire*. Isn't that what always got me in trouble? My *sins*, as my mother would say. Maybe. Definitely. But right now I don't care. The desire is too strong. I picture it: stalking across the room, waking him from his slumber by biting his collarbone or gripping his hair in my fist, drawing a cry of pain. I'm not in a healthy place mentally, but I'm with it enough to know that my wanting to inflict pain, on Mr. Sawyer's son of all people, is *fucked up*.

Maybe I'm more Jocelyn right now than Elizabeth, and I want revenge. There have to be a million psychological reasons for me wanting to *hurt* Noah Sawyer, but I'm not willing to stop and analyze any of them.

I unzip my dress, slip it from my shoulders, leave it in a pile by the door. The cool night air sends goose bumps over my body. I exhale, walk to the bed, slowly lift a knee and climb on, feeling the plush fabric of the comforter against my skin.

I'm just about to straddle his hips when Noah's eyes flicker open. A rush of adrenaline races through my body. His lips curve into a cocky grin.

He knew. He knew I'd come tonight. Probably left the door unlocked because he was *that certain* of himself.

And from that smile, I'd say he's pretty damn happy he was right.

I settle my knee, finish straddling his hips, and drape myself over him, pressing my lips to his. His hands come up, cup my jaw, pulling me closer. As we kiss, Noah reaches down, grabs my hip, and starts to move me, taking control.

But that's not how this is going to go. Not today.

I smack his hand away, catch his wrist, and press it to the bed. A rush of power floods me as I pin it at his side. My other hand reaches for his jaw, caresses its way down to his throat, where my fingers splay wide. When he tries to sit up, to push me back, I bring my weight forward, onto my hand at his neck, and *squeeze* his Adam's apple. My heart slams against my rib cage as his face starts to turn pink.

A half laugh comes from his throat, and his eyes light up—excited—as he gives in and settles beneath me. *Good boy.*

I make my way down his body, raking smooth skin beneath my nails as I go. When I reach the waistband of his boxers, I stop, wait until our eyes meet, then slide them slowly down, peeling at the elastic until he springs free.

My hand wraps around his girth. "Is this what you want?"

Noah's eyes close, his lips part, and he inhales soft, shallow breaths. It takes him a moment to come back, to look at me, to nod fervently.

"Good," I say. "But too bad . . ."

And then I stop and climb off him.

"What are you—"

"Out of bed." I stand, snap my fingers, then point to the ground. "On your knees."

He watches me, trying to figure out what the hell I'm doing. But then that intoxicating grin comes back, the one that has reeled me back time and time again, and he slides out of bed, onto his knees, gazing up at me like he's ready for anything, like he trusts me.

Just like I trusted his father.

But Noah doesn't know what he's in for, not yet.

"Don't look at me." I grab his hair, force his head down. "Eyes on the ground."

"Yes, ma'am," he drawls. But he sneaks one last look—and in those eyes, I don't see Noah. I see *him* . . . And for a breath, I want to do something awful. And then I think, *Why not?*

I walk around to his back, run my nails across his skin until welts appear. "Lean over the bed," I command.

He complies immediately, still on his knees, big hands

bracing himself against the fabric. I look around the room—
a pair of pants hangs over a chair in the corner, and I grab
them, whip the belt through the loops, and wrap it around my
fist, bringing it down in a firm smack across his ass.

A grumbling laugh comes up from his chest. "Elizabeth,"
he whispers, not upset, but *more* excited. Suddenly, an image
flashes in my head—me on my knees in that dimly lit hotel
room. I'd liked those first smacks. They were more playful
than painful, until they weren't anymore.

"Quiet," I hiss.

And I do it again, and again, and again, using all my might.

Eventually, after he's stained with marks, swollen with
welts every which way across his flesh, we end up in bed. Me
on top, his hands tied to the bed frame. I ride him until he's
about to come, and then I stop. Pull away. He groans in pain,
and I smile.

"Did you enjoy your punishment?" I undo the knots at
his wrists.

"I liked you riding me. But what was I being punished for?"

"Your sins, of course."

"Well, I got plenty of those." Hands free, Noah rubs one
wrist, then the other, before reaching for me. "Now come
here, let me finish what you started, darlin'."

I step back. "Sorry. But we're already finished. At least
for today."

CHAPTER

33

I hate sitting in the front row.

Hated it in school, but church is far worse. It feels like the statues are all staring at me, and there's nothing to distract myself with watching—no kid sneaking to look at his phone, no God-fearing dad checking out the ass of another man's wife as she walks a few pews in front of him, no mother with pursed lips ready to listen to a homily about acceptance while judging the length of every young girl's skirt when they walk in.

I check the time on my phone. One minute after nine. Why haven't we started yet? A voice from behind me makes me jump as my head comes up.

"Is that seat taken?"

Noah.

He smiles like he's *not* in church, like it's last night and he's looking at me naked. It makes my cheeks heat. Noah doesn't wait for me to respond. He brushes past me and sits so close, we're shoulder to shoulder in the pew.

"What are you doing here?" I whisper.

"Figured I'd keep you company. You don't seem like the type to enjoy coming to church."

I raise a brow. "Why is that? Because I like sex rough and out of wedlock?"

He grins. "Actually, I assumed you weren't fond of the

place because last time I saw you here you were outside in the car waiting for your mom, rather than sitting next to her." He leans toward me and lowers his voice. "But if I have to choose between premarital sex and being a Catholic, I'll be going down the block to the Episcopalian place from now on."

A few minutes ago, I couldn't wait for the service to start. Now I'm disappointed when the church organ begins playing and all heads turn toward the back. Father Preston makes a grand entrance, leading the procession, followed by three altar boys—the one in the middle carries a giant cross above his head, and the two on either side carry poles with candles. In the back is my mother's glossy red oak casket, being carried by men from the funeral parlor.

Noah reaches over to my lap, takes my hand into his, and squeezes tight. My gut reaction is to pull away, but any fight I have is quickly forgotten when the casket passes by and a man in a suit is right behind it.

My eyes grow wide.

Sam.

What the hell?

He smiles at me like I've been expecting him and couldn't wait for his arrival. But the corners of his lips quickly wilt when he notices the man next to me has his fingers laced with mine. Sam's face turns stern. He clears his throat and leans over to speak quietly. "Do you want to move down, or should I sit on the other side of your friend?"

I tug my hand from Noah's and catch his eye. He scooches over without being asked. Sam unbuttons his jacket and takes a seat at the end of the pew. Jesus Christ, I wanted a distraction, but not *this* hot mess waiting to explode. Sam stares ahead at the altar, the muscle in his jaw flexing like he's trying to send silent Morse code. I wait until the priest starts talking to lean over and whisper, "What are you doing here?"

Sam's eyes bounce between Noah and me. "You texted me

your mother died. I thought you might need some support, someone to lean on."

"When have I ever given you the idea that I wanted to lean on someone?"

He pins me with a fiery glare. "Not now, Elizabeth. Have some respect."

My blood feels like it's boiling in my veins. Have some respect? For whom? Him? A man who shows up uninvited and unannounced? This organized cult that pretends it's a church? Or for my mother—a woman who believed it was okay to leave me alone at seven years old to go off with men because she went to confession after?

I suppose the one good thing about these two showing up is that I'm too preoccupied to be upset that this is the last hour I'll ever have with my mother. Not that she's here anymore, but her body—the wake, the funeral—still tethers me to her. This morning, I woke with a hollow feeling in my chest, knowing that would end today. But there's no hollow space now; I'm filled with anger.

The service goes by in a blur—all three of us staring straight ahead like strangers. Father Preston says his closing remarks, then steps from the altar and stops by my pew to give me his condolences one last time.

I force a smile. "Thank you. The service was lovely."

I don't bother to say anything to Noah, nor do I wait for the man to my right to step out of the pew. Rather, I climb over Sam's legs and start up the aisle alone behind the casket. At the door, the funeral director catches me.

"We'll drive over to the crematory now, if you'd like to follow."

I shake my head. "I don't think that's necessary."

He looks horrified. But I need this to be over. "Thank you for everything."

I march down the marble church steps and head across the

parking lot. Sam catches up to me as I reach my rental car. He goes around to the passenger side.

I look at him, but say nothing.

He frowns. "I Ubered here. My flight was delayed, and I didn't want to be late for the service."

I climb into the car, unlock the passenger door, and pull out of the parking lot so fast that Sam barely had time to get in. I would've left tire marks in front of the church if this rental had any treads left. I drive for a while in silence, but I'm not even sure where I'm going. Sam's face is red with anger as he stares straight ahead. A few miles down the road, I pull into the parking lot of a boarded-up Burger King. Not even a fast-food giant could make it in this town.

I shift in my seat to face Sam. "Say whatever you want to say, because I'm at a loss for words right now."

His jaw is rigid. "Fine. Are you fucking that guy?"

I throw my hands up in the air. "That's none of your business. We've never had an exclusive relationship."

Sam shakes his head. "I was trying to do the right thing."

My eyes close, and I soften. This is all my fault. I should've cut things off with him when he admitted he wanted more. But instead, I *used* him.

I sigh. "I'm sorry, Sam."

"Sorry you're fucking someone else or sorry that it upsets me?"

I shake my head. "I'm sorry that it's going to end this way. On a bad note. You've been nothing but kind to me, but we don't want the same things."

"What is it that you want?"

That's a good question. I look down for a long time, trying to come up with the answer. When I do, he couldn't possibly have any idea how much one word means to me right now. "Freedom. I want my freedom, Sam."

He looks into my eyes, searching. Finding whatever he's looking for, his eyes close briefly. When they reopen, the anger in his face is replaced by disappointment. "Will you drop me off somewhere? A bar or a place I can wait for an Uber back to the airport."

"I'll drive you to the airport."

The twenty-minute ride is quiet, but I'm not sure what else is left to say.

I pull up at the little terminal and put the car in park. "Thank you for coming."

"Sure." He frowns, grabs his backpack from the floor, and unzips the front. Pulling out a folder, he holds it out to me. "You might as well have this."

I take it. "What is it?"

"I did some more research on your missing friend, widened the search to the US. There's a sheet there on every Jocelyn Burton that came up. Consider it a parting gift."

CHAPTER

34

I give the thick file a sideways glance as I stop for a light. Multiple sets of papers clipped together are visible from the side. Various Jocelyns, no doubt, scattered throughout the country, none of them knowing that someone with their same name went through what I did.

As soon as I get home, I head straight for the overflowing trash can in the kitchen. The smell of garbage permeates the whole room. It probably hasn't been taken out since before Mom was hospitalized.

I open the trash can, hold the file above it. But something stops me from letting go.

Curiosity pings around in my brain. I'll just take a quick look. I remember asking Mr. Sawyer why he chose that name for me, *Jocelyn*. He'd said it was his mother's, and I always wondered who in their right mind would want to screw someone they'd named after their mother. Not that Mr. Sawyer was in his right mind, come to think of it.

At the table, along with an overly sweet bottle of moscato from Mom's collection, I flip the file open. Jocelyns are in California. Montana. Kansas. But then I find one from *here*. Or rather, the next town over. The hair on the back of my neck rises with a tickle as I slide the pages out from the file folder and start reading.

Born in the 1930s. Raised by her grandmother. That fact alone is a red flag. Where was her mother? Did she take off? Get arrested for abusing her? Die? There aren't too many positive scenarios that end with your mother not in the picture.

I scroll the fact sheet, take a long pull of the wine.

The second page holds the answer. Multiple arrests. Child removed from her care. Another swallow. *Child abuse.*

I pause at that, wonder what she must have done in the 1960s, when Mr. Sawyer was born, that would have been considered child abuse. Mom used to brag about the punishments she got when she misbehaved, like it was a rite of passage or something—spankings with a wooden spoon, slaps across the face, sometimes she'd be locked in a closet for hours at a time. Things that today would never fly, but back then would have been fairly commonplace.

So I have to wonder what the real Jocelyn was doing to her child in the 1960s.

I turn more pages. Drink more wine. My head starts to go fuzzy, but then it comes back into sharp focus with an entry dated 12/25/68. *Christmas.*

Horror grows within me as I read.

The real Jocelyn beat Mr. Sawyer nearly to death, badly enough that he was hospitalized, placed in foster care. There's a mug shot, black and white and shades of gray, so fuzzy I can barely make out her features. But somehow, the eyes stand out—Mr. Sawyer's eyes, *Noah's* eyes.

On Jocelyn, they look cruel, hardened. Like she never knew a happy day in her life.

Mr. Sawyer's looked hardened, too.

But Noah? His eyes have always been soft.

For a moment, I wonder if Mr. Sawyer dying was a blessing to him. He got to have maybe not a *normal* childhood, but one free of abuse. If he'd been raised by Mr. Sawyer, I can't imagine he'd have turned out the way he is now.

That's when it hits me—why Mr. Sawyer would have given

me the name Jocelyn. In a way—a fucked-up way that wasn't
remotely fair to me—he was abusing his abuser.

A coldness settles in my belly. *Not unlike what I did to
Noah the other night.* I gulp down more wine, hoping to numb
it, hoping to numb *everything*. But alcohol alone won't do it.
I stare down at the papers strewn over the table and decide
they need to go. The garbage isn't good enough, so I sweep
together a pile, shove all the Jocelyns back into the folder, and
march outside. At the back of the yard, near a fence that's long
fallen down, a rusted metal ring sits in the soil and scraggly
grass. Beneath it, the earth is dark, the remnants of regular
scorching.

I pause long enough to wonder what Mom burned often
enough that the ground is still fallow. But I suppose it doesn't
matter now. Once upon a time, we burned garbage here—
Mom and me—before there was organized trash pickup, and
then for a while, even after there was. We couldn't afford to
pay someone to pick up our *trash*.

I return inside long enough to dig for a box of matches.
Finding some, I use a bit of kindling from the waning wood
supply stacked against the house. I start a fire, let the orange
embers flicker, and think of my mother's body at the cremato-
rium. The funeral director told me I could pick up her ashes
in a few days, suggested I purchase one of his overpriced urns
for my mantel. But the idea of keeping a powdered version of
Mom's body in my house doesn't sit right. I could dump them,
but where? Most people do it somewhere meaningful, somewhere the person loved. The only things Mom loved were
men, alcohol, and the church.

Nausea sweeps through me as the flames come back into
focus. My mother—my *mother*, who sucked as a parent, but
who some part of me still loved—is being turned into nothing
but dust. Will she feel it? What if when we die—

I force myself to stop. Obsessing over the what-ifs never
changes anything. Instead, I open the folder and strip off one

piece of paper, then another, slowly feeding them to the fire. It builds to a blaze, burning all remnants of Jocelyn, just as is being done to my mother. Both will be nothing more than a memory.

The fire eventually peters out, so I go back inside. Though too much adrenaline is pulsing through my veins to sit down and relax. I could drink more wine, but I don't want to be here in this house right now. Instead, I grab my purse and my keys, stare out the window, and wonder, *What now?*

I could leave. Just go, and ask the church to deal with her stuff. They might. Or they might say it's my responsibility, and I'd have to come back again.

No, when I leave here this time, I'm never coming back. *Never ever.*

Maybe a distraction, then. That's what I need.

I get in the car, decide to take a ride. Twenty minutes later, I'm crossing a bridge, driving with the woods on both sides of me. But there's even less to occupy my mind out here than at Mom's, and my thoughts start to wander to a dark place again. Without warning—I'm lucky there's no one behind me because I never even looked—I slam on the brakes, pull to the side of the rocky dirt road, and cut the wheel sharply. Not long after, I'm heading back through town. A quick glance at the bar's parking lot tells me Noah's not there, and suddenly, I'm not meandering anymore—I know where I'm going.

I pull into the driveway, park, sit there to the count of ten, debating.

But then I step out of the car.

Turns out, I need a different kind of distraction. A different kind of *ride.*

CHAPTER

35

The front door is open again.

It makes me wonder if he knew I'd come, knew I'd need to work out my frustrations after the funeral today. Though if that's the case, it's pretty cocky of him, considering Sam showed up at the church.

The door creaks open. It's dark downstairs. Quiet enough that I might think no one is home if it weren't for the truck in the driveway. My heels clack against the wood floors as I walk, the sound echoing off walls since there's no furniture to catch it. I could take my shoes off, but why? I have no reason to hide that I'm here. Then again, maybe he has company already. A woman. With those cavernous dimples and the way he gives a woman his full attention, I'm certain there've been many visitors taking this walk. My pulse pounds as I climb the stairs.

The second floor is dark, too, except for a streak of light spilling out into the hallway from the master bedroom. I briefly debate getting undressed like I did the other night, but decide shimmying my underwear down my legs is quicker.

I stop a few feet from the door when I see him. Noah sits on the bed shirtless, his back propped against pillows, engrossed in whatever he's typing fervently into a laptop. The soft glow of the screen illuminates his features, highlighting his chiseled jawline. He really is a good-looking man. His hair is tousled, like he's run a hand through it a few times. But it strikes the perfect balance of mess with his otherwise flawless features. And he's wearing glasses tonight—horn-rimmed, perched on the bridge of his nose like something out of a Ralph Lauren ad. I like it. *A lot.*

"Did I get you in trouble with your boyfriend?" he asks without looking up.

I step to the door and push it open halfway, staying inside the doorframe. "Don't have a boyfriend."

He looks up. "Because of today?"

"Because that's the way I like it."

He smirks and shakes his head. "I'm glad you came."

"Did you know I would? Is that why the front door wasn't locked?"

"The lock is broken. It's always open. But if it weren't, I would've left it open for you. Wasn't sure you would show. I was hopeful, though."

I lift my chin, gesture to his laptop. "What are you working on so intently?"

"A book. Thriller. Started it a few years ago. Had to set it aside a while back. Writer's block."

"I take it you're feeling *un*blocked?"

The corner of his lip quirks up, causing a positively charming dimple to pop out. "I'm feeling inspired lately."

I tilt my head. "I'm feeling . . . something right about now, too."

"You didn't know he was coming today, did you?"

I shake my head. "No, I didn't."

"He's a little old for you, isn't he?"

"I didn't realize there was an age limit on the men I spend time with."

"Is that what you do? You 'spend time' with that guy?"

"I used to."

"When did that end?"

"Officially? Today."

Noah chuckles. "Note to self, call Elizabeth before dropping by in the future."

"Aren't you going to invite me into your room?"

"You didn't need an invitation to let yourself into my house."

"True." I push the door the rest of the way open and take a few steps inside.

Noah's eyes rake up and down my body. "How long were you with the old guy?"

"Do you really care? I don't want to talk anymore, Noah."

He smiles and sets his laptop aside. "I'm happy to use my mouth for other things, then."

The room feels charged, sexual energy arcing between us. I can't wait to dig my nails into his back, claw his skin. I stalk over to the bed, climb on, get ready for whatever the night brings us. Noah's eyes glitter with anticipation as I straddle his hips and press down to find he's already rock hard. My eyes close, roll back into my head. *This.* This is exactly what I needed after today.

"You're ready for me." I groan.

"I'm ready for whatever you've got for me today, Elizabeth."

I lean down, lick a line from his Adam's apple to his chin, kiss the underside, then trail my way to his ear and bite. *Hard.*

"Fuck," he hisses. His fingers dig into my hips. His other hand trails up my spine, winds my locks around his palm, tucks a wad into a fist. He yanks so hard, my head jerks back. Noah leans forward, sucks along the delicate skin of my pulse line, traveling up to my ear. When he reaches my lobe, he bites back. But I don't feel like Noah wants to top me from the bottom. He only wants to give me what he thinks I want.

We make out for a few minutes, nibbling and sucking, biting and bruising. But he still has pants on, so I wrench my lips from his and start to unbuckle. Something shimmery catches my eye as I work, and I freeze when I realize what it is, sitting near the hollow of Noah's throat. My racing heart comes to a screeching halt, and I bolt upright. "Where did you get that?"

His face wrinkles. "Get what?"

"That pendant around your neck."

Noah reaches up, feels around until he finds the silver charm. "Oh, this? It's Saint Agnes."

"I know what it is. Where did you get it?"

"I don't remember. Why?"

"You weren't wearing it the other day. You haven't had it on any of the times we were together."

He shrugs. "I guess I took it off when I was doing some work and forgot to put it back on. It dangles, so I take it off when I'm using the table saw and stuff. Safety hazard." Noah reaches for me, like we're going to pick up where we left off. But we aren't. We *definitely* aren't.

I pull back, climb off the bed. "You just *happened* to put it on today?"

"What are you doing? Where are you going?"

How could I be so stupid? Noah Sawyer, the son of a man I killed, *happens* to walk up to me at the bar, and he just *happens* to be a writer, and *happens* to wear a Saint Agnes pendant? This man has been playing me from the start. I narrow my eyes at him. "What are *you* doing, Noah? What kind of sick, twisted game are you playing?"

Before he can answer, I'm already running. Out of the bedroom, down the hall, taking the stairs two at a time, and crashing open the front door. I don't stop until I'm in the car, doors locked. My hand is shaking so much I can't get the stupid key into the ignition. It clanks to the floor, and I curse, trying to scoop it up while keeping my head high enough to watch the front door. But Noah never comes out. At least not that I see from my rearview mirror as I hightail it the hell out of there.

CHAPTER

36

I'm out of trash bags. I curse as I tie off another one filled with Mom's clothes and glare at the chest of drawers, which still contains far more stuff than I've bagged up to drop off at the church.

Boxes? Maybe there are boxes somewhere. Mom was a bit of a hoarder, and she often left the liquor store with so many bottles they'd have to give her something sturdy to carry them all. I look around her bedroom once more. I've barely made a dent. It hits me that my mother knew she was dying and took the time to plan her own wake and funeral for me, yet didn't bother to sort out her life. Somehow, it seems fitting for our relationship.

I check everywhere for more trash bags or boxes—the kitchen, the laundry room, the closets, even the shed outside. The only ones I find are already filled to the brim. *More I need to go through.* Eventually, I collapse on the bottom step of the staircase, gazing up at the ceiling and wishing I were anywhere but here. My mind circles back to where it has spent most of the last twelve hours. *Noah.* That damn Saint Agnes glistening on his neck, staring up at me.

He had to know, right? Had to know about the necklace Jocelyn—*I*—was given. Was it possible Mr. Sawyer gave them to everyone? Perhaps . . . But why would he give his *son* Saint

Agnes, the patron saint of *virgins* and *victims of sex abuse*? It didn't make sense. It did make sense, in a sick way, why he'd given it to me. But not to his son. And why did Noah suddenly start wearing it? A month has passed since we met, and he's never worn it before. My stomach churns, thinking about it, thinking how vulnerable I've made myself to Noah.

And he said he was working on a novel—a *novel*.

Could he be Hannah Greer?

I bite my lip hard, like I bit his just last night, dig my teeth into the meaty flesh until I taste blood and the shock of pain jolts me from my thoughts. It's too much to be a coincidence. Way too much.

Besides, it doesn't make sense that Hannah is anyone else. Now that I think about it, hasn't it been *obvious* all along? Sam has helped me—found information on Jocelyn, been there for me in a way that quite frankly I didn't deserve. And last night he wouldn't have left so easily if he had something. Or if he *wanted* something. What he wants, more than anything, is me. At least until yesterday.

I force myself to my feet and wander into the kitchen. I grab the coffee carafe, dump out the cold, burnt coffee, and begin the process of making more. *Who else?* Father Preston. But he hasn't been sniffing around, either. Now that Mom's dead, he's rinsed his hands of me. Probably, he's glad for that. I sure am.

In the cupboard, I shuffle around for the coffee, for the oversized plastic Maxwell House container Mom bought at Walmart. When it's not there, I crouch down to search the lower cupboards, pushing aside expired cans of soup and boxes of mac and cheese. This will all need to be sorted, too.

But who else? Who else? The chief has been oddly absent in all of this after his constant appearances, but I'll take that as a positive sign. And why would *the police* not arrest me if they knew the story? Enrolling in my class, sending haunting chapters—no, it's personal to whoever is doing this.

That leaves Ivy. Ivy who, as it turns out, was more involved than just helping me cover up my crime. I still can't get over that she slept with Mr. Sawyer, too. Maybe she only told me *part* of the story and the real truth is that she was in love with him. And now she wants *revenge* on me for what I did. It's possible, isn't it? Lord knows anything is in this crazy mess. Then again, she has so much to lose. She was there that night, too, and she has more at stake than I do, what with her family. So as much as finding out she's kept secrets from me for twenty years leaves me unsettled, it doesn't change that I'm almost certain it's not Ivy doing this to me.

With a sigh of frustration, I abandon my attempt to make coffee. I need more bags or boxes anyway, so I'll just pick up my caffeine fix while I'm out. Plus, I could use some fresh air. So I find my purse, my keys, take a long look through the window—no red pickup truck—and hurry out to my car.

The hardware store is nearly empty. It's a local one, run by a couple who lives at the edge of town—or maybe their kids own it these days. I take a cart and wander through the aisles, finding coffee and trash bags, a pallet of moving boxes stocked eye-high in the back. I load up an armful and head down the cleaning aisle. I haven't inventoried what's at the house, but Mom probably doesn't have anything besides Comet and Windex, and the place is going to need a good scrub.

I'm halfway down an aisle when my phone buzzes. I lift it and see Lucas's name on the screen, a short text below it.

Lucas: Lunch? Would today work?

I hesitate. I like Lucas, apparently always have. And I told him we'd get together after Mom's funeral. I also can't remember the last time I ate. But there's no point in having lunch with him. My goal is to clean out Mom's house, wrap up whatever loose ends need to be dealt with here, and get the hell back to

New York—far away from whoever is messing with me. Or
rather, far away from Noah.

I shake my head. I'll just grab a sandwich and eat while I
work—anything to get done and get out of this town. But before I can slide my phone back into my jeans pocket, it buzzes
again.

I look at the screen and go still.

Lucas: Wait, don't put the phone away! I'm more fun
than that mop—promise!

The mop in question sits upside down in a caddy just in
front of me. I was debating the merits of two different styles
and had mostly settled on the cheaper, foam-padded one. I
lower my phone and twist around, finding none other than
Lucas grinning at me from the end of the aisle.

I don't expect the response that floods me—warmth, happiness to see him. But a second later, suspicion follows. It is a
small town, but . . .

Then I spot his cart. It's nearly overflowing with household goods, things that make sense to purchase—paper towels,
grass seeds, flower starters from the garden area.

"I thought that was you." He comes down the aisle and
parks his cart to one side, approaching me with arms wide,
offering a hug.

I suppose it's normal after someone's parent dies to em-
brace them. Lucas wraps me in his arms, holding me against
his chest, and I can't help notice he smells good. Woodsy, with
a hint of leather and . . . something else. I think it might be
sawdust? Though I suppose we are in a hardware store.

"So, what do you say?" he pulls back and asks. "Lunch?"

Half of me wants to say no. The other half is happy to
see him.

"Come on." He squeezes my shoulder and motions to my

cart. "You're going to kill my ego if using *that* is more enticing than my invitation."

I smile. Screw it. It might be nice to spend time with someone who knew me before, when I was still *me*. Plus, when was the last time I had a conversation with someone who wasn't on my suspect list? "Sure."

––––––––––

There are only two places in town to sit down and eat. Luckily, Lucas chooses the diner over the bar. Inside, we sit in a booth in a corner. Without realizing it, I put my back to the wall, keeping my gaze on the front door, like Noah's going to walk in here. It occurs to me that maybe I should get a different rental car, so I'm not as easily spotted. Of course, that wouldn't solve the problem. He knows where I'm staying. And he doesn't seem to want to hurt me, just . . . screw with me.

Lucas is talking about work, about how he never thought he'd work in medicine, but how he finds it very satisfying. "It doesn't always end well, of course . . ." He gives me a humorless smile, clearly meaning my mother. "But I do help a lot of people. And I like that. Even when we can't save them, at least I can bring them comfort. Your mom had plenty of visitors, but not everyone does."

I sip my coffee, grateful for the long-awaited caffeine. "My mom had a lot of visitors?"

"Oh, and I wanted to say," Lucas continues, "I'm really sorry again that I called you out of the blue after she died like that, and didn't call you earlier. She'd been going downhill for a couple of nights, and I suggested to her that I call you. But she wouldn't let me. I have to respect my patients' wishes, but . . ." He sighs. "I should have called anyway. I'm sorry I didn't. I wanted to come to the wake, pay my respects and tell you that, but I had to work."

I'm still stuck on "plenty of visitors."

"It's okay. You were doing your job." I sip my coffee again, trying to seem casual. "Who visited my mom?"

"Some of her church friends came by on their own. I offered to call whoever she wanted, but she only had me call two people to come see her. Father Preston and Noah Sawyer."

I go still, the coffee halfway to my mouth. "Noah Sawyer? Why him?"

Lucas spreads one arm along the top of the booth. "No idea. She was asleep the first time he visited, so he came back a second time, the night before she passed."

Silence settles between us.

"Did they talk?" I ask.

"I'm not sure. I left shortly after he arrived. My shift was over. I wasn't working a double for a change."

Lucas and I chat some more, and he finishes up eating while I get my caffeine fix. He's good company, or at least he would be if I were able to stop thinking about Noah visiting Mom in the hospital. It's a small town, and sure, they attend the same church—but it's strange. Unless Mom knew we were fooling around and wanted to chew him out about it. But I can't imagine she did, and *why the hell wouldn't he mention that to me if he wasn't hiding something*?

The bill comes, and Lucas pays before I can object. I dig for cash, but he presses a hand over mine, grins. "I got this, Elizabeth. If I have the pleasure of your company for another meal, you can pay next time, if you want. Fair?"

I hesitate, but Lucas paying feels different from when Sam or some other man I dated paid. "Okay. Thank you."

We step outside together. A misting rain has begun, slowly turning the world gray and foggy. Lucas pulls up the hood of his sweatshirt. "I almost forgot. I wanted to ask if you've picked your mom's things up from the hospital. Sometimes people don't bother because it's just more to sort through, but your mom had rosary beads with her. They seemed important to her."

"I didn't realize I needed to."

Lucas frowns. "The hospital should have called. But they're so short-staffed lately, a lot falls through the cracks. Everything should still be there."

"Thank you." We give each other another hug.

"I hope I get to see you again before you leave."

"I'd like that," I say. And I mostly mean it.

"I'll text you."

"Okay."

"Be careful driving. The back roads still get slick when they're first wet, especially the country roads where your mom lives."

"I will." Though I already know it won't be an issue. Because Mom's house is not where I'm going.

CHAPTER

37

"Hi. Can you tell me where I go to pick up a person's belongings, a patient who died?"

The volunteer in the pink smock leans forward over the desk and points down the hall. "The clerk's office in the admissions department should be able to help you out. You make a right after the elevator bank. They're doing some painting in that area at night, so the floors are covered in brown paper, and it looks like you've made a wrong turn, but you haven't."

"Thank you."

I head in that direction, but when I reach the elevator bank and one of the car doors slides open, I make a last-minute decision. I step inside and push a button on the panel. It's pretty crazy to think that barely over a month has gone by since my first visit up to the ICU, when I found out just how sick my mother was. It feels more like a year. The last few weeks have really taken a toll on me. At the fourth floor, I step off and walk to the nurses' station.

"Hello. My mother was a patient here in the ICU, Theresa Davis. She passed away last week, and I didn't think to come collect her things until now. Is this where they would be kept?"

The woman smiles sadly. "I'm very sorry for your loss.

Theresa was more than a patient to me. We both belong to Saint Matthew's. She was such a lovely person."

"Oh, thank you." My eyes drop to her name badge, and I dig deep for what I hope will come off as doting daughter. Lord knows, it doesn't come naturally. "Oh, you're Margaret! My mother talked about you. She was so nervous when she was admitted. She told me you brought her comfort." I shake my head and look down at my feet. "I was devastated that I wasn't here with her on her final days. I teach college up in New York and went back after her last hospital stay thinking . . . Well, I guess I misjudged how much time she had left."

The nurse reaches out, touches my hand. "She wasn't alone at the end. I was right there with her. I hope that brings you some peace."

Peace is the last thing I'm feeling these days, but her comment does give me the perfect opening. "Thank you. It's comforting to know she had good people around her. Noah Sawyer, for example, came and visited her a few times."

The nurse nods. "I was here when he visited. Lovely young man, from such a wonderful family."

It's hard to keep the facade up after that comment, but somehow I manage a pleasant smile. "Yes. A friend of mine is a PA here. He was on duty the first time Noah came to visit. Sadly, Mom wasn't awake. But he thinks she got to talk to him the next morning when he came back."

"I'm sure that made her happy."

"Did you . . . happen to see Noah when he visited the morning my mother died?"

"Yes, I was here."

"And Mom was awake?"

She nods again. "It's actually common that very sick patients get a burst of energy and feel more alert in the hours before they pass."

"So Mom did get to talk to Noah then?"

"I believe so. I work seven to seven, and I remember he was here toward the beginning of my shift. Mrs. Davis was awake when breakfast was served. She ate a little that morning."

"Did you . . . happen to hear what they spoke about?"

Nurse Chatty pauses. I must look too anxious to hear her answer, because she clams up. She smiles, but it's gratuitous now. "I'm sorry. I didn't." She points down the hall to the elevator bank. "Your mom's personal belongings would've been sent down to the admissions office. They have a place where they lock things up until the family comes to collect them. It's down on the ground level."

"Oh. Okay."

She picks up a file, hugs it to her chest, and waits, subtly letting me know our conversation is over. I lift my hand in a half-hearted wave and head back to pick up Mom's belongings—more stuff to go through and add to the donate or garbage piles.

Downstairs, the clerk gives me a clear plastic bag, makes me sign for the contents. I've never been in prison, yet I walk out of the hospital feeling like a person who just got sprung carrying everything she owns.

In the car, I toss the bag on the passenger seat. Mom's purse catches my eye, and I slip it from the plastic. The smell of stale smoke wafts from the tattered leather satchel. Inside are three different inhalers, a string of rosary beads, and a pack of Marlboros. *Great combo, Mom.* There are crumpled tissues and a few singles, coins, and loose tobacco confetti the bottom of the lining. Her wallet is the only thing of interest. It has eleven dollars, a few credit cards that are likely maxed out or cut off because of delinquent payments, and her Louisiana driver's license. I'm not sure what I was looking for, but whatever it was is not here, so I stuff everything back inside. As I do, I notice there's a zippered interior compartment. So I unzip and dig around, coming up with a business card. My heart stutters as I read the words printed.

NOAH SAWYER
Columnist
Louisiana Post

The bottom left side has an address a few towns over. The right has a telephone number and email. I run my finger over the lettering, thinking. What the hell did these two have going on? What reason could she possibly have to call him, request that he come visit her in the hospital while she was on her deathbed? She didn't even call *me*—her only child—during her last days. Yet Noah came to visit her twice that I'm aware of, and she's carrying around his business card.

My mind races all over the place, but the car grows too hot, the Louisiana heat forcing me to make a move, start the car. I could go home and search for more clues left behind by a dead person, or . . . I look down at the business card in my hand and nibble on my bottom lip. Or I could learn more about Noah Sawyer firsthand. Apparently, there's a lot he hasn't shared with me.

My stomach growls. I should've had more than just coffee at the diner with Lucas this morning. But my appetite has been nonexistent lately. Plus, I thought I was headed home soon. Who knew my one-hour errand would turn into lunch with Lucas, a visit to the hospital, and a three-hour stakeout at the corporate headquarters of the *Louisiana Post*? And who knew so many people would be here on a Sunday afternoon? Though I suppose the news never stops, never takes a break.

I rifle through my purse for a protein bar. There's usually always one in there, but of course there isn't when I need it. When I look up, I gasp. Noah is walking to his truck. Instinctively, I slink down in the seat as much as possible, while still being able to watch him. He's swinging his keys, looking like he doesn't have a care in the world. I'm parked four rows away, partially blocked by a light post. Noah doesn't seem to notice anything unusual as he gets into his truck. I've been sitting here for more than three hours, mulling a million things around in my head, yet for some stupid reason, I never considered what I was going to do when he finally came out. But when his pickup pulls out of its parking spot, it only seems logical to follow.

I trail a safe distance behind, so safe that I almost lose track of him on more than one occasion. Noah drives fast, twenty miles an hour over the speed limit. So the forty-minute drive back to Minton Parish takes only thirty. It's uneventful, predictable even. Noah turns left at the second light off the highway, then right, and when the two cars between us go in different directions, it's too obvious for me to follow anymore. I pull to the side of the road and let him go the rest of the way home alone. After ten minutes, I figure he should be inside by now, so I do a drive-by to make sure that's where he went. Sure enough, the red truck is parked out front.

I pass, blowing out two disappointed cheeks full of air. *What a waste of an afternoon.* I could sit around, wait and see if he goes anywhere else tonight, but I suddenly don't have the energy. So I keep driving until I pull into my mom's driveway. Noah's business card still lies on the passenger seat on top of Mom's things. I leave the car running and pull out my phone, type *Noah Sawyer* into the Google search bar. I have no idea what took me so long to do it, but a bunch of stuff pops up. I scroll through the garbage—Whitepages, Classmates, LinkedIn, Facebook—a bunch of articles with high school baseball statistics. Apparently, Noah was a pitcher. At the bottom of the first page, I click on something interesting—Publishers Marketplace, an announcement about the sale of a book.

> Debut author Noah Sawyer's *The Secret,* in which a decades-old secret leads a struggling reporter to realize he never really knew his family, to Rena Kline at Umbrella Books.

My heart pounds. Family secret? A reporter who never knew his family? Is this what he's writing? My story? *Our* story? Is it the chapters I've been reading? Is that what he's planning on *publishing*? My entire body is shaking.

My phone, which is still in my hand, vibrates, and it scares the shit out of me. But it's only a text coming in from my boss, my department head at the university. I need the distraction, so I swipe over and read.

> **Maryellen:** Hi, Elizabeth. I'm sorry to bother you at a time like this. But I emailed you a few days ago and haven't heard back. I just wanted to find out if you have an idea when you'll be returning so I can work on getting coverage extended. No rush. Take as long as you need. If you could please just shoot me an email and copy HR whenever you have an opportunity, I'd appreciate it. I hope you're doing well.

Ugh. It isn't like me to shirk my responsibilities. I've been so wrapped up in the mess down here that I haven't checked my work email since before I left New York. I texted Maryellen and told her my mother died and I needed to take some time off, and that I'd check in when I knew more. But I never did.

I immediately swipe over to my work email, to do as Maryellen asked. There are a dozen new messages. I scan them, freezing when I get to the last one.

Hannah Greer.

And there's an attachment.

CHAPTER
38

I stare at the email for a long time—long enough that the screen goes dark and I have to swipe and let it recognize my face again to reread the message. It's dated almost a week ago—the day before my mother's death. And it's just been sitting here, waiting for me this whole time. My boss's request forgotten, I jab at the attachment, opening it as the car's air-conditioning hums away.

I take a deep breath when it flickers open, wishing I had a whiskey or two to fortify myself. I could run into the house, pour something, but my heart pounds, the anticipation too strong, and I can't do anything but sit right here in the driver's seat.

It's another chapter. Of course it is. I knew it would be.

I imagine Noah in his house, sitting on his bed wearing his glasses, smirking as he hits send from a fake email address. I exhale and start to read.

Chapter 6—Hannah's Novel

Jocelyn didn't hesitate this time as she drove up to the parking lot, parked the car, strolled into the motel office. She paid with cash and gave her fake name, then went to the room to wait. Mr. Sawyer wouldn't arrive for some time. That was how they stayed safe, how no one found out what they were doing. And she didn't want to give him any reason to put a stop to it. She lived for these nights with him, the one person who noticed her, who took time to help her.

As she waited, she wandered the room, opening shelves and drawers. Sometimes she found surprises—things people had left, the people who stayed here on the nights they didn't have the room. Once, she'd found a pack of gum, though she wasn't about to chew some stranger's gum. This time, she found a Bible. A nice one. Freshly placed there. The spine hadn't even been cracked yet. Jocelyn ran her fingers over the cloth exterior, but didn't dare open it. She'd gone to church, knew the scripture, and didn't feel the need to read more about God or Jesus, especially not on the nights she was at the motel.

From behind her, the door creaked. Jocelyn whipped around and hurried over. Probably it was Mr. Sawyer, and he needed to be let in. Usually, she left the door unlocked, but maybe she forgot to this time. Maybe—

She swung the door open, but no one stood there. She stuck her head out, looked left and right, but there was only humid air and a cracked parking lot. Not even another car besides the guy's who worked the front desk. *Odd.* She could've sworn someone had opened the door, or at least rustled it.

She blew out a breath, shut the door so she wouldn't be seen, and went back inside to wait. Finally, twenty minutes later, the man she'd been waiting for burst through the door.

"Running late," Mr. Sawyer muttered, though notably, there was no apology. "On your knees." He pointed to the spot where he always had her kneel, and she rushed to obey. "Don't have much time tonight. Have to get home to . . ." The rest of his words were a mumble she couldn't quite make out, but she knew better than to speak when she had not been asked a direct question.

Jocelyn knelt there for some time before he came over, running his fingers over the back of her neck, twisting them through her hair. The rest of the evening went as it always did—he gave her commands, and she obeyed. They undressed. They had sex with her up on all fours, facing the wall and not him. But today it was faster than usual. Mr. Sawyer was brusque, ordering her around.

"Hurry up," he said when they finished. "Get dressed."

Jocelyn tried to, but one of her stockings snagged, making it impossible to pull up. She reached to fix it, but before she could, he was right there. Shoving her.

"I said *hurry up*."

But Mr. Sawyer's tone only made Jocelyn more nervous. One second she was standing on one foot, fixing her clothes, and the next she was on the ground, blinking.

"Shit," he said.

"What happened?" She reached for her head. The spot where her hair met her forehead ached and felt hot and wet and—

"You hit your head. Why are you so clumsy? Here, let me look." Mr. Sawyer crouched down, frowning in the dim motel light as he examined her.

Jocelyn was confused. She didn't remember hitting her head, didn't remember what happened. Not exactly anyway. But when she looked up and around, she knew she'd hit the corner of the nightstand. She'd fallen, and on the way down, bashed her head on it. When she pulled her fingers away, they were covered in blood.

"You need stitches."

Jocelyn's mouth gaped open. That was a problem, wasn't it? She couldn't afford a visit to the doctor, much less stitches. Neither could her mother. And besides, if she went, they'd ask what happened. She couldn't tell them. Yet she also couldn't imagine lying to a doctor.

"Let's go," Mr. Sawyer said. "There's a clinic in the next town over. No one will recognize you." It was as if he could hear her concerns.

He helped her pull on the rest of her clothes, then

gathered his own belongings, shoving his keys and wallet back into his pocket. Jocelyn watched him, dazed, processing. She was about to say something—she already couldn't recall what—when out of the corner of her eye, she caught a flash of motion in the window. A face, eyes peering through—

Grabbing the dresser to steady herself, she took two steps and opened the gaping curtains wider. But there was no one. Again.

"What?" Mr. Sawyer asked.

"I thought I saw someone."

"You hit your head. You probably have a concussion and are seeing things."

Jocelyn nodded without replying. She always agreed with him. That's what he expected of her, how he taught her discipline—but she was sure someone had been looking in.

Out in the parking lot, Jocelyn walked toward her mother's car.

"You can't drive right now," Mr. Sawyer barked. "Get in my car. In the back. Lie down so no one sees you."

But she couldn't help wonder if someone already *had* seen them.

———————

The clinic was quiet, clean. Much nicer than the last time she'd gone to the doctor her state-funded insurance covered. The nurse did all the normal doctor's office things—checked her pulse and her blood pressure, took her temperature, handed her a specimen cup to give a urine sample.

"You're here alone?" the nurse asked, taking notes on a clipboard.

"My . . ." She almost called him her boyfriend. But he wasn't that. He was *more* than that, in a way. "My dad dropped me off," she managed. "He had to get to work." Jocelyn felt proud of the quick lie. It worked, too, just in case someone had seen Mr. Sawyer leaving her at the curb.

"I see." The nurse peered at her once more, then nodded. "Okay, the doctor will be in shortly."

Jocelyn sat on the exam table, swinging her feet, the paper crinkling beneath her. She grew dizzy, gripped the sides with her hands, felt it bunch, then relaxed.

He'd pushed her.

She remembered now. She'd been trying to hurry and get dressed, do as he asked, but he *pushed* her. Jocelyn pressed her lips together, tried not to think too hard about what that meant. She let him do a lot of things that caused her pain—but those usually caused a good pain. This was different. And now she needed stitches.

She knew what Mr. Sawyer had done to her was wrong, knew she should probably not go to that motel to meet him anymore. Not just her mind knew it, either. Her palms were sweating, and her throat felt tight—like the inside was swollen. The same thing had happened before, when she'd done things with Mr. Sawyer that made her uneasy. Yet she kept going back. This time, though, she would be stronger.

Fleetingly, she thought of her mother—what she'd tell her happened. She could simply say she fell. It was true, after all. Hell, her mother might not even notice a head wound with stitches.

"Jocelyn?" A woman tapped at the door. She was tall, young, and wore a white coat. "I'm Dr. Nye. I understand you have a cut that needs tending to."

"Yes, ma'am."

The doctor was quick and thorough. The most painful part was when she injected something she called lidocaine to numb the area. But after that, Jocelyn didn't feel anything other than a little pressure. "It'll wear off," Dr. Nye said. "But you can take some Tylenol or ibuprofen, and that should help. You'll have a scar, but since it's at the beginning of your hairline, it won't

likely be noticeable, unless you're looking for it." She
snapped off her rubber gloves and tossed them into the
garbage can. "Can you wait here just a moment?"

Jocelyn nodded, and the doctor left. She stood up
and peered at herself in the mirror behind the sink.
A gauzy bandage had been placed over the stitches.
This was going to be hard for anyone to miss, even her
mother. And why did her damn palms kept sweating? She
twisted the knob on the faucet and ran cold water over
them, blotting them dry with a paper towel.

"Jocelyn?" Dr. Nye came back into the room and beck-
oned for her to take a seat. "We took a urine sample when
you came in. Standard procedure."

"Okay." She nodded.

"For female patients, part of that screening is a
pregnancy test."

Jocelyn tilted her head, waiting for more. Perhaps
the doctor was going to tell her all the different tests
they'd run.

"Jocelyn, your pregnancy test . . . It came back
positive."

CHAPTER
39

I *was pregnant.*

    I can't believe I didn't remember that. At least not before I read that new chapter last night. After, though, I couldn't stop the memories from flooding back. At 5 a.m., I gave up on trying to sleep and brewed a pot of coffee. Caffeine didn't help. Certainly not the four cups I drank. It only made my heart race faster and my head spin so violently that I had to sit down so I wouldn't fall.

I was pregnant.

Pregnant.

With *his* child.

The thought makes my stomach roil, and the coffee threatens to come back up.

I've gotten used to the idea that Jocelyn and I are the same person. But *this* . . . this I will *never* get used to. No way. Not possible.

Every time I closed my eyes last night, vivid memories rushed back. One in particular felt so real that at one point, I barricaded the bedroom door with my dresser.

It was the week after I'd gone to the clinic. I went to meet Mr. Sawyer at the motel at our usual time. I'd been anxious about telling him I was pregnant, afraid of what his reaction might be. He had a wife, a small child. I couldn't imagine he would want a baby with me. But he surprised me, told me he was happy, that we could run away together and raise our family. We wouldn't have to hide anymore. Texas, he said— Galveston, a small coastal town where you caught a breeze in the summer, unlike this suffocating part of Louisiana.

It was my dream come true. He was so gentle that night, so caring and warm. We made love for the first time. Of course we'd had sex before—the dirty kind, the kind where he called me a whore as he pumped inside me from behind. That's what he liked, what got him off. But that night, I was on my back. He looked into my eyes and told me I was beautiful, how beautiful our child was going to be. It was such a drastic change. I should've known it was too good to be true. But the most dangerous lies are the kind an innocent person *wants* to be true.

That night, we walked out of the motel room together, something else we never did. I remember smiling, thinking it was the beginning of a fresh start, one far away from Minton Parish and my alcoholic mother. But then . . . I felt it. A hand at my back, a forceful shove. And all of my hopes and dreams went flying along with me, down the sixteen stairs that led from the second floor to the parking lot below.

I remember lying on the blacktop, him kicking me and telling me to get up.

I remember the pain in my arm and head, a bloody chin.

Somehow, I drove Mom's car home anyway. My vision was so blurred from tears, it was a wonder I made it. The next morning I woke to blood-soaked sheets. The cramps were so bad that I walked doubled over in pain. Mom hadn't come home from the night before, and I didn't want to explain what had happened to anyone else, so I went back to the clinic a few towns over alone. I'd miscarried. I also had a concussion and a fractured ulna, but nothing hurt more than the betrayal I'd suffered. That day was the beginning of the end. I just didn't know it yet. Because like most abuse victims, I went back for more. I took the flowers he brought the next week. I accepted the apology and promise that it would never happen again. I believed him when he said he would change.

I blink back to the present moment, pulling myself from the past, only to realize I'm holding my stomach. It hurts. *Cramps.* My period must be due. Or maybe the line between reality and illusion is blurring so much that I'm manifesting pain. I don't even know anymore.

I force myself into the bathroom, turn on the shower, and let the hot water sluice over my knotted shoulders with my eyes closed. My mind wanders. But not far. Now I'm back to wondering how anyone knows about the pregnancy. I've never told a soul. Not ever. Not Ivy or my mother. I'd been too ashamed to admit the truth. To this day, I lie when I go to the gynecologist for a checkup, and I scribble a big fat zero in the box on the medical history form that asks how many times you've been pregnant. The only person who knew was *him*. I suppose the people at the clinic knew I'd miscarried, too. But that place was fifty miles outside of town and twenty years have gone by. It *has* to be Noah. All roads keep leading back to him. Maybe his father kept a journal? Wrote down the sick shit he did to me? Nothing else makes sense.

I dry off, get dressed, and decide I need some fresh air. The house has no food, and I can't remember the last time I ate. So I drive over to the bakery in town and order a buttered roll and an orange juice. A few minutes later, I hear the woman behind the counter.

"Ma'am?"

I blink a few times. She's looking at me funny, so I think maybe it's not the first time she's tried to get my attention.

"Sorry, yes?"

"I said, that'll be six dollars, please."

"Of course. Sure."

I dig money out of my purse and pay, wait for the woman to hand over the white bag. After, I sit in the car and force half the juice down, eat a few bites of the roll. I'm just about to start the engine, figure out where I'm going next, when I look up and spot a red truck. *Noah*. At least I think it's him, though plenty of people have pickups, especially in the South. It's parked a block up at the Shell station, next to the pump. I hold my breath and wait. Sure enough, thirty seconds later, Noah ambles along. He climbs back into his truck and starts to pull away. I rush to follow.

Is it a coincidence that he's here, where I am? There's only one gas station in town, and it is about the time most people leave for work. But nothing is what it seems with the Sawyers. Either way, I follow. Or maybe I'm being led. I don't know anymore. But I wait until two cars are between us and he's already a half mile down the road before pulling out. The route he takes is familiar. It's the same one I took yesterday. Noah must be heading to his office.

As I drive, I stare straight ahead. I can see the back of his head through the rear window, and I keep asking myself the same question over and over.

How does he know?

How does he freaking know?

The exits in this part of the state are spread miles apart. I'm about to pass the last one before he'll get off for his office, when I make a rash decision to get off the highway. Crossing two lanes, I ignore the car horn blaring behind me and swerve to make the exit ramp. I catch one last glimpse of the red truck up ahead before I lose sight. My heart races as I pull up to a red light at a four-way intersection, a plan already taking form.

The next exit is at least fifteen miles. Noah can't get off until then. Even if he turns around immediately after getting off, he'll still be thirty miles behind me. That's twenty minutes, minimum, even at the hurried speed he drives. And chances are, he's not turning around the second he gets off. He's going to work, probably will stay awhile.

The light in front of me turns green. I make a left and another sharp left and then nail the gas to merge back on the highway going the opposite direction I just came from.

I need to know what *else* he knows.

I need to get a step ahead, figure out what he's got planned for me next.

CHAPTER
40

The lock on the front door is broken. He told me that mere days ago. If I'm lucky, he hasn't gotten around to fixing it. Given the state of my life, I'd say I'm *not* lucky, yet still . . . Maybe the universe owes me a little something.

I pull into the driveway and cast a quick glance in the rearview mirror, as if somehow he might have managed to catch up with me. But all I see is a long, empty road. Good. He's still stuck on the highway. I swing out of my car, slam the door, and stride across the drive to the front of his house.

I reach for the doorknob and—and nothing. *Motherfucker*. He *did* fix it. Or it was never broken to begin with. I stare at it for a long moment, wondering if he knew I'd play right into his plans, that I'd follow him home, wander through this very front door. He literally tried to fuck me while *fucking me*. I let out a short, staccato exhalation of anger, and kick the door. Well, *fuck him*, too. I'm going to find out what he knows, one way or another.

Stepping back, I sweep the front of the house with my gaze, searching for where he might have hidden a key. That's what people with houses do, right? Especially if they live alone, no spouse to rescue them if they lock themselves out. I search beneath a flowerpot filled with weeds, overturn several stones in the side yard. I even stretch and reach up high, running my fingers along the top of the doorframe.

Nothing. Like Noah knows he'd never lock himself out. Or he's better at hiding things, which is absolutely true. He's hidden so much from me.

I look back at the road again. I have to hurry. If he did see me on the highway, if he is turning around, suspicious I'd come here, he'll be back soon. I edge around the house, stepping around construction material—a sawhorse, roof shingles on a pallet, piles of brick. The backyard grass isn't cut like the front, and I have to wade through calf-high growth to try the back door. It slides open easily. Satisfaction rolls through me as I enter, closing it behind me. I stop and look around, searching for clues like they'll be out in plain sight. But that's dumb. I'm going to have to search, look places I wouldn't see wandering through the house. The obvious place to start is his bedroom. I climb the stairs two at a time, rushing to get there. Once inside, I drop to my knees and look under the bed—nothing. It's neat, tidy. Not a single dust bunny, even.

His closet stands open, and I go for it next. It's a walk-in, and I turn a slow circle once inside. But there are no shoeboxes for storage on the top shelf, no bins pushed to the back. Not even a single book to page through. I clench my jaw, gazing at shirts hung neatly on hangers, arranged by color. It almost looks like my closet, and knowing what he's done, what he's *doing*, that irks me. His dresser holds only clothes—socks matched and underwear folded. What is he, a sociopath?

Maybe. He just might be.

It makes me question his ultimate goal—to punish me? To hurt me?

My eyes land on the last piece of furniture in the room, a wide nightstand with several drawers. It's so big it's nearly a small dresser. I drop to my knees in front of it and go through the clutter on the surface—eyedrops, some coins, a candle, the glasses he was wearing the other night, what looks like a homeowner's insurance policy, a couple of books, and . . . his laptop.

I grab that first, set it on the bed, flip the top open. I pray it's not locked. I see students with unlocked laptops all the time, like they're the most trusting idiots in the world. But one touch, and the password prompt pops up. I sigh. Back to the nightstand. The books are books on writing, story structure. Still, I flip through them, but find only notes he's taken in the margins, a couple torn-off pieces of paper serving as bookmarks.

The first drawer pulls out easily, but it contains nothing but tissues, a bottle of melatonin, condoms, and a spare phone charger. The second drawer is empty. I expect the third drawer to be empty, too, but when I yank it out, there's a box. A small, old-fashioned gift box, crafted in purple and yellow. It looks more like something that would have belonged to his mother than something that belongs to him. I pull it out, open the top, and freeze.

Photographs.

Polaroids, to be exact, a thick stack of them.

My stomach bottoms out, another memory rising to the surface. Mr. Sawyer, hair blowing in the wind. A blocky camera in his hands, him raising it with a grin to snap a photo of Jocelyn—*of me*. I blink, and the vision dissolves. I'm not sure if it was real or my imagination coming up with something. But I empty the box of photos into my trembling hands.

The first several are women I don't recognize. Or maybe "women" is an exaggeration. These are girls, no older than I was. Years are scribbled at the bottom of each. All before I was even in high school. I swallow back bile and keep flipping until I stop at a familiar girl, all legs and arms, in a bikini.

Jocelyn. *Me.* On a local beach.

The memory from before hits full force—he was kind that day, asked if I wanted to do something different. We met in a parking lot the next town over, and I got to climb into his car with him, got to sit in the front seat beside him. He planted his big, strong hand on my bare thigh, and we rolled down the windows for the whole drive there. I felt so happy—like he was really my boyfriend, like we were together, like we had a future.

At the beach, he spread out big towels and offered me watermelon. We sat together for a long time, and he pulled out a well-loved book of poems, read many of them aloud to me. I lazed on the towel, feeling like things had changed, things were going to be different from now on. Afterward, I stripped down to my bikini, and he gazed appreciatively at my body before asking if he could snap a photo—"Gotta remember a beautiful girl on a beautiful day," he said. I blushed, so pleased he thought I was beautiful. Of course he could take a photo.

I posed for a couple, in fact, rolling on my stomach and glancing what I thought was seductively over one shoulder.

Now, I flip to the next photograph, and there it is—my ass hanging out of my bikini bottoms, looking about twelve years old. I think I might vomit. Might lose my tiny breakfast.

I swap the photos around again, look at the next in the stack. This time, it's a different girl. She's posing in front of a motel room.

A motel room numbered 212. It, too, is dated before he met me—five years before, in fact.

"How many girls did you do this to?" I murmur and realize my hands are wet—the photos are wet—and it's because I'm crying, big fat tears rolling down my cheeks. How dare he? How dare he do this to *me*? How dare he do this to all of them? Are they all out there somewhere, going through the same thing I have? The thought angers me, makes me wish I could wrap my hands around his throat and squeeze.

I freeze when I get to another photo of someone I recognize. *Ivy.*

I let that photo and some of the others slip from my hands and scatter over the carpeted floor. It's a mistake, though—half a dozen innocent girls' gazes staring back at me, trusting me like they trusted him. It's overwhelming, and I rock back on my heels, holding back sobs. One man hurt so many girls.

"What the fuck are you doing?" A booming voice shouts from behind me, a voice that for a moment, I think is Mr. Sawyer's. I twist around, panicked.

But it's not him. It's his son. *Noah*.

CHAPTER
41

My entire body shakes.

But it's not fear. It's *rage*, raw anger searing through my veins.

"What *the fuck* is wrong with you?" I scream. A few Polaroids are still in my hands. I clench my fists and crumple them into a ball. "Do you get off on it? Reminding women who've finally moved on what was done to them?" My eyes widen, a horrible thought occurring to me. "Oh my God. Are you doing this to *all* of us? All the girls in the photos?"

Noah's eyes drop to the floor, to the splatter of Polaroids strewn all over the carpet. His face changes. Anger morphs into something else—a moment of indecision, almost confusion. He opens his mouth, but says nothing as his pupils dart between the photos and my face. "What are you talking about?"

"Give me a fucking break! I'm not buying the innocent act anymore." I gesture to the photographs littering the floor, hold up the several still in my hand. "He *deserved* to die. He preyed on young girls who were *desperate*, who needed love and attention and would take it however they could get it. So I'm *not* sorry. Not even a little. I'm *glad* he couldn't do it to anyone else."

Noah shakes his head. "I don't understand . . ."

"How did you know about the pregnancy? Is there a journal somewhere?" I turn, ripping everything out of the nightstand I've already gone through, tossing the contents over my shoulder as I go. The first drawer empties, so I whip open the next, but it's still empty. Desperate, I run to the nearby dresser, open it, and keep flinging things. When there's nothing left in those drawers, I turn. "Where is it? I know it's here somewhere!"

"What journal? What pregnancy?" He just stands there, pretending he doesn't have a clue what I'm talking about.

I laugh maniacally. "Oh, you're good. Almost as believable as that sick fuck of a father of yours. But I'm not a little girl anymore. And you've both taken so much from me, I have nothing left to lose." I march toward Noah, brush my shoulder with his as I round the bed to the other side. He stays in place as I yank open the second nightstand, pull out everything, just like I did the first. After, my eyes flit around the room, looking for more places to search. "Where is it? *Where the fuck is it?*"

"I don't have any journal."

"Is it a notebook, then? An electronic file? What did he leave behind that you've used to write the chapters you've been sending me, *Hannah*?"

His forehead creases. "Elizabeth, I can see you're upset, but I really have no idea what you're talking about."

"Nice try." My eyes land on a book on top of the dresser, and it reminds me . . . books, shelf—*the office*! Why didn't I start there? I bet that's where it is. Without another word, I run out of the bedroom and bolt down the stairs.

Noah chases behind me. "Where are you going?"

I march into the office and start with the bookshelves, tearing each book, one by one, from the neat rows. *"Where is it? Where the fuck is it?"*

Noah comes to a stop in the doorway, watching me as though he's afraid to come in. *Smart man.* Because even I don't know what I'm capable of right now.

"I'm not sure what's going on, but why don't we sit down and talk about it? Clearly you're upset . . ."

This is taking too long, so I wipe the second shelf clean by reaching in and sweeping everything to the floor. Then I do the same to the third and fourth. The case is empty, but that's not good enough, so I pull at it, trying to bring it down. When it doesn't budge, I lift a leg, press my foot against the wall on the side for leverage, and yank harder.

Noah puts a hand on my shoulder. "Elizabeth, stop. It's screwed to the wall."

I jump back. *"Don't touch me! Don't fucking touch me!"*

He holds his hands up, actually looking nervous. "Okay, okay."

I move on and empty the contents of two more tall shelves while Noah watches. There are piles of books knee-deep now, and I try to trudge through them to get to the other side of the room, but I trip and fall two steps in, landing on top of the pile.

Noah rushes over. He reaches out a hand to help me, but I slap it away. This time, he doesn't back off. Instead, he secures my hands in front of me and wraps me in his arms while I kick and scream, trapping me against him.

"Shhh," he whispers. "It's okay. Let me help."

"I don't want your help! Get off me."

He holds me tighter. "I'm not letting go until you calm down, Elizabeth."

"I fucking hate you!"

"You can. I don't care. But you're scaring me, and I don't want you to get hurt."

"I'm scaring *you?* Are you fucking kidding me? You turned my world upside down by pretending to be *my student* and sending me that sick shit you wrote!"

Neither of us speaks for a moment. My breaths are coming fast, harsh. I'm hyperventilating.

"I can tell you're not going to believe me, but I have no

clue what you're talking about right now. Whatever you think I'm doing to you, you got the wrong guy."

I keep trying to get out of the hold, but he's bigger and stronger. *Just like his goddamned father.* Eventually, I settle into an eerie calm.

"Let go of me," I grit through my teeth. "I'm fine."

He loosens his grip, but doesn't release me. "Will you talk to me? Tell me what you think is going on here?"

I don't respond, but after a moment, he slowly lets go, lets his arms fall away a little at a time. Eventually, he takes a step back, giving me space. The crumpled Polaroids that I brought down here, still in my hands, are now on the floor. Noah bends and picks them up. He unfurls the plastic and stares down for a long time.

"This is you, isn't it?" He swallows. "You were one of his girls?"

He's almost believable. But I'm not falling for the Sawyer men's crap anymore. "I think we're past pretending. Why don't you just tell me what you want from me, Noah?"

"I don't want anything from you. I only wanted to get to know you."

"Why?"

He shrugs. "I don't know. Because I like you. Because you seem to know what you want and not be afraid to take it. I found that refreshing." He looks into my eyes. "I swear, I had no idea that you . . ." He trails off. "I only recently found out about my father's affairs with his students."

"They weren't *affairs*. 'Affairs' implies two consenting adults. I was a child, and your father was my abuser—both physically and sexually."

Noah rakes a hand through his hair, blows out a full breath of air. "I had no idea. I really didn't. After my mother died, I decided to remodel the house. When I took down the drop ceiling in the bathroom, I found the Polaroids. I recognized my father's handwriting, and, well, it was par for the course with him."

"How so?"

"Well, he wasn't a good guy. His hobbies included writing poetry and beating my mother four nights a week. Me, too, once I turned six and tried to stop him the first time. Sad to say, but discovering he kept a stash of photos of young girls wasn't too shocking." He frowns. "I'm so sorry he did that to you."

For a half second, I almost buy it—believe he's sincere and just another innocent victim in this mess. But I'm done being gullible. "Where's the journal, Noah? Your father must've kept a journal."

"If he did, I didn't find it."

"Then how did you know all the details you wrote in the chapters you sent me?"

"I didn't send you anything, Elizabeth, I swear."

I look over at the desk, at the bookshelves I haven't checked yet. "I'm going to keep searching."

He shrugs. "Have at it. I'll give you some space and go wait in the kitchen. It's the least I can do."

Noah leaves, and I finish rummaging through the office. I don't rip the books from the shelves or upend the drawers, but I do a thorough search—every book, every piece of paper in the desk. Twenty minutes later, I walk into the kitchen empty-handed. Noah sits at the table with a bottle of whiskey and a glass.

"You want some?" he asks without looking up.

"No."

He shrugs. "Find anything of interest?"

"I assume you know I didn't or you wouldn't have let me finish searching. You have it somewhere else."

He shakes his head. "Is there anything I can say or do that will make you believe I had no idea who you were when you walked into the bar that night? And I had no idea what you went through until you just told me?"

"Probably not. What did my mother want?"

His brows furrow. "Hmm?"

"You went to visit her in the hospital. Why?"

"Oh. She had a nurse call me. I was curious, so I went. The first time she was sleeping, so I went back the next day. She asked what my intentions were with you. I told her not to worry, they were all good. She was in and out of it after that, so I left her to rest." He knocks back the amber liquid in his glass. "Can I ask you something?"

"What?"

"You accused me of sending you stuff. So you, what, think I was stalking you or something?"

"Yes."

"Why would I do that? Even if I had known about you and my dad. Why on God's earth would I want to bring up shit that happened twenty years ago?"

"Revenge?"

"Revenge for what?"

I don't answer right away. Instead, I wait until Noah looks up and our eyes meet. "Revenge for killing your father."

Noah's brows shoot up. "You strangled my father?"

"Strangled? No. I hit him over the head with a lamp to keep him from punching me more on the night of my graduation."

Noah's eyes flare. "Well, then you didn't kill my father. Because he died from asphyxiation, not a head injury."

CHAPTER

42

The days pass in a blur, one after another.

Mr. Sawyer died from *asphyxiation*.

The morning after Noah caught me in his house, I woke to an envelope slipped under my door. Inside was a death certificate. *His* death certificate. An original, with a raised county seal. Of course, Noah could've made it. Technology is pretty advanced these days. But it looked pretty damn real. Even the envelope it was tucked into had the county seal and return address.

I unfold the thick paper sitting on the kitchen table for the millionth time, and my eyes drop right to the bottom.

Cause of death: Asphyxiation by strangulation

Ivy and I were both too terrified to go near a dead body, but it sure *looked* like Mr. Sawyer was dead. There was *so much* blood around his head. And we were in the room for a long time, trying to make sure we'd wiped down anything I'd touched and making it look like a robbery. He'd never moved. But I suppose it was *possible* he was only unconscious. Though if I didn't kill Mr. Sawyer that night, who did? And if I'm innocent, why would someone be haunting me with those chapters? Who haunts a *victim*?

I pace my mother's house day and night, subsisting on coffee and wine. But sometimes it's wine for breakfast and coffee late into the evening as I wander aimlessly, trying to figure out how all of it, how *any* of it, makes any goddamn sense. I ignore the phone calls that come in, don't even consider checking my email.

The rest of the world can fuck off.

In the good moments, I manage to stuff knickknacks in boxes to take to Goodwill and separate tattered clothing to go to the dump. But mostly, I stare off into space, thinking—thinking of Noah, his wide eyes, swearing up and down he didn't know what I was talking about. Letting me destroy his house to search for evidence. Why did he let me do that? Has he cleaned it up?

And the Polaroids, those sick-in-the-head photographs . . . I should have taken them. Should have burned them to protect the other the girls, to protect me. I could go back, find an unlocked door when he's not home, break a window if I have to, and take them, if he hasn't hidden them again. There's a reckless desire to send the photos of the other girls to the police, to tell them what he did, to sully Damon Sawyer's name forever so he's not remembered as the honored schoolteacher anymore. But those women have been through enough.

It's Thursday—or maybe Friday? I don't know—when a knock comes at the door. It's not the first knock this week. Sometimes casseroles are left on the doorstep from Mom's church friends, all of which go uneaten. Because I have no appetite at all.

I stop halfway through the kitchen, a coffee mug in one hand, an empty wineglass in the other. I'm trying to decide which to fill next. Or if I should instead heat up some food. My stomach feels queasy from all the alcohol and caffeine, but it's been that way for days. I'm almost used to it. Is this how Mom felt all the time? I look at the door. Maybe whoever is knocking has some fresh food, and I won't even have to turn the oven on.

When the knock comes a second time, I set down the cups and peer through the curtain.

There's a man. He's wearing a suit, with his back to the door, looking out at the driveway. It doesn't look like Noah, but I can't be certain it's not. So I step back from the window and yell, "Can I help you?"

"Hi. Umm . . . I'm looking for Elizabeth Davis? I'm an attorney. I did some work for her mother."

I've grown suspicious of everything and anything, so I go back to the window and look again. The man is facing forward now, hands in his pockets, no casserole. *Not Noah.* Probably not from the church, either.

"Shit," I mutter. "Okay, I'm coming." I take a minute and attempt to pat down my hair, straighten my disheveled clothing, but I'm a wreck inside and out.

He smiles when I open the door. "Hello. I'm Dennis Freeby. Are you Elizabeth?"

I nod.

He reaches into his suit pocket and takes out a business card, passes it to me. "May I come in?"

I examine it, yet still hesitate. The house behind me is even worse than when I arrived. It's a goddamn mess.

"I've tried calling. Left a few messages. I prepared your mother's will and have a few things to go over with you. It won't take too long, and then I'll take my leave. Promise." He smiles.

I'm still wary, but I sigh, open the door wider, and take a step back to let him in. It's best I get this over with anyway. When I do leave Louisiana, I'm never coming back.

"Sorry for the mess," I say. "I've been having a hard time lately."

"Of course. I understand. Loss does that." He peers

around, and I clear off a seat covered by knickknacks at the kitchen table.

"Sorry. I'm sorting through things."

He smiles as he sits. "No worries. You should see the piles in my office, and I don't have an excuse."

I take the seat opposite him and fold my hands to stop myself from fidgeting.

"So, like I said, your mother left a will, along with a few requests."

"Requests?"

He unzips his leather briefcase and pulls out a file, flips it open, and extends a small stack of papers to me. "This is your copy of Ms. Davis's last will and testament. You're welcome to follow along, but I'll list the main points." He turns a page, settles glasses on the bridge of his nose, and begins. "Your mother left her house and car to Saint Matthew's Church, but with specific instructions that you can use them as long as needed to grieve and clean them out."

At least one thing in my life is reliable—my mother giving me work and leaving me with absolutely nothing in return. But that's fine. I don't want anything; the fewer ties to Minton Parish, the better. If I could wipe my memory clean of it all and move on, I would.

"Your mother would like any clothing in good condition donated to Christ House Thrift Shop." He continues on, listing out the particulars of what my mother wanted after her death—people to contact, where other donations should be made, even how she would like her ashes handled. She wants them spread on a beach, the one we went to once that I have warm memories of. Memories I'd started to doubt were real. That makes my heart squeeze.

After another ten minutes, the attorney wraps up by reaching into his suit jacket and pulling out a sealed envelope. I eye it warily but extend my hand and accept it.

"What's this?"

"Your mother wanted me to give you this letter. I don't know the contents. It's just for you. She also asked me to urge you to go to confession."

I snort-laugh. "Of course she did."

To his credit, Mr. Freeby doesn't react. Just gives me a polite smile, stands, thanks me for my time, and shows himself out.

I breathe a little easier once the door is locked and I'm alone again.

But his visit is a wake-up call. I take a long look around the house. At the rate I'm going, I'll be here forever. And that's the last thing I want. I need to get more organized. It's time I pull my shit together. Hell, I may never know some answers—like who's been sending the chapters. It could be it's Noah, and he's a very good liar, or someone else entirely. Either way, I need to let go, move on, and put the past behind me, even when others try to stop me from doing that.

I look down at the envelope still in my hand. There's no time to start like the present. Whatever my mother had to say is the past, not my future. The last thing I need is to read a posthumous lecture on going to church and asking God for forgiveness for my sins—sins I don't even think I committed anymore.

So I toss the envelope where it belongs: in the trash can.

CHAPTER

43

The following morning, I drag garbage cans from the garage to the end of the gravel driveway at 6 a.m. It's still dark out, and low fog hovers just above the grass, giving the house an even more ominous feeling than usual. Headlights up the road catch my eyes, momentarily blinding me. It's probably the garbage truck, and since there are still at least six bags to put out in addition to these metal drums that are missing lids, I hurry back up the driveway and grab two more. The rumble of the truck is close. When I'm halfway to the curb, it stops and idles. I look up and find it's not the garbageman.

It's a red pickup.

I drop the bags, freezing in place, and stare.

It's too dark to see inside the cab, but I know it's Noah. Neither of us moves for what must be close to a minute, until the window on the truck rolls down.

"Can I talk to you?" he yells.

"What do you want?"

"I just want to ask you a few questions. I haven't slept in days."

I scoff inwardly. *Days? That's nothing.*

I'm still mulling how to play this when Noah points to the driveway. "I'll just pull in. I won't get out of the truck if you don't want me to."

I have questions of my own, so why not? What's the worst that can happen? He kills me? At least then my eyes would shut for more than ten minutes, and I'd be put out of my misery. "Fine. But I'm only answering your questions after you answer mine."

I turn and walk toward the house, not bothering to hang around for his response. Noah waits until I reach the front porch before pulling in. He parks ten feet from the door and kills the engine.

"What can I answer for you?" he says quietly.

"For starters, you can tell me where the journal is."

He shakes his head. "I wasn't lying. There is no journal. Or if there is, I don't have it."

"How do you expect me to believe you when you had pictures of me and told me you didn't know who I was when we met?"

"I had no idea one of those girls was you. It wasn't like I spent a lot of time staring at the photos. They're fucking creepy. But I did go through them after you left." He reaches over to the passenger seat and holds a Polaroid outside the window. "Is this you, too?"

It's dark, but the porch light shines enough to see it. I can feel a storm brewing inside me, yet I swallow. "Of course it is."

"Why does it say Jocelyn underneath? They're all labeled with that name. I never understood that."

I'm supposed to be asking the questions, so I ignore his. "If I didn't kill your father, then who did?"

Noah shrugs. "I always wondered if maybe it was my mother. Couldn't blame her after what that bastard did to her. Though I never asked, and she never mentioned it. We just went on with our lives—my mother fell into a deep depression, and I tried to make the best of it after he was gone." He shakes his head. "But it seems like there were plenty of people who had good reason to kill him."

"How is it possible that I didn't know someone strangled him?"

"Did you ask anyone questions about what happened?"

I shake my head. I'd left Minton Parish for New York the very next day, with a whopping $600 saved from my shifts at McDonald's. But the homeless shelter I stayed in until I landed a job was better than this place. "No, but it was on the news."

He shrugs again. "I remember seeing it. Georgina Cobb was the reporter, a pretty brunette. She wore a blue dress on the news that day. I'm not sure why I remember that, but I suppose there are some things that stick with you forever. She said my father had been killed in a homicide, during a robbery. Don't think they reported the specific details. But I'm positive they called it a homicide, because I asked my mother what the word meant. After, she unplugged the TV and told me not to turn it on for a while."

I hate that I want to believe him. It makes me feel like the same dumb little girl who believed his father time and time again. I fold my arms over my chest. "I want all of the Polaroids. Not just the ones of me, but of all of the girls."

"Okay. You can have 'em. What will you do with them?"

"Light them on fire and watch them melt. They should've never existed."

He nods. "I'll deliver them, or you can come by the house and pick them up. Whatever you prefer."

My mind is a tangle of random thoughts. I don't bother to try and organize them before spitting each one at Noah. "What's the book you're writing about?"

"Three estranged brothers wind up on vacation at the same resort twenty-five years later. They haven't seen each other in more than two decades, so they think it's a coincidence at first. But when one of them dies, and the body is found tied up in the exact way a young girl was found when they were teenagers, they realize there's more to their getaway than meets the eye."

He's either one hell of an off-the-cuff liar, or he's telling the truth. I shake my head, unsure what to believe anymore, and go quiet.

After a few minutes, Noah speaks. "If you're done, can I ask you a few questions now?"

"What?"

"Why are all the photos labeled Jocelyn?"

I frown. "That was the name he made me use to check into the motel where we met. I didn't know about any of the other girls until I found the box, but I assume he did the same with them."

"Do you know why he had you use that name?"

I meet his eyes. "Do you know anything about your grandmother?"

Noah's eyes close. "Fucking hell." He shakes his head. "I was afraid that might be your answer. I don't know much about my real grandparents. I was always told they died when my father was little. He had a foster mother I vaguely remember. That was his biological mother's name? Jocelyn?"

I nod.

"I'd never heard the name mentioned before I saw it written on those Polaroids. But when I took out the autopsy report and death certificate the other day, his mother was listed as Jocelyn. I wasn't sure if that was his foster mother who adopted him or his actual mom. The last name is . . . something with a *B*."

"Burton?"

"That's it. I take it my father wasn't put into foster care because his real mother died, like I was told?"

"No, she abused him. The same way he abused others. She went to prison."

Noah swallows. "Is it all right if I get out of the truck? I think I'm going to be sick."

I nod.

Noah hops out of the pickup and jogs around to the back.

He bends over, hands on his knees, and empties the contents of his stomach. After, he dry heaves for a long time. Eventually, he wipes his mouth on the back of his hand and walks back to the still-open car door. "I don't know what to say. *Sorry for my fucked-up family* doesn't seem like enough."

"If you're not sending me the chapters, then who is?"

"I wish I knew. I'd help you if I could. I swear I would. You've been through so much already." He rakes a hand through his hair. "You have any other questions for me?"

I'm certain I do, but my mind is too jumbled to do this anymore, so I shake my head.

Noah nods. "Will you be home if I go get the Polaroids and come back?"

"Yes. But just leave them in the mailbox."

He smiles sadly and nods as he climbs back into his truck and pulls the door closed. Noah starts the ignition but then turns it off again. "Hey."

I look up.

"It's probably not the right time to say this. In fact, I know it's not. But I get the feeling this might be the last time I get the opportunity, so I'm going to say it anyway."

"What?"

He smiles, and his adorable dimples make an appearance. "I really did like you, Elizabeth. That's why I was paying you attention. You're different from other women."

I shake my head. "I'm different because I'm fucked up, Noah. And that's because your father made me this way."

CHAPTER

44

It's time to go home. Past time, really.

Two days later, the house cleanout is nearly done. My bedroom is the biggest task left, but I took anything of importance when I ran out of here two decades ago. Anything still remaining is going to the garbage, so it won't take me long. Mom's mattress and box spring still need to go, too, along with the set in my room, and a dozen bags in the garage.

When I sit down to book a flight, the earliest I can get is tomorrow in the late afternoon. *Perfect.* I hit purchase and enter my credit card. I'll clear out my room and be done by tonight. Then I'll get back to my life. Speaking of which, I need to text my boss and tell her I'll be back in two days. I miss my job. In some ways it's never seemed like much, but after these last weeks, months of realizations, it now feels like so much more—like it saved me. I really did escape this place and start over, thanks to Mr. Hank and my career. I think I'll go see him next weekend, bring a box of donuts and bask in his smile while he enjoys them.

I stall for an hour before finally making my way to my bedroom. When I do, I sit on the decades-old carpeting, feeling hollow inside my chest. This place is untouched since I left at seventeen, from the pink comforter to the posters on the wall, secured with thumbtacks. There are even stuffed animals still lining a little toy chest I have a vague memory of someone handing down to me.

I settle in front of the bed and reach beneath it. The first box I pull out has Valentines from grade school. I nearly smile—for some reason, I kept these. Maybe because they were claims that people cared about me: *Please be my Valentine* and *Sweet on you*, along with two-decade-old cheap candy. I toss the entire thing into a trash bag and reach for the next box.

Stacks of photographs.

It momentarily rocks me, thinking about the Polaroids I burned in the backyard yesterday. But these aren't photos like that. These are photos of me and Ivy and Lucas—hanging out in a parking lot, wandering by a stream on the outskirts of town. Ivy and me hugging in a classroom, wearing ridiculous clothes we thought were cute and sexy back when we were teenagers. Our hair was straightened so much it looked frayed, and we were so incredibly skinny, I now realize. But we looked happy, innocent—little idiots who had no idea what the world was about to throw at us. These memories aren't bad, but they're my past, and that's staying here. So I crumple the photo in my hand, add the entire box to the bag of trash. When I go back to New York, I'm going back to pretending my life started when I was eighteen.

There are half a dozen more boxes under the bed—there wasn't money for storage containers—and I slowly sift through the history of all the shoes I wore in my childhood, each box filled with more mementos. I throw away papers I was proud of, art I did in grade school. I can't bring myself to throw away my favorite books, though, so I pile those up to go to Goodwill. Maybe some other little girl will find comfort in them. After the last of the bags is tied up and at the curb, I drag my twin mattress out. The only thing left is mom's set, which I left, knowing it would be heavy and awkward to carry.

Her room is dark now, since the lamps were tossed days ago. I open curtains that have probably been closed for a decade and let a little sunshine in. The bed still has bedding on it. It's old and ratty, so it's all going to the curb with the last bag of trash. I strip the comforter and top sheet, then walk around to tug the fitted sheet from the corners. When I pull at the third corner, something pops partially out from between the mattress and box spring.

Something yellow, something *familiar* . . .

I crouch down for a better look, gripping its spiraled side to pull it out.

The butterfly on the front. My *journal* from back then.

But it can't be. It's probably just another yellow spiral-bound notebook with a butterfly on the front. One my mother wrote in—though I can't really see her doing that. I flip it open, then go still, my whole body trembling in shock.

It *is* my notebook. The one I wrote every last secret in. *Me*, not my friend Jocelyn.

And my mother had it all this time, hidden between the layers of her bed.

I sit down, heart pounding at what I hold in my hand. I flip it open and skim the entries. It starts with simple things—*I have a crush on Lucas. He's so cute*—and details about Ivy and me. I've even pasted in a photo of us, wearing what we thought were fancy gowns, going to some dance at the school. We couldn't have been older than fifteen, before everything happened.

But I know what else is in this notebook.

I turn page after page, searching for what comes later.

It doesn't take long to find. My writing changes, turns to scribbles as I hurry to get the details down. There are entries about Mr. Sawyer. Entries about kneeling. Entries about having *sex* for the first time. Entries about the beatings. Then . . . *an entry about my pregnancy*. I made the words bold, going over them repeatedly with my blue, ballpoint pen. *I. AM. PREGNANT.* I hadn't known how to feel about it. Shocked. Frightened. As crazy as it sounds, happy. I detail how I plan to tell Mr. Sawyer. How I hope he's not mad. How I hope it doesn't mean I'll be stuck in Minton Parish for the rest of my life like other girls who got pregnant too early. I speculate what might happen—will he leave his wife? Will we go away together? Am I special enough that he would do that for me? Tears form in my eyes, reading all the hope I had. I wanted him to save me from this place more than anything.

The next entry is about the miscarriage. About how he pushed me. The clinic. How I went back to the motel after I was strong enough, and we had a fight. The first and last time I ever fought back. *Because I thought I'd killed him.*

I don't move for a long time, staring down at the scribbles, the one place I told the truth back then.

Then it hits me.

My mother knew all the details that are in the chapters . . .

I'd pretty much ruled her out after that pregnancy chapter came in. Because while I might've told her I'd been involved with Mr. Sawyer the night everything happened, might have told her the things he made me do, I *never* told her about the pregnancy. I'd never told anyone.

But she knew.

She had my journal.

I drop the notebook, get to my feet, race to the garage. *The letter! The letter!* It can't have been in one of the bags I took out. *Please, God, no.* There were so many damn bags of trash, and only three of them made it to the curb before I was interrupted by Noah showing up on trash day—a dozen more still have to be put out. I yank the first one open, turn it upside down, and dump the contents before shuffling through. *Nothing.* I rip the next one wide and sift through garbage I cleaned out of her kitchen, her dining room. *Nothing.* My heart pounds. I'm afraid it's too late. Afraid it was one of the three I dragged to the curb that day.

But I keep going. I've lost track of how many bags are strewn across the garage floor, but I think it might be bag number nine I find it in. The thick envelope her lawyer brought is now smeared with coffee grounds, but otherwise intact. I rock back on my butt and rip it open.

The handwriting is shaky and barely readable, but it only takes ten seconds to get to the line that makes my blood run cold, makes me draw a hand to my mouth in shock.

> *Dearest Elizabeth,*
>
> *I know I don't have long now, and as you are very aware, I am a true believer. There is one sin I have yet to confess, and you are the person I will confess it to. In the Old Testament, Book of Exodus, 21:23-24, it reads:*
>
> *"And if any mischief follow, then thou shalt give life for life, Eye for eye, tooth for tooth, hand for hand, foot for foot . . ."*
>
> *You know the scripture.*
>
> *Perhaps it excuses what I did. Perhaps not. But I did what I had to.*
>
> *He took the life of your baby, my grandchild. So I took his. And I do not regret it. That night you'd fought back and gotten away. Next time you wouldn't be so lucky.*
>
> *I might have been a shit mom to you. I didn't have the best examples myself growing up, and the drinking and pills didn't help. Probably, I failed you in every way. But no one was going to hurt my grandchild, no one was going to hurt you and get away with it.*
>
> *I'll say this here, so you may keep it always, because I suspect you may not believe it otherwise. I love you.*
>
> *I would ask for your forgiveness, but I am beyond all of that now, if you are reading this.*
>
> *So I will just ask for you to go to confession. Cleanse your soul. My reminders didn't work, so I pray that your mother's dying wish might start your journey with God over.*
>
> *Love,*
> *Mom*

I swallow back a mix of so many emotions I'm surprised I'm not choking. My body feels as though it's vibrating as I read the letter again, and then again. I picture Noah in the driveway the other morning, how he said he didn't know who killed his father, how he suspected it might have been his mother.

But it wasn't his mom after all.

It was mine.

Because she loved me.

CHAPTER

45

Ten months later

H ow was your week this week?" Dr. Sterling folds her hands on top of her notebook, the one that's always on her lap.

"It was good. I slept through the night twice with no sleeping pill."

"Oh, wow. That's a big deal."

I nod and smile. "It is."

Ten months ago, when I returned from Louisiana, I expected things to improve—things like my mental health and insomnia. Minton Parish was behind me, and there were no more chapters coming in since Mom was gone, and, well, dead people take their tales with them. So I assumed I'd settle back into the way life had been before Hannah had thrown it into a tailspin. But too much has changed. I'm no longer only Elizabeth Davis. I'm also Jocelyn Burton—she didn't stay down south like I'd hoped. Neither did my mother. I've felt a lot of guilt for not being with Mom at the end, when it turned out she'd done so much for me. So instead of my mental health getting better, things got worse. I wasn't hungry and couldn't sleep. My ability to concentrate was virtually nonexistent. Grading exams for a class of forty students went from taking me two hours to almost two weeks. And then there were the physical manifestations of stress—heart palpitations, muscle fatigue, and the worst heartburn.

I went to the doctor a few times. But with all the new symptoms, she wanted me to see a psychiatrist or a therapist—get to the root of the problem. I'd yessed her at my visits, like I was going to look into it. But after she wouldn't prescribe me sleeping pills anymore, I had no choice but to actually do it. So I made an appointment with Dr. Sterling. I figured she already knew I had some pretty big issues, so she wouldn't be a hard sell to get what I needed. I had no intention of letting her dig into my psyche, but I did need someone to prescribe me those pills so I could sleep. As it turns out, she's done a lot more. I think she's actually helping me.

"So tell me about your week," Dr. Sterling says. "You're finished with classes now, right?"

I nod. "Thursday was my last day of the spring semester."

"Will you teach any summer courses?"

"Not this year. It will be the first time since I started teaching that I have three full months off."

"I think it's good you're taking a break. Do you have any plans for the summer?"

"Not too many. I'm mentoring a student who just completed my full-year novel-writing seminar. She's shown a lot of promise, so I'm going to keep reading the chapters she writes and giving her feedback until she finishes. I really think she has something, and the book could sell to a publisher."

"That's wonderful. It must give you a sense of accomplishment to see your students succeed."

"I guess." I look out Dr. Sterling's window, my mind already wandering to a new topic. "I went into a church the other day, Saint Paul's."

Her brows lift. "Really? Tell me how that came about."

"I'm not sure. My hairstylist moved, so I had to take the train uptown to her new salon for my appointment. After, I decided to walk home since it was so nice out. I passed this small church, the door was open, and I just wandered in. There wasn't a mass going on, and I didn't talk to anyone or anything. But I sat in the back pew, watching people go in and out of the confessional for an hour."

"You've mentioned your mother urged you to go to confession. Did you consider going in yourself?"

"Maybe for a second." I smile. "But instead I decided to go to the local bar and pick up a guy to take my mind off my sins."

Dr. Sterling chuckles. "Whatever brings you peace, I suppose."

"I met a guy who was just my type—older, a corrections officer, burly and tough. But I didn't wind up going home with him."

"Why didn't you?"

"I don't know. Maybe he reminded me of my ex too much." I stare off once again, thinking of Sam. I never heard from him after the funeral. Not that I can blame him. He dropped everything and flew 1,500 miles to support me, and I turned him around and delivered him back to the airport. He was a nice guy. Decent. Just not right for me, at least at the time. "I've always been attracted to a certain type of man—older, self-assured. I'm not the psychiatrist here, but even I can see there's a reason for that."

Dr. Sterling nods. "It's called trauma bonding. Abuse victims form a distorted perception of what a healthy relationship is and find themselves drawn to people that remind them of that relationship. In your case, you might not have been able to recall the details of what happened for almost two decades, but the pull to a certain type of partner could still stem from what your mind perceived as an idyllic mate. Sadly, victims who escape one abusive relationship often find themselves in another abusive relationship."

I sigh. "I guess I'm lucky I didn't do that. But now that I'm aware of the tendencies I've had over the years, I'm making an effort to date a different type of man." I nibble on my bottom lip. I've been keeping something from Dr. Sterling, and I'm not sure why. She already knows the ugly parts. "I've actually been . . . talking to someone."

"A man?"

I nod. "He doesn't live in the city, so it's mostly been texts and phone calls. But he's coming to visit for the weekend. He arrives tonight."

"Is this someone that you think might have potential as a partner?"

"Maybe." I shrug. "I'm not sure. But the more I talk to him, the more I like him. Though the long-distance thing probably wouldn't be easy. Or maybe that would be ideal— planned visits every once in a while rather than the expectation of seeing someone on a daily basis."

"Tell me about your prior relationships. We've talked about Sam, but have you ever had a long-term relationship with a man, perhaps committed to exclusivity or lived with one? Someone you grew close to and maybe leaned on and he leaned on you?"

I shake my head. "I never dated anyone for more than a couple of months. Sam was probably the longest."

"Do you think that perhaps you've never had a serious relationship because the men you pick *are* older and self-assured and that relates back to your abuser?"

"I don't know." I smile. "Can't you tell me that?"

Dr. Sterling laughs. "I definitely don't have all the answers. But talking about things, giving a new perspective to consider, can help *you* figure it out." She tilts her head. "Do you think you'd like a long-term relationship with a man someday?"

I smile. "I already have one. Mr. Hank."

"That's your old neighbor, right?"

I nod. "He's always been there for me. And I've been trying to do a better job of being there for him since I got back from Louisiana. He's older than my mother was, and I guess her dying was a reminder that he won't be around forever, either."

"That's wonderful that you're visiting him more. But what about a relationship with a man your own age—a romantic relationship of some kind. Do you see that in your future?"

I stop, really considering the question. It might be the first time in my life I have to take a moment. Because the answer for two decades was always *absolutely not*. But now . . . I shrug. "Maybe?"

Dr. Sterling picks up her pen, scribbles a note in her notepad. "That's good. Progress. You've been let down by more than one person you placed your trust in—your mother, a teacher. It will take time to open yourself up, to allow yourself to trust someone new."

"But how do I fix something I didn't break?"

Dr. Sterling smiles warmly. "You're already doing it. You're here, and we're talking about it. Acknowledging you've been hurt is the first step, and it's a big one. You're doing great, Elizabeth."

———

I'm nervous. But it's a different kind of nervous than I've been plagued with this last year. These nerves are the *good* kind, anticipation instead of dread. I can't remember the last time I looked forward to a date. Is tonight even a date? I'm not sure. But I've shaved my legs and have on lacy panties—not that I'm certain I'll be having sex, but a girl can never be too prepared, and, well, old habits die hard.

My buzzer rings at ten till eight. For once, my heart races with excitement. I push the button for the intercom to make sure it's him, then open the downstairs door lock remotely and check my face in the bathroom mirror.

It's just a date, Elizabeth.
Relax.

A minute later, there's a soft knock on my apartment door. I take a deep breath before wiping my palms on my pants and opening it.

He smiles. "Hey."

"Hi, Noah."

CHAPTER

46

Noah
One hour earlier

I really think readers are going to love this as much as I do.
I can already see this sitting on *The New York Times* list."

"Oh yeah? Well, if it does, you'll have to let me take you
out to celebrate."

"The team would love that."

"Was kinda thinking it could be just me and you, darlin'."

My editor blushes. "How long are you in town?"

"Just a few days. I'm visiting an old friend."

"Do you come to New York often?"

"I think I'm going to be here a lot in the foreseeable future. I have some business to take care of." I look at my watch.
"Speaking of which, I should get going."

Rena stands and extends a hand. "I'm really glad I got to
meet you in person."

I take it but lift it to my mouth, drop a kiss on the top.
"Not as glad as I am."

She walks me out to the lobby, to the revolving door at
the front entrance. "I almost forgot to ask—at the end of the
book, the protagonist finds her notebook in her mom's house.
So it was her mother sending the chapters all along?"

I wink. "Maybe . . . or maybe the antagonist was a really good liar and wanted revenge for the twenty years of suffering his mother went through after her husband was killed and she found his journals."

Rena laughs. "You're really not going to tell me?"

"Gotta keep you curious so you'll want to read book two."

"Will you at least give me a hint about what's going to happen? With the new ending, I'm sure readers will be curious whether the son gets together with his father's old victim or he's just seeking revenge."

I smile. "That remains to be determined."

She laughs. "You authors are so secretive."

"That we are . . . *that we are.*"

It's a beautiful afternoon, so I decide to walk to pick up my date. I stop at a florist and grab a bundle of wildflowers, then pop into a liquor store for a bottle of wine. My cell phone rings two blocks from my destination. It's a local number, so I answer, thinking it could be her.

"Hello?"

"Hi, is this Noah Sawyer?"

"It is indeed."

"This is Helena Esme from Saint Paul's Church. I work in the office."

"What can I do for you, Ms. Esme?"

"Well, first I want to say thank you for your donation. It arrived today, and it's absolutely beautiful. Our parishioners are in for a treat."

"I'm glad you think so. Someone special to me visited your church a few weeks ago, and I'm hoping she comes back and gets to see it. It'll be sort of a surprise. Saint Agnes has a special meaning to her, and I think she's really going to appreciate it."

"I'm sure she will. And I personally love it. All the staff feels the same. We're excited to put it on display for everyone to enjoy. That's actually why I'm calling. Would it be all right if we put your name on a small plaque on the base of the statue? We like to put the donor's name as a thank-you when we receive such generous gifts."

"That's very kind, but I prefer to keep the donations I make to the church anonymous. I'm not looking for attention."

"Oh, okay. I understand."

A thought crosses my mind, makes me smile. "Actually, on second thought, would it be okay if I put it in my sister's name? She passed a long time ago."

"Of course. We can put *donated in memory of*, if you'd like."

"That would be perfect."

"Let me just grab a pen, so I can take down the name and make sure I get the spelling of your sister's name right."

"All righty."

Helena comes back on the line a minute later. "Okay, I'm ready. What is your sister's name?"

"Hannah. *Hannah Greer Sawyer.*"

ACKNOWLEDGMENTS

Thank you to Emily Bestler and her publishing team for taking a chance on a romance author who felt it was time to start killing characters. And to Hannah Wann and Becky West for bringing *Someone Knows* to the UK.

To my agent, Kimberly Brower—thank you for always being there to support me and steer the ship to new adventures.

Behind every woman who succeeds is a tribe of successful women who cheer her on, have her back, and encourage her to do scary things. Thank you to my tribe leader, Penelope Ward, who is always by my side, and to Cheri, Luna, Julie, Elaine, Jessica, and the 26,000 smart ladies in my amazing Facebook Group, Vi's Violets.

To my family—Chris, Jake, Grace, Sarah, Kennedy, and Kylie—thank you for putting up with having to repeat yourselves often, because I'm always lost in my head thinking about a story.

To you—the *readers*. Thank you for your support and excitement. Whether we are meeting for the first time, or you've been with me for more than a decade reading my romance novels, I'm so grateful you took a chance on this story.